D1261009

SUNSET TERRACE

A NOVEL BY REBECCA DONNER

MacAdam/Cage Publishing
155 Sansome Street, Suite 550
San Francisco, CA 94104
www.macadamcage.com

Library of Congress Cataloging-in-Publication Data

Donner, Rebecca.
    Sunset Terrace / by Rebecca Donner.
        p. cm.
    ISBN 1-931561-34-6 (Hardcover : alk. paper)
    1. Los Angeles (Calif.)—Fiction.  2. Apartment houses—Fiction
3. Young women—Fiction  4. Violence—Fiction  I. Title.

PS3604.O6365 S86 2003
813'.6—dc21

                                                    2002153579

Manufactured in the United States of America.
10 9 8 7 6 5 4 3 2 1

Book and jacket design by Dorothy Carico Smith

# SUNSET TERRACE

A NOVEL BY REBECCA DONNER

# MacAdam/Cage

For Mia

They sit in their room
pinching the dolls' noses, poking the dolls' eyes. One
time they gave a doll a ride in a fuzzy slipper but that was too
far, too far wasn't it.

—Anne Sexton, Sixth Psalm

# CONTENTS

# I. MAY

There was no terrace and you couldn't see the sunset but that's what the building was called all the same, *Sunset Terrace*. In front there was a garden of sorts—a small, dirt-packed area wild with dandelions and the occasional cluster of ice plants, enclosed by a low wall of rocks cemented together, freckled with specks of mica that winked in the sun like secret jewels. At the far end of the garden stood an old cactus, one side of it caved in and looking chewed, next to a wrought-iron post where the Sunset Terrace sign hung from curlicue hooks.

Sunset Terrace was rent-controlled and governed by single mothers. There were six apartments in all, one through three on the bottom floor, four through six on the second. The bottom-floor apartments featured an L-shaped cinderblock wall that partially enclosed a rectangular patch of Astroturf, where tenants could set out a lawn chair or a few flowerpots. Most of the time, though, only yellowing newspapers and trashcans could be seen there, making the mothers who lived on the second floor shake their heads when they walked past, calling it a waste of a patio, jealous since all they had was a balcony so small and narrow it could barely accommodate a stool.

The apartment doors were all painted the same muddy

color. Centered on each like a small, unblinking eye was a peephole that looked out to the elementary school playground next door with its rusty monkey bars, swings with cracked rubber seats, all of it fenced in by chain-link.

Among the kids in the building the garden out front was known as The Graveyard, ever since one of them dug up an old shoebox under the Sunset Terrace sign and found inside a gerbil skeleton and a silver crucifix with a chain just long enough to fit around a little girl's neck. From then on it was where the kids buried their dead pets, the youngest among them whispering about the ghosts you saw—a floating menagerie of hamsters and guinea pigs and cats and dogs and even goldfish—if you spun around backwards three times exactly at midnight and hunched behind the dumpster.

Walking down the pathway that ran along the bottom-floor apartments you stepped on names and messages etched in the cement by kids who had once lived there. *Ruben '68,* and underneath in bigger letters, *Josh '74* and *T. M. sucks C. L.'s dick* on one square by the mailboxes. In between apartments one and two was *SxMx,* and on the square next to it a kid named *Danetta* had written her name in cursive, with a heart and *1962,* the oldest date on the pathway. Farther down past number three was *RD+JS=4-Ever* and *Hot Tuna Rocks!* In front of the laundry room, the last door before you reached the parking lot, was a newly paved-over square. There, etched in boxy letters, was *Bridget '83.* The name belonged to a scrappy nine-year-old girl who lived in number one.

She'd had her eye on the spot in front of the laundry room since the day she moved in to Sunset Terrace. A root from the eucalyptus in the playground lay directly underneath, and thin cracks cobwebbed the old cement, yielding to the pressure. Every morning Bridget checked the root's progress, hoping the cracks would buckle so the square would have to be repaved. It had tried her patience, waiting for the root to do a job she figured she could very well do herself, which is how she came upon the idea of marching out of her apartment one morning with her foster mom's boyfriend's bowling ball. Her twiggy arms shook as she raised it above her head. Gritting her teeth, she hurled it down onto the cement. Six tries it took in all to loosen a chunk.

Just ten minutes later, the widowed Mrs. Grover in apartment three tripped over the chunk as she marched to the laundry room in her satin slippers with the fancy puff at the tip, her wicker basket flying out of her arms. A scraped knee and jangled nerves were her only injuries, but she marched right back into her apartment and called Warren Wilkes, the landlord of Sunset Terrace, and threatened to take legal action if he didn't immediately fix the problem. Warren was known to the residents of the building as a penny-pincher, who'd hem and haw under the direst of circumstances—a busted pipe spraying water into your bedroom closet, or an infestation of roaches the size of rodents—until you mentioned lawyers.

That afternoon Bridget sat on a bus-stop bench, right in front of the gas station on Pico Boulevard, crying her eyes out. A middle-aged man in jogging shorts filling the tank of his black Audi spotted her. Concerned, he approached, thinking she was a boy at first, with her tomboy clothes and her mangle of short blonde hair. But then he saw a smear of bright pink lipstick, and realized he was mistaken.

"I lost my bus money," she blubbered. "I can't get home."

"Here," he said, gently, pulling a crisp one-dollar bill from his wallet. She mumbled a tearful thank-you as she snatched the money out of his hands.

She waited for his car to pull out of the gas station and merge with the traffic on Pico. Then wiped the phony tears away and ran a half a block to Jan 'n Joe's, the corner store. Inside, she bought a cherry popsicle with the dollar, deftly slipping two

Milky Ways and a pack of Fruit Stripe gum into her shorts pocket while the tan old man behind the register fumbled with change.

She raced back home, three blocks in all, and arrived in the nick of time: the shy Mexican laborer with the missing front tooth who Warren always hired to do maintenance work was stooped over in front of the laundry room, finishing the job on the broken cement. As he worked, he whistled through the gap in his teeth.

"Hola!" she called to him.

He stopped whistling long enough to answer "Hola" in a soft voice, without looking up.

She edged past him and slipped into the laundry room, leaving the door open. It was a closet-sized space, just large enough for the washer and dryer. She climbed into the dryer and peeked out its little circular window, watching him scrape the gritty wet cement with a putty knife over the hole she'd made with her foster mom's boyfriend's bowling ball. Someone's clothes had been left in the dryer, warming her as she merrily sucked on her popsicle. Her plan had worked out perfectly.

When he was gone, she licked the wooden popsicle stick clean and climbed out of the dryer. Squatting down, she stuck the tip of the stick into the wet cement and made her mark: Bridget '83. Then she guarded the area for the rest of the day and into the night so no other kids in the building could share the enviable distinction of having their name preserved for posterity on the Sunset Terrace pathway.

So far 1983 hadn't been a particularly eventful year at Sunset Terrace, except when Rich Jr. in apartment six got sent to juvie for stealing the mail and Davy in number four broke his arm doing 180s on his skateboard by the dumpster. Up until now nothing of any consequence had happened to Bridget that year, which was maybe why she'd had the idea of smashing the cement with her foster mom's boyfriend's bowling ball in the first place. But later that night, something did happen: a new girl moved into the building, into the recently vacated second-floor apartment, number five, along with her mother and her little sister.

It was just past nine or so. Bridget was sitting in her favorite spot, straddled over the top of the chain-link fence in the driveway that separated Sunset Terrace from the apartment building next door, where she had a bird's-eye view of everything. She'd been doing what she always did while she was up there, listening to the clanging sound her heel-kicks made against the chain-link, when she heard the advancing cough and rumble of an old car engine. A beat-up Datsun pulled up to the curb, right under the only streetlight on the block.

The driver's door swung open, and a travel-worn woman climbed out, dropping her keys. With a sigh, she picked them up, then wearily made her way around the car and opened the passenger's door. Out tumbled a little girl, clutching a blanket and whining. The woman lifted the girl into her arms and thumped on the back windshield with her elbow. "Hannah, let's go."

The back door opened, and Bridget saw a girl around her age—nine or ten—emerge. Pale and thin, with sleepy eyes and frizzy hair, stumbling into the streetlight's bright pool of light. The girl didn't even bother to look around at her new surroundings. Just placed her palm flat on her forehead, a gesture looking almost like a grown-up's, before letting it drop.

Bridget kicked her heels against the chain-link, keeping a steady beat. Here was a girl who harbored a secret burden just as she did. Bridget knew it the instant she laid eyes on her.

*California California California*

Hannah's mother liked driving away from places when it was dark. After Spokane, Hannah counted eleven moves in three years, eleven sleepy tumblings into the Datsun, eleven apartments, eleven teachers. Still, her mother had an ability to invest hope in whatever destination she chose as their new home, and Hannah felt an odd tingle, glitter under skin, when the car pulled away from the curb and gathered speed. She'd wait for her little sister Daisy to fall asleep, then lean her forehead against the cool glass of the windshield and count the gas stations, then the hubcaps, then the dead animals that whizzed by, letting the strange new word warm her lips. *Taos.* Then *Florence. Casper. Amarillo. Helena. Duluth. Aberdeen. Appleton. Yakima. Joplin. Odessa.*

Once they arrived, her mother would look for a cheap motel room with a kitchenette. Her mother wasn't choosy about where she worked, and it took her a week at most to find a cooking job in a nearby diner or coffee shop. On nights her mother worked a late shift, Hannah and her sister would entertain themselves by making appetizers, each piling a plate with bread and cheese cut into little shapes and decorated with whatever spices the previous guests had left behind, mysterious jars of dried-up green leaves, red flecks, fine golden powder. Later, her mother would return from her cooking job, exhausted, stumbling into the room with a stack of styrofoam to-go containers in her arms, kicking the door shut with her heel. Her mother called them her dinner surprises, the greasy styrofoam with the evening's mistakes: a tuna melt when the customer had ordered it without tomato, or a Salisbury steak cooked too long. Hannah knew enough to eat whatever her mother had brought home, even though her stomach, by then, was stuffed.

Wherever they went her mother made friends with the waitresses, and once she learned their names, she'd get them to talk about their hometowns. After her cooking shift, late at night, she'd stretch out on the motel bed with her feet high on a stack of pillows and thumb through her dog-eared *Rand McNally's Road Atlas*, trying to figure which waitress's hometown was closest to where they happened to be right then. Hannah watched her mother's forefinger trace over the routes. "We're going to Oregon next," her mother would murmur dreamily. "Judy says it's beautiful there, lots of forests and water." By the time Hannah's records arrived at the local elementary school, the three of them were long gone, in another town already.

It was always at night, after Hannah and Daisy had gone to sleep: "*Off we go,*" came her mother's whisper, and Hannah would wake, clutch her pillow and stumble out the front door with her sister in tow. There, the idling Datsun would be waiting for them, already packed, rumbling in the dark.

They rarely stayed in any one place longer than three months. The waitresses' hometowns were never like they described them, usually smaller, colder, dustier. For Hannah, the classrooms swirled together, losing distinction. Kids with the same sizing-up stares. On playgrounds, shouting. In hallway huddles, with their quiet backs. Their intricate codes, games, hands deft with their manipulations of string, marbles, pennies, folded paper.

Every school had a quiet spot on a far corner of the playground, and it was there that Hannah learned she belonged. There, far away from all the shouting and shoving and laughing, she played with ants, blockading their paths with a glass shard or a leaf, entire worlds in the asphalt cracks. Sometimes she'd capture one, close the tips of her fingernails over a wispy leg and watch it limp away. Then she'd rescue it and straighten out its leg, although by that point the ant was usually dead. Girls, here and there, edged toward her spot on the playground, giggling as they sniffed around her, surprising her with hair yanks. Once, a raven-haired girl in Taos who liked to steal Hannah's barrettes surprised her with a present. Hannah flinched, waiting for the quick hot burn on her scalp, when the girl handed her a turtle.

That night they left Taos, the Datsun heading north for Florence, Oregon, Hannah cupped the turtle to her throat, watching the yellow painted lines on the highway whiz past. From one waitress's hometown to the next, her turtle remained her only companion. She kept it in a shoebox, fed it insects, stroked its cool, leathery head.

Her mother hated leaving Hannah and Daisy alone when she had a cooking shift, saying she wished she could tuck her babies in her pocket and take them with her. Her kitchen apron clenched in her hand, she'd open the motel room's front door, then reel around and rush back to smother their faces once more with kisses, squeezing their bodies together in a fierce hug so her lips could move easily from forehead to forehead, nose tip to nose tip. But by the time they'd reached Odessa, something in her mother, Hannah observed, was changing. The grip in her was gone, as if all that hugging had left her limp. Mornings, when Hannah watched her fill a cereal bowl with cold milk, she saw that her movements were stalled, more careful; even the milk seemed to pour out in slow-motion. And when her mother ambled around the motel room, leaning over to pick up a stray sock, it seemed like her whole body was heaving one long sigh.

It was time to put down roots, settle things, her mother quietly announced one morning. No more of these motel rooms, greasy spoons—Annie at the Steak Shack said her father in California had a vacancy in one of his rent-controlled buildings. How do you like the sound of that? her mother said, stirring her cereal, putting on her hopeful smile.

And so, the final move one night. The Datsun rattled down the highway, heading toward Sunset Terrace, its headlights casting two shaky beams into the advancing darkness. Her mother whispered promises about their new home: oranges and oceans and light. On the highway, broken yellow lines streamed past. Daisy slumped in the front seat, blinking, shivering, still clutching her pillow. Hannah sat in back, looking out, her forehead tipped against the cool glass, trying to freeze a yellow line with her eyes before it was gone. *California. California. California.*

The sun was blazing by ten. Hannah and Daisy lay sweating in sleeping bags in the middle of a small, empty room. A Sunday calm settled until a little girl's voice, clear and loud as a church bell, pulled her from the folds of sleep:

*Mother-fuckin', titty-suckin' two-balled bitch*
*Momma's in the kitchen cookin' red hot shit*
*Daddy's in jail, sayin' go to hell—*

Hannah slid out of her sleeping bag and stepped over Daisy, careful not to wake her. Peering out the open window, she saw a wild head of hair, short and blonde and matted, like a straw nest. A small girl, about her age—nine or ten, she guessed—was down below, straddling the top of a chain-link fence that bordered the apartment building. The girl kicked her heels against the fence, making it ripple.

*Mother-fuckin', titty-suckin' two-balled bitch*
*Momma's in the kitchen—*

The girl stopped suddenly, took a long, deep breath, craning her neck as her chest filled with air. Hannah crouched down so the girl wouldn't see her, then peeked out the corner of the window. The girl started up again where she'd left off:

*—cookin' red hot shit*
*Daddy's in jail, sayin' go to hell—*

Hannah heard gentle clinking sounds in the kitchen, the creaking of her mother's weight on uneven floorboards. She smelled something cooking, or burning, maybe. Looking down, she saw that her little sister was wide awake, watching her. Daisy lay there a moment more, then wriggled out of her sleeping bag and dashed out the bedroom door. Her voice receded down the hallway, bouncing with her steps. "Mo-o-o-o-mmy!"

Her mother was in her nappy terrycloth robe, bent over the sink, scraping the charred bits off a pile of burnt toast with a butter knife. On the stove, a trickle of steam rose from a teakettle's spout.

Daisy plunged her face into her mother's robe, whimpering guinea pig sounds. Her mother looked down and smiled.

"You hungry, Squeaky?"

Daisy burrowed back into the robe, said "Mmm-mmmm-mmm," the inflections hinting the words.

"What do you mean 'You don't know'?"

Daisy shrugged, then dashed into the living room and scrambled inside a large, empty cardboard box.

Hannah hoisted herself up onto the kitchen counter. The teakettle started a low whistle, crescendoing into a wail. Through the walls, Hannah could hear Elmer Fudd stuttering on a neighbor's blaring TV. Somewhere in the distance, a lawnmower stopped.

Her mother turned off the burner, and the teakettle gave another quick shriek when she lifted it. "Did you sleep okay, Hannah?"

Hannah shrugged. Her mother had finally taken notice of her, and she was embarrassed by her sense of relief. Part of her wanted to do just what Daisy always did—burrow her face into terrycloth and rock back and forth, feeling her mother's thin fingers stroking her head. But no, she was nine years old, too old for babying, she decided.

Daisy was huddled inside the empty cardboard box, her

hands turning an imaginary steering wheel, saying *Rrrrrrrrr! Rrrrrrrrrr!* Hannah slid off the counter and walked into the living room. As she passed the box she gave it a little kick, got the desired shriek.

"*Stop!*" Daisy wailed.

Her mother turned, holding a mug of tea. Her other hand clenched the braid at the nape of her neck. She dragged her hand down its length, pulling it out to the side. When she reached the rubber band at the end, her arm was fully extended, the braid taut. It was a sign that she was losing patience, that she wanted peace.

"Hannah, get the jam, would you?" She let the braid go, and it swung behind her back.

Hannah opened the refrigerator door. There was a dry, sour smell. On the rusted wire shelf stood a jar of raspberry jam, a clear plastic tub of deli pickles from the trip, a half-chewed one bobbing in the brine, and the same dented orange box of baking soda her mother had put in the mini-refrigerators of all the motel rooms they had lived in over the past three years.

Hannah put the jar on the shag carpet in the living room, where her mother had arranged folded paper towels and toast cut into triangles. She sat down cross-legged and picked up a toast triangle, examining it. Her mother was a good cook and never burned things unless she was in one of her distracted moods—when she nodded like she was listening but really her attention was flitting in and out, lucky if you could catch it.

Daisy bit into her toast, her face scrunching up. She looked down miserably at the charred crumbs that showered onto her paper towel.

"Yummy, Daisy," Hannah said softly, wickedly. "Pancakes."

Daisy, changing tactics, reached for the jam and scooped an enormous spoonful onto her burnt toast, then another. "Yummyumm," she said, and let out a giggle, two dimples indenting her pale cheeks like milk drops.

Hannah joined in, in spite of herself. They spooned huge mounds of jam on their toast, their laughter infectious, the two of them choking, breathing in crumbs.

Her mother set her mug on the carpet and sat down, smoothing her bathrobe over her knees. "A picnic with my sillies," she said.

Somehow, her presence spoiled the game. In the silence that followed, Hannah forced down the jam-sweetened, charred mouthfuls, watching her mother thinly spread her toast triangle with jam. A bus outside screeched its brakes; moments later, the engine grumbled up again, and the kitchen window trembled. The neighbor's TV hummed through the walls, now a game show, the applause like instant rain.

"Mom?" Hannah said.

"Mmm?" Her mother reached for a burnt crust Daisy had left on her paper towel and popped it in her mouth.

"When are we going to unpack the rest?"

"Soon, honey. Right after breakfast."

"Mothermothermothermother," Daisy babbled.

"My little silly silly sillies," her mother replied, smiling over the rim of her mug. She kept smiling until Daisy spoke again.

"Motherfuckin," Daisy babbled. "Motherfuckin motherfuckin motherfuckin."

*Where did Daisy learn those awful words?*

But Elaine did not have time to pursue the thought—someone was knocking at the front door. Flustered, she jumped to her feet and fumbled with the doorknob.

"Hello?" came a man's grizzled voice.

"I'm so sorry, I can't seem to—"

It dawned on her that the door was locked. She recalled the precise moment when she'd turned the oblong knob of the deadbolt: after leading her girls into their bedroom and coaxing them into their sleeping bags, she'd wandered back into the living room to shut out the light. It was then that she realized the door was not only unlocked, but ajar. *I must be more careful,* she'd thought, realizing that she'd grown accustomed to motel doors that automatically locked when you shut them.

"You all right in there?"

"Yes—yes, I'm sorry." There was a solid metal click as she turned the deadbolt's knob.

It was Annie's father with the lease, holding a battered briefcase. Her landlord. An enormous, weathered man, well over six feet tall. Elaine forced a smile through her agitation: he'd told her that he would come by late in the afternoon, maybe the evening, but here he was, interrupting her breakfast with her girls.

"Warren Wilkes, pleasure to meet you." He held out a large, hairy hand.

She shook it, astounded by the lack of family resemblance. Annie was a little elf of a waitress—five-foot-three at the most.

"First thing I should tell is you don't have to worry about the Mexicans. Your kids won't catch anything from them—they all get tuberculosis tests at the school. Plus, the Mexicans stay on their side of Pico."

"Pico?"

"The major cross street, just north of here." He fingered the top button of his polo shirt, where tufts of curly gray hair sprouted out. "That's where they all live—five kids, five cousins, five second cousins all crammed in under one roof. I weed 'em out if they apply, it's hard to get 'em out once you got 'em in. Now, understand that the rent here's what the city tells me to charge, I've got to dot every 'i' and cross every 't' with all the regulations I have to follow and not that I'm complaining but it's hard, it's expensive, the upkeep, you understand, the price isn't market and I'm the one who has to foot the bill."

Elaine hoped he'd come to the end of his train of thought. His words had washed over her; whatever reservoir of attention she had left had been drained by his ramblings. Her bathrobe, she realized, had indiscreetly flapped open below her waist, exposing her bare thighs. She yanked the ties tight. "I'm sorry— I'm—I'm embarrassed I'm not more presentable. We got in very late last night."

"Nooooo." He flicked his hand up, as if shooing away a fly. "If you barged into my house in the morning," he began, eyes twinkling, "you'd be lucky if you didn't catch me naked."

Elaine fought the urge to cringe. "Let me just run and get a pen."

"No need, got one right here." He pulled out a gold pen from the side pocket of his sweatpants and offered it to her with a hairy pinky in the air.

"Well, thank you. So, Annie mentioned that you used to be a Hollywood actor for MGM."

"RKO," he corrected. "Stand-in's more like it. Years ago, no use mentioning it now." Frowning, he squatted down with a *Hrrrrrrruh,* his knees cracking, and clicked open his briefcase. He poked through a jumble of papers and produced a manila folder. "I deposited the money order you sent, so you're all set once you sign and date the lease. You keep one copy, you know, and *hrrrruh*"—he rose to his full height again—"I keep the other."

Elaine opened the folder and skimmed the first page of the lease. What the stipulations were didn't matter—this was where they would put down roots, this would be their home. But she inched Warren's gold pen down the margin anyway, wanting her new landlord to see her as the careful consumer she was, knowing all along she wouldn't have any objections to whatever contract she was signing. She wanted this apartment. It was that simple.

"There were eight inquiries about the vacancy. Did my daughter tell you that? I told her I wanted to put some good people in for a change. Annie, she's what you'd call a firecracker, all lickety-split when it comes to making decisions. But she's got good sound judgment."

"I'm—I'm sorry," Elaine said, opening the door wider. "Would you like to come in? I don't have any furniture yet, we can just stand, I guess."

"Well, fine," Warren said, ducking his head as he stepped into the room. Hannah and Daisy, still sitting on the shag carpet, peered up at him. He returned their appraising stare. "You two won't have far to walk to school. And you've got a playground out there for a backyard, that's one of the advantages of this location." He wiggled his pinky, then gave it a surprising, violent tug. He moved down his hand, cracking the knuckles of each finger, and started on the pinky of the other hand. When he finished, he laced his fingers together and stretched his arms above his head with a "*Gaaaaa,*" almost touching the ceiling.

Daisy's eyes widened. She bolted across the room, and within seconds Elaine found her daughter nuzzling her face into the folds of her bathrobe. Elaine shot an urgent look at Hannah, hoping her older daughter would understand the tacit meaning: *Say hello, show Warren that we are nice, polite tenants.* But Hannah simply stared back at her—with incomprehension or defiance, she didn't know.

"So ah, Annie said you were the best cook they had at the Steak Shack in years. How'd you like Odessa?"

"Actually we—we didn't stay long, we were just passing through. Annie probably told you." She hoped Warren would leave soon.

But he wasn't in any hurry, she saw. He strolled into the kitchen and fiddled with the oven, turning the knob on and off. Then he opened the oven door and stooped down to peek inside, as if he expected to find something in there.

"The folks who lived in this apartment before came in from Utah six years ago. Two kids, had three more while they were here, would you believe. All crammed in a two-bedroom." Grimacing, he closed the oven door. "Screaming babies and a dog barking all day and night, you can imagine the complaints. She's the sister of the little Mormon in apartment four right next to you, name's Tanya. A welfare-collecting grocery store clerk with four kids she doesn't exactly have a handle on, if you know what I mean."

"Four?" Elaine said mechanically, "goodness." Oh, she was exhausted by this meddling old man, by her girls—who she couldn't help but see through his eyes: Daisy, babyish, maybe too much so for her age, and Hannah, rudely glowering and distant. Hardly the picture she hoped to present to him, of two sweet, obedient daughters standing beside their proud mother.

Once again, she regretted confiding in Annie. It was during that blissful half-hour after the last customer had left—after she'd scrubbed the grill clean with a stiff bristle brush and the urgent hum of the dishwashing machine gave way to the clinking of plates and cups and silverware being put in their place for another day—when she sat in a booth with Annie, swallowing down stale custard pie with lukewarm coffee. Elaine blurted the whole story—or most of it, anyway, skipping over what happened to Roger. She just stuck to the consequences. About her daughters being suddenly fatherless, about their three years on the road living in motels. Annie had taken pity on her, which was why she was here today, in Annie's father's apartment building, ready to sign a lease. Still, how filled with *shame* she felt just thinking about how Annie must have told him everything. What did he see when he looked at her? A pitiful, down-on-her-luck woman with misbehaving children, a charity case?

"Well," she said, forcing a bounce into her voice. "I guess you need my signature."

"That's what I'm here for," Warren said.

"Honey, Mommy's got a lease to sign." She peeled Daisy off her leg, closing her eyes to the guinea pig squeals.

The first neighbor Hannah saw was a woman in apartment one, leaning out her window to smoke a Virginia Slim. Her hair was long and frosted blonde and wavy, like Farrah Fawcett's. When Hannah walked past the woman didn't say a word, just stared at a spot of nothing in front of her face, exhaling two streams of smoke out her horsey nostrils.

As they unpacked the Datsun, Hannah saw some of the other kids in the building. Two girls drew hopscotch lines in blue chalk on the sidewalk. Another one, younger, sat in the shade of the dumpster, picking at her dirty toenails. The boys circled around them on skateboards, shouting, smashing rocks against the stucco walls, one of the boys swinging an arm with a cast on it like a propeller. They all tried to look absorbed in activity, but Hannah caught their sideways glances when they thought she wasn't looking.

Hannah speed-walked across the sidewalk, trying to get the unpacking over with as quickly as possible. But Daisy milked it, wanting to inspire jealousy. Eyebrows arched, she strolled by the kids with her grubby Barbies like an exotic bouquet, legs like stalks in her fist. None of them bothered to look except for the one picking her toenails by the dumpster, a little blubbery girl with red punch stains around her mouth, who seemed to sniff the air as Daisy passed her.

Hannah and her mother had emptied the car by the time Daisy finally made it upstairs, the punch-stained girl in tow. Daisy had let her hold Skipper, the flat-chested Barbie, which the girl, wheezing now, was undressing as they walked through the front door.

"Well, hello there!" her mother sang from the kitchen. The girl gazed up, letting her sausagey tongue, also punch-stained, loll out of her mouth.

"Everybody this is Mim," said Daisy, suddenly bossy.

Mim looked down at her bare feet. Said "Hi" as if she were greeting her dirty toenails.

Daisy grabbed her by the wrist and they disappeared into the bedroom in back. "Watch, watch Skipper do the splits, watch," she said, and the bedroom door clicked shut.

* * *

The rest of the afternoon, her mother busied herself with unpacking and cleaning. Hannah occupied herself in the living room, making a home for her turtle in a practically-new shoebox she found by the dumpster. One by one, she took out the pebbles that were scattered on the bottom of her turtle's old dented shoebox and arranged them in a pile in the corner of the practically-new one. In another corner she neatly stacked three bottlecaps; she'd never seen her turtle sleep like a person, but she liked to imagine that it secretly turned over on its shell at night and used the bottlecaps as a pillow, after the lights were off and no one was looking. While she worked, she could hear the distant shouts of the other kids from the building, now in the playground. They were involved in some sort of game, shouting "Safe!" and "Busted!" and "Allie Allie All Come Free!"

"Looks like your turtle needs some fresh air," her mother said, shaking Comet onto the kitchen counter.

Hannah knew the message behind the words. It wasn't her turtle her mother was worried about staying cooped up all day long in the apartment. "I don't like California," she said.

Her mother wrung out her sponge. "We just got here. Why don't you go find a friend? Daisy's already found one."

Hannah shook her head. Kids were the same wherever she went. Boys with their shoving and pinching. Girls with their split-second switches—one minute their warm breath was in your ear, telling you secrets, the next they were wrinkling their noses at you, saying you were never their friend.

"Come on, sweetie. There are lots of children who live here. I'm sure you'll find someone you like."

She remembered the girl on the fence, yelling her dirty song at the top of her lungs. Her mother wouldn't like her at all. The thought of meeting the girl made Hannah's stomach flutter. She grabbed her turtle and headed for the front door.

Down the stairs she went, holding her turtle with one hand and the railing with the other, careful to place her foot on the black tar strip glued to the edge of each stair. She did not want to slip, so she held her breath the whole way down.

*Allie Allie All Come Free!*

On the other side of the chain-link fence, a boy in the playground stood next to the rusted monkey bars, cupping his hands around his mouth. The other kids from the building emerged from their hiding places—one from behind the thick, peely-barked trunk of a eucalyptus tree, another kid crawling out of a dented metal trashcan. The two girls she'd seen playing hopscotch this morning were among them, but the girl she was looking for wasn't there.

Maybe she was farther away, off by herself somewhere in the playground. But Hannah did not know how to climb a chain-link fence.

Defeated, she walked past the laundry room and into the parking lot. The sky made bluish rectangles on the car windshields, and specks of broken glass glinted on the ground. The asphalt was spray-painted with white lines and numbers, six in all. She set her turtle down on the rusty roof of a VW bug parked in the number three spot.

She hadn't heard the footsteps, but a sudden awareness that she was being watched made her turn around.

It was the woman with the Farrah Fawcett hair. Two streams of smoke shot out her nostrils.

The woman brought the cigarette up to her mouth and squinted, her long fingernails hovering over her lips. Five pointy daggers. She looked Hannah over, took in every inch.

Hannah stood there, heart pounding, watching the quick jerks of the woman's moist eyeballs in their sockets—then grabbed her turtle and fled.

"Yoo hoo!"

A short woman peeked through the front door, dressed in an orange polyester uniform with white lapels. Her hair was in pigtails and was peroxide blonde, except for a dark strip down the center of her scalp where her hair was parted. "I'm Tanya," she said, "your next-door neighbor."

Elaine set her sponge down and looked around for something to wipe her hands on, settling for her old jeans. "Hello," she said.

"I'm throwin' a party on Sunday and I wanted to come by and tell you you're invited. No special occasion or anything. Just a little rabble-rousin' after church. It's potluck."

"Well, thank you, we'd love to come," Elaine said. "I'll bring deviled eggs."

"Good, then I'll give you a tip on grocery shopping. Lucky's is the closest store. Plus it has the sweetest cashiers this side of Pico." Saying this, she dusted off some imaginary dirt from her shoulder, calling attention to the store name stitched in cursive on the breast pocket of her orange uniform.

"Oh, you work at—"

"Three to eleven-thirty every blesséd day of the week, except for the Day of Rest."

The Mormon, Elaine realized, remembering Warren's complaints. "So, you had had a sister who used to live in this apartment?"

Tanya frowned. "Warren's got a story to tell about every one of us, nothin' to do all day long but sit in his air-conditioned condo in Marina del Rey and cast judgment on his tenants. He say anything nasty about her?"

*Screaming babies and a dog barking all day and night.* They were Warren's words, but Elaine couldn't bring herself to repeat them to Tanya. "No," she said, "just that she used to live here."

"What about me, what'd he say?" Tanya twirled a blonde pigtail around her finger, waiting.

*A welfare-collecting grocery store clerk with four kids she doesn't exactly have a handle on.* "Just that you have four children," she said.

"You're just being nice," Tanya sniffed. "Give him two minutes he can cram in more dirty laundry than a Mexican and her cousins at the corner coin 'n wash."

Elaine smiled uncomfortably. Tanya nudged a pinky under her pigtail for a quick scratch. "Listen, I got two girls your daughters can play with, Sandi and Sue-Sue. I got two boys, too, Danny and Davy. There's other kids in the building, too, they're always out and about. Just tell them to keep their distance from Bridget."

"Bridget?"

"Yeah, you met Joan yet? Lives downstairs in number one, leans out her window smoking cigarettes? Joan's her foster mother. She's got two other kids, too, besides Bridget. Ned and Mim, from two different men, and she wasn't married to neither of 'em. I don't believe in casting judgment, but they're a sad bunch. You met any of 'em yet?"

Elaine recalled the little girl with the punch stains around her mouth. "Mim," she said. "She's made friends with my younger daughter."

"Well Mim you don't have to worry about. It's Bridget that's the problem. Now, I don't like to gossip, and I don't like to judge, neither. 'Judge not, and ye shall not be judged,' is how I look at things. So I'll just say this. Joan gets checks from the government for taking care of Bridget—if you call getting drunk on Bloody Marys in the middle of the day taking care of a kid. Bridget's ma abandoned her in a Von's parking lot in Del Mar when she was just a baby. Got kicked around from foster home to foster home until Joan took her in. Most nights Bridget sits on the fence by herself, singing all sorts of crazy songs. You get what I'm saying?"

Elaine nodded, though she wasn't sure what she was agreeing to. Abandoned in a parking lot as an infant? Kicked around from foster home to foster home? Bridget sounded like a poor, lost child. Which this gossiping woman didn't seem to understand.

* * *

That night, Hannah burrowed into her sleeping bag, curling up into a tight ball at the bottom. The air inside was warm and dense. It was pitch dark, except for the pinpoints of light through the zipper. I could stay here, she thought, and never come out. She listened to the electric crackling of the power lines through her open window. Closer, there was the sound of water—Daisy taking her nightly bubble bath, and her mother washing the dishes.

Hannah stayed inside her sleeping bag until the warmth became hot hot hot, and she had to poke her head out and gasp for air.

Gazing up at the ceiling, she blurred her eyes, making the stucco smooth. Back in focus, the clustered bumps re-emerged— haphazard, like sloppy Braille. Her eyes, she imagined, were her fingertips, like a blind girl's, feeling the ceiling for the message of this room with its thick smells, its mingling of hot paint and old carpet.

If her father were here, he would tell her what the message meant. He'd guide her fingertips over the bumps, testing her (*And what does this say?*), then whisper the answer in her ear if she didn't guess right.

The memory of him was so vivid she could feel the tickle of his breath in her ear, could smell the cocoa-buttery whiff of his scalp. But he seemed so distant, too. So unreal, as if he were someone else's father—as if his daughter were some other girl who had once lived in Spokane. When Hannah closed her eyes, she could see that girl spinning around and around in the living room, dancing while her father played the cello, or sitting on his lap in his study with a musty, leather-bound book while he drilled her on the names of planets and bones. The girl stuttered words that had no meaning, *Uranus, tarsus, patella*, wanting so much to please him. Sometimes her father was jokey and kind, wiggling his fingers an inch above her belly, saying *Creepy crawley spider*, like he might tickle any moment.

It was hard to believe that the girl had been her. That she'd lived in a house where she had her very own room. That she'd had a father who lavished his attention on her in his study, quizzing her, wanting her to be smart. Who would reach out and grab her mother as she laid a casserole on the dinner table, making her shriek with pleasure. He'd run a hand through her mother's hair, chuckling *The crazy mane of sweet Elaine*, his eyes softening. Her mother would dip her chin, embarrassed. *You silly,* she'd say, setting the casserole down.

Then there were memories of her father that didn't seem to fit. The times his eyes didn't match the rest of his face, his pupils narrowing to pinpricks of rage while he grinned. When he stopped wearing clothes because they were radioactive, saying that people were trying to poison him, and watched TV all day long, writing lists in his spiral notebook of all the W-words the people on TV said—*war, women, win, west, wage, want, watch, warning, Washington.*

The arguments started, then. He roared *Goddamnit Elaine*, while her mother winced at his door slams, soothed him with her sobby *Shhhh shhhhh, nonononos.* Hannah locked herself away from it all in the bathroom. Once, water trickled in from their bedroom, the waterbed razor-slashed. Later, she heard her mother's delicate rappings on the door (*Hannah? Fresh batch of date bars getting cold*), bribing her out of the bathroom when he was back in his study.

Some nights Hannah awoke to the sound of her mother's muffled crying. Hearing it took the breath out of her. A hush blanketed the house, silencing everyone except Daisy, just a baby then, with her screeching and gurgling. Instead of pot roasts and mustard chicken, they had warmed-up cans of soup or boiled hot dogs for dinner. Her mother always set a place for him at the table, just in case, but he never came out of the study. After dinner, her mother would cover his plate in Saran Wrap and set it on the bottom shelf of the refrigerator. And late at night, after they were all in bed, Hannah would hear the study door creaking open downstairs, followed by her father's heavy footsteps—would hear him walk into the kitchen, the refrigerator humming louder when he opened its door.

He was sick, her mother said. The doctors had given him pills that he refused to take. "It's not a sickness that you can see, honey, like a cough or the chicken pox," she explained, "it's in his head."

Hannah felt a trickle of sweat run down her thigh, but her legs felt too weak to kick off her sleeping bag. The air hung heavy in the room, felt too thick to breathe, like she was under water.

*Miss Mary Mack Mack Mack*
*All dressed in black black black*

It was Daisy, singing one of her hand-slap songs as she splashed around in the tub. Hannah closed her eyes, wondering what drowning felt like.

The other memory snuck in then. The day she got first place for the best science project in the class—"The Lengthening Days of Winter," it was called. Her father had come up with the idea, helping her make a graph of the shadows a dandelion cast on the sidewalk. After school she ran home, clutching the blue satin ribbon, slamming through the front door in a flurry of excitement.

Thinking *he'll be so proud*, making a beeline to his book-crammed study.

Opening the door.

Seeing him slumped over his desk, head to one side, his arm dangling down.

Seeing what little remained of his blown-off face: the stony glaze of an eye, the hideous splatter of blood.

And then after: hiding under her bed, huddling into a ball, hearing her mother's key in the front door, her mother's clip-clopping clogs on the wooden floor, then her mother's screams.

Now, lying in her sleeping bag, Hannah replayed the scene in her head, over and over again, until she had to blink it away.

But there was another, and another.

The uniforms: policemen in dark blue, paramedics in green. And later, people in black: relatives, friends, strangers at the wake in the living room, milling around with their styrofoam cups of coffee and crumbling slabs of banana bread on white cocktail napkins. Her mother pale and statuesque in her long black dress, with her wiry hair pulled back into a tight braid that snaked down her spine, jiggling Daisy on a raised hip.

Yes, Hannah remembered all the details now. The murmuring voices, the touch of her mother's hand, cold and dry. Remembered what she knew then—that her mother wasn't paying attention to any of the people, that she wanted them all to go away.

*Mommy! I'm done!*

Hannah heard Daisy's shouts, the wet slap of her feet on the bathroom floor. A hot breeze came through the open bedroom window, the crackling of the power lines sounding even louder. There was the *pat-pat* of her mother's advancing footsteps on the shag-carpeted hallway.

"All clean, sweetie?"

Then came that girl's voice again:

*Hot hot pussy's*
*What I want Lady Lynn*
*Hot hot pussy's*
*What I want lemme in—*

Hannah slid out of her sleeping bag. She crept up to the open window and looked down. It was dark outside but she could still make the girl out, straddling the chain-link, swinging her legs.

There were bells in her voice.

Her blonde scramble of hair looked like a nest—a rat's nest, her mother would call it. Hannah would perch herself there if she were a bird.

What grade was she in? Was she afraid of anything?

*Thomas*

Elaine crept out the front door once she was certain her daughters were asleep. Walking down the stairs, she made sure to step only on the toes of her clogs so they wouldn't slap down with a loud *clomp*.

The bar was dim and warm, an inviting cave. Soon, she would be face to face with her dead husband's brother, whom she'd never met. One hour, she decided, was all the time she had to spend with him; her daughters were safe at home, but she'd start to worry about them if she stayed too long.

She was aware of people milling around her, but she couldn't look for him yet. A few more moments was all she needed, just to breathe, breathe and surrender herself to this room and what it held for her. There was the murmur of voices, the dull gleam of lacquered wood, the clinking of glasses as the bartender rinsed them in his sink. A ruby glow there, there and there. They were candles, she realized, touching one: a delicate flame inside a globe of red glass. A whiff of lavender—she turned and saw the source: a flutter of pale silk receding into the room, earrings swinging. Another woman brushed past, a thick braid of silver resting on her naked collarbone. And a fireplace, of all things! Elaine held her hands over the fire, thinking *In the middle of summer!* Several feet above the creamy marble mantelpiece was a great oak-framed mirror, which held the shadowy reflections of the figures in the room. It was tilted down, giving the room an illusion of bigness: she could see the tops of people's heads, while at the same time she seemed to be standing below them. The confusion of perspective made her stomach tighten.

She rubbed her palms together and held them once more over the fire, hoping to warm the jitters out. Bright orange flames burned under the logs, licking the sides of the wood, and as she gazed into the fire she felt a thawing within. She heaved a grateful sigh, reflecting on how nice it was to take a break from things, even if all she was given was just this one small sliver of time. The warmth spreading through her body kindled her courage. This wouldn't be so bad, meeting Thomas.

One minute more, she decided, and then she would be ready to face him. She stood there rubbing her palms together, until it dawned on her that the flickering flames seemed mechanical, almost cold. Oh, what a featherhead she was, how foolish. The fire was electric.

Four carpeted steps led down to the sunken section of the bar, which featured low tables and wine-colored leather chairs studded with brass rivets. She made it down the first two steps, but that was as far as her legs would take her.

She saw him, sitting alone at a table in the far corner of the room. His back was turned; he was saying something to a cocktail waitress. She didn't need to see his face. Not even the telltale hair color, so blonde it looked almost white. His fingers were what gave him away: elbows rested on the armrests of the chair, his forearms hanging down, they were twitching ever so slightly.

Too stunned to take another step, she watched Thomas from afar. His fingers kept at it: playing, she knew, an invisible flute. For Roger, it was only his left hand—the cello was his instrument. And she was transported back to the hospital room in Spokane of all places, when she was holding Hannah, just hours old, a precious wrinkley red-faced bundle in her arms, and had just spotted Roger's hand thrumming on the starched white hospital sheet as he sat beside her. Maybe it was the hormones, or the fact that she was so young—just eighteen when Hannah was born—but she'd started to sob, saying that he didn't care about this beautiful pure moment, his mind was obviously on one of his concertos. Roger cleared his throat and insisted he did care, of course he did—he was merely going over a difficult fingering pattern, it was just something he did without thinking. Why the hell did she need one hundred percent of his attention one hundred percent of the time? He got up in a huff and she sobbed harder; it was always that way.

"Elaine—?"

Even the voice was Roger's. He stood up, straightened his gold-flecked tie. And there is the proud forehead, she thought, there the sharp carved jaw: the family resemblance was unnerving.

When she reached the table she thought: should I kiss his cheek, hug him, shake his hand? He offered an upturned palm for her to shake. Glad that the decision was made for her, she laid her hand in his. His fingers were surprisingly cold. "Thomas, hello," she said.

"Well, well," he replied.

They sat down in the padded leather chairs, which seemed to Elaine the most luxurious feature of the place, more suited to a living room than to a bar. She reached into her purse, then reconsidered and quickly withdrew her hand.

Now was not the time to show Roger's brother pictures of Hannah and Daisy. Thomas had never laid eyes on his nieces—thrusting them into his hands now might be too much too soon. Better to pace herself, wait until they'd gotten to know each other a little better. Then, once he saw the pictures—once he was reminded that there were other members of his family (*yes, given the circumstances, it's understandable that you'd pushed it out of your mind, Thomas, don't feel bad*)—she could discreetly ask him for the money that was rightfully theirs.

As an icebreaker, Elaine said, "This is a nice place."

"Yes, I just ran into it one day." He leaned back in his chair. "Literally. I was on my way home from work. I'd been up for thirty-two hours, and I was falling asleep at the wheel, it was a catastrophe. I had all the windows rolled down and I was chewing gum and drinking coffee at the same time. No use. Smacko—my fender and their front door. One way to make an entrance."

"Were you hurt?"

"My wallet was," he replied with a wry grin. "But me? Not a scratch. Lucked out."

The cocktail waitress returned with his drink. "And for you, ma'am?"

Elaine cleared her throat, caught off-guard. "Oh," she stalled, racking her brain. "Oh, anything is fine." The cocktail waitress arched a razor-thin eyebrow.

"I mean," she revised quickly, "whatever he's having."

Thomas looked amused. "A Scotch drinker?"

"Well no, but—but oh, why not," Elaine said.

The cocktail waitress nodded and sashayed to the bar. Thomas's eyes lingered on her before turning back to Elaine, his face beaming. "This place is famous for its waitresses," he said.

"It's a nice place," Elaine offered, not knowing what else to say. Then she hoped he hadn't heard her.

"I believe you already said that."

All she could do was smile.

When the cocktail waitress returned with her drink, Thomas said "On my tab" and waved her off.

"Well, thank—" Elaine began, but he waved off the rest of her sentence with the same hand. "No expression of gratitude necessary. This is a treat for me." In the brief silence that followed, Elaine looked down at her hands, stung with self-consciousness: he was studying her.

"So tell me, Elaine," he said finally. "Where are you from? I know it's a dull question, but we might as well start with the rudiments."

"From? Originally?"

"Yes yes, from," he said impatiently.

"Portsmouth, New Hampshire," she answered, "or just north of there. Salmon Creek. It's a little town."

He let out a sharp "Hah!" that made her flinch a little. "I was always curious about what kind of woman would marry my little brother."

"Well, here I am," she said, feeling foolish.

"Here you are, yes, here you are. You must have had to endure so much. What a lunatic he was," he sniffed.

She wanted desperately to change the subject; if she let herself think any more about Roger she'd lose her composure. "Roger never mentioned what you did," she said, forcing a brightness into her voice, "or do, I guess."

"Computer animation."

Elaine touched her chest, impressed. "Really?"

"No," he said.

He chuckled and leaned back luxuriously in his chair. "But if I could start all over again I think I'd enjoy sitting by myself doodling around with cartoons all day. That or be a priest. An itinerant priest, traveling alone, dispensing wisdom to the multitudes, offering counsel to wayward souls. No. Not a priest—people's problems are so boring. A profession that embraces solitude is what attracts me. Solitude, solipsism. Singularity. My soliloquy." He bowed his head. "But listening to soliloquies is just as boring as listening to people's problems, I suppose. I apologize, I get carried away. So he never mentioned anything?"

"Excuse me?"

"Nothing about a family business? Kierson and Sons? Or Kierson and *Son*, as it turned out. Not ringing any bells? Not a one?"

"I just thought," she explained, "that maybe you'd changed careers."

He fixed his piercing eyes on her. "Why would I do that? I have a responsibility to my family. Does that sound so unusual?"

"No-no, not-not really," she stuttered, unnerved by the aggression in his voice.

"I'm sorry, I just made up all that nonsense about bashing into this place with my car. You'll have to forgive my penchant for tall tales. I can't explain it, sometimes the opportunity is just so irresistible. What I mean to say is, when you made that comment about this place being so nice—the first time, that is—and I heard myself say 'I just ran into it one day' I just got a vision of bricks flying. I can't explain it. So as the wife—switching gears again—did you see it coming? Wait. Don't answer that, another dull question if there ever was one. Let me hazard a guess first. I would say…yes. Oh yes! The signs were there, the odd reclusiveness, the ennui. But you didn't know what to do, you felt helpless, no doubt, what with a toddler and a terminally unemployed husband. Who could you turn to? Not his family, of course, since you knew he despised us all and would exact some retribution if he found out you'd contacted us. You knew that this was not merely an existential angst, no, this was pathological, you realized at some point, some point when you took off your rose-tinted glasses. Speaking of glasses, do you know, the first year or so of high school he refused to wear his glasses? Did he ever tell you that? Did he?"

He wanted an answer from her. She didn't want his anger directed at her. All she could do was nod.

He took a satisfied gulp of his Scotch. "He liked the distance blurry, he claimed it helped him focus on what was right in front of him. There's irony there somewhere, I just don't feel like ferreting it out. A year later he was wearing his glasses again but had started to watch television nine hours a day with a notepad in his lap, counting the number of times someone said a certain word—"cash" or "coin" or "capital"—then six months or so later he abandoned the project for another. Lucid dreaming, I think it was. If he could control his dreams then he could control reality, I believe he shouted once at the dinner table when our father castigated him for his failing grades. Don't get me wrong, it's not as if Roger has occupied my every waking thought, of course, but on Christmas and other holidays whether you like it or not you think about your family. And when your little brother drops out of college after knocking up some naif— pardon me, I'm speculating, but I'd put money on it—and he moves to Spokane and hide nor hair is seen of him—not a goddamned word—you can't help but wonder. I won't deny it. I've wondered about him for years. So you can't imagine my glee when I received your telephone call. Here is my chance, I thought." He twiddled his fingers above his head devilishly. "To ask all the questions I'd been dying to ask. To get some insight on my brother, The Nutcase."

Elaine had stopped listening, and was in a kind of slumber, letting his words blend together so they wouldn't register anymore—but his twiddling fingers roused her.

Right then it came to her: Not the flute. The *clarinet*. Thomas plays the *clarinet*—it was one of the only things Roger had ever mentioned about his older brother, so deep was his contempt for him—for all his family, really. Thomas once whacked his clarinet against Roger's cello in an envious rage. Something about Roger getting into a youth orchestra Thomas was rejected from—she couldn't remember the details anymore, but she knew Thomas had hated Roger for his brother's superior musical talent.

"Your kids must be nutcases too," Thomas said dryly.

"Ex—Excuse me?"

"No offense, of course. Just an objective observation about genetic inheritance." He tossed back his head and shook the last drops of Scotch into his open mouth.

"I don't know what you're trying to do here, Thomas." She struggled to keep her voice steady, but a tremble was creeping in. "I don't know what you—why you want to do this to me, but I'd appreciate it if—"

"Hold that thought." He signaled the cocktail waitress for another drink. "I'm sorry, you were saying?"

"I was saying," she pressed on, furious now. "I was in the middle of saying that I'd appreciate it if you'd leave my girls out of this. They have nothing, absolutely nothing to do with—I mean they're good children, they've been through so much. I've done the best I could given the circumstances and I'm not saying that I'm not to blame for all they've been through but with no money—that's why I came, in fact. There must be something—"

"Something?" he snorted. "My father cut him out of the will when he turned his back on us. I'll tell you who's been through so much. My father. He had a heart attack, you know, when we heard about Roger's suicide."

"So that's why none of you came to the funeral?"

"Roger made that decision for us. Years before he pulled the trigger."

*That's no excuse,* Elaine wanted to say, but she restrained herself. She was, after all, asking the man for what she hoped would be a hefty check.

"I need the money for my children," she pleaded. "*Roger's* children. I have some savings, but it won't last through the summer. As soon as we get settled, I'm going to look for a job, but—"

"Roger broke my mother's heart," Thomas continued, ignoring her. "No, let me amend that. He broke her heart when he dropped out of school and ran off with you, without a word about where he'd gone. She knew he was a nutcase, but she was hoping he'd come to his senses sooner or later. In the proper environment, he could have amounted to something. He was a fine musician, you know."

Elaine felt suddenly protective of Roger, a feeling she didn't know she had for him anymore. She had grown so accustomed to the anger she felt toward him, which intensified into a panicked rage when he shot himself and left her alone with two young children to raise.

Looking down, she saw that her drink was untouched. She sipped it once, just so Thomas couldn't accuse her of being rude.

Then she said "Excuse me," and walked out of the bar.

On the drive home, she pressed her palm against her mouth and cried into it, steering with her left hand, letting the sobs out only when she had to shift gears. She was never good at fending off people's cruelty, Roger once told her. But then he'd been cruel too. Hammering into her the same way Thomas just had; tuning it out was her only defense. She felt a surprising, fresh surge of anger at her dead husband for putting her through this.

Then it faded. *Roger, Roger.*

"Ooo!" her mother said, and she slammed on the brakes so fast Hannah's seatbelt took the wind out of her. Her mother was always on the lookout for yard sale signs, wherever they went. This one was hammered into a splintered telephone pole at the corner intersection, a lone square of white cardboard with brisk writing, all capitals. The eye-level area of the pole was studded with hundreds of bent rusty nails; many signs had been posted here. Hannah read the address out loud while her mother lunged over her for the map book in the glove compartment and flipped through the index, murmuring the street name over and over until it sounded strange to Hannah, *Fir Fir Fir Fir Fir Fir*. The telephone pole, with its rusty nails, looked to Hannah like a sad old porcupine.

"Fir Street, found it," her mother said.

As they drove, the neighborhood transformed. The street narrowed, and cars parked along the curb became newer, shinier. Saplings with tentative trunks sprouted up. Apartment buildings gave way to bungalows with red-tiled roofs and lawns. Oncoming cars hummed past with glinting windshields, as if each possessed its own sliver of the sun.

Her mother rolled down the window. She steadied the steering wheel with her knees and crawled her fingers down her braid, loosening her hair. Long, frizzy strands streamed out the window. She let her arm dangle out and mused aloud about the future, about the restaurant in California that maybe one day she could be part-owner of.

"Smell, Hannah. The ocean."

Hannah unrolled her window. A thick rush of wind. They drove in silence, heaving in the salty air through their noses, their hair flying.

The yellow light ahead turned red. They screeched to a halt, and the rushing in Hannah's ears stopped. A woman in sunglasses and shorts appeared at the curb. She marched across the street, followed by a line of girls wearing brown caps and brown dresses.

"Brownies," her mother said, dreamily stroking her throat. "Once upon a time that was me in one of those uniforms."

As the Brownies marched past, Hannah looked for the girl her mother would have been. She studied the line leader, who chewed a gob of gum in time with her steps. There was a fearlessness in the girl's eyes—no, Hannah thought, my mother wouldn't have been her. Next came a girl with a cloud of frizzy hair, violently swinging her arms—no, not her either, even though her mother had the same hair. Three girls all wearing ribbon-threaded braids followed, a frail girl with milky skin and large eyes among them. And there were still more Brownies coming: a shy girl with knobby knees, a girl singing *Make new friends, but keep the old, something-something-something-other's gold*, a wide-mouthed, waddling girl who reminded Hannah of a duck, the two tiny redheads—sisters, maybe even twins, a girl with a sharp chin and long sheets of blonde hair who Hannah decided was stuck-up, and the last, wearing blue bobby socks, blowing out her cheeks. Hannah thought of the old picture her mother had once showed her. In it, her mother was a little girl, sitting on a porch swing with *her* mother. The frail girl with the large eyes, Hannah concluded—*that* was her mother in the picture. She scanned the line of Brownies, looking for the little girl's ribboned braids, but the girl was already gone, marching down the block, lost among the brown caps bobbing up and down.

A white car behind them honked.

Her mother struggled with the gearshift. There was a bracing metal sound: the violent unzipping of something. The car shuddered.

"Comeon-comeon-comeon-comeon," her mother said.

Their car lurched forward and stalled just as the white car swerved around to the lane beside them, the driver a shadow behind smoked windows. It let out an angry, drawn-out honk as it zoomed ahead.

Her mother cupped her hand over her mouth. There was a line of honking cars behind her now. A man poked his head out his sunroof.

"Come on lady move-move!"

"Mom?" Hannah said.

Her mother nodded, face reddening. When she took her hand away, her lips were pressed together, and Hannah wondered if her mother were about to cry. Honking cars streaked past in the lane beside them, making their stalled car shake.

"Mom? Are we going to go?"

"Yes," she said. But she didn't make a move to press the gas pedal. Instead, she touched Hannah's cheek. "From now on we're going to be all right, honey, okay? I promise."

"People are honking," Hannah pleaded.

"Okay," her mother said at last. She turned the ignition key and the car lurched forward. They drove on, the car clacking every time it shifted gears.

And then they saw it, up ahead, a line of blue, shimmering in the sun. The ocean. The air was so light, you could fill your mouth with it, crunch it like a salty wafer.

"Fir! Fir!" Hannah shouted.

"Good, now addresses," her mother said, turning onto Fir Street. The car slowed down to a crawl.

"Ooo, chi-chi," her mother said, admiring the houses.

Hannah leaned out the window. Trees with peeling bark and great leafy branches lined the sidewalk. The numbers by the doors were all different styles, black pewter curlicues, gleaming brass, some hand-painted on cozy wooden plaques and decorated with little flower petals. Hannah tilted her head back and closed her eyes. The sun took turns with the trees on her face, bright warmth then sudden cold splashes.

"Addresses, Hannah."

"I'm *looking*," Hannah insisted, quickly opening her eyes. "1378, 1382, 1389, 1393…"

"Good, we need 1401. Almost there!"

They parked in the shade of a tree, several houses down from the yard sale. Her mother yanked up the emergency brake and slammed the car door; yard sales made her so excited, her every move quickened.

Hannah stumbled out of the car and ran down the sidewalk to catch up with her.

A woman in a string bikini top and bright white shorts squatted on a small lawn, folding a pair of jeans. The front of the house was ablaze with rich, crackling reds and yellows from a crawling bougainvillaea.

"Hello," her mother said.

The woman looked up and gave her a toothy, languid smile, mouthing "Hi," although no sound came out. The woman returned to her task, arranging the folded jeans on a sheet that displayed neat stacks of clothes separated by category, T-shirts, long-sleeved shirts, shorts, pants. A small chrome garment rack on wheels displayed blouses and dresses. She stood up and stretched her head back until her spine formed an elongated arch. Her shoulder blades glistened with suntan oil. "Gorgeous day, right?" she said.

"Mmm," said her mother, running her palm along the top of a dark wooden dresser. She wanted it—Hannah could tell by her mother's frown. Frowning was her way of getting a better price.

A collection of small glass bottles caught Hannah's attention. She looked underneath a slender, ridged one for the price tag. One dollar. She had thirty-five cents in her pocket. Hannah picked up another bottle, then a smaller one, and grimaced: all the bottles were the same price. She knew she couldn't talk the price down like her mother could. Her mother always bargained at yard sales, a tactic that both embarrassed and impressed Hannah. Once her mother assembled a pile of things she wanted, she'd approach the yard sale woman with a coy smile, and Hannah would watch the shrewd charmer in her negotiate a package deal—her mother's secret self that only surfaced, it seemed, at yard sales.

Hannah set the bottles down, and resolved to slip one into her mother's pile right before the bargaining started.

"You like those?"

Startled, Hannah looked up and saw the woman approaching, tightening the bikini top strings around her neck.

"They're empty perfume bottles, aren't they sweet? You can still smell the perfume." She unscrewed the top, a thin shard of glass, and held it to Hannah's nose. Her hands were tanned and oily.

Hannah flinched, confronted with the sudden intimacy of the woman's fingers nearly touching her mouth.

"Smell," the woman urged.

Hannah inhaled, although she couldn't detect anything except a stench of coconut and sweat as the woman drew her arm away.

Her mother had a pile by her feet already—cereal bowls, a milky blue tablecloth, and an assortment of pans. Head tilted back to one side, her mother examined the jeans the woman had been folding earlier. In a moment, Hannah knew, she would do her trick to see if they'd fit.

"You want to try them on in the bathroom? I always rip the tag out—I think they're size eight."

"Oh, no need to go to any trouble," her mother replied. She shoved her elbow into one side of the waistband and brought down her forearm so her knuckles touched the other side. "Perfect," she said.

She tossed the jeans into the pile. Hannah slipped the perfume bottle underneath, but she wasn't fast enough.

"Honey," her mother said. "No."

"It's only a dollar," Hannah begged.

"We can find used bottles by the dumpster for free. Put it back."

Hannah groaned, turned away. Her mother pointed to a sewing machine. "Excuse me, does that work?"

"My mother used it right up until the day she died," said the woman. "It's just been sitting in the garage."

"You know *my* mother, before she passed away, she sewed all the time, too. I didn't have a single store-bought piece of clothing until I went to college. Well jeans, I guess. Jeans she bought me. She even made my prom dress. From a Vogue pattern—those are the hardest, all those darts and pleats."

Hannah wandered to the edge of the curb and leaned against a tree. Yard sales made her mother tell strangers long stories. Her mother was warming up, she knew, for the bargaining that was coming next. She dug her fingernails under a thin curl of bark and stripped it off, listening.

"I'll tell you another funny little story. I used to lie in the bathtub in cold water with my jeans on, so when they dried they'd be extra tight around the rear end. One time they were on so tight the zipper got stuck and my mother had to cut them off. Was she furious! When she found out I was planning on wearing them out on a date with a boy, she made me say twenty

Hail Marys and fifteen Our Fathers."

The woman was smiling, but she looked bored.

"Well, anyway," said her mother, looking down at the pile at her feet. She knotted her hair in a bun, using a pencil to keep it in place. "So. How about twenty and we call it even?"

"Twenty dollars? For what now?"

"That's thirteen for the sewing machine, two for the card table, for the bowls and pans, oh, another three let's say, that makes seventeen, then this old tablecloth and jeans, fifty cents each, so we're at nineteen"—and here she handed the woman a ten and a five and counted out the singles—"one, two, three, four and I'll throw in one more for good measure, that makes twenty."

"Those jeans are Jordache. I paid seventy dollars for them— I can't sell them to you for fifty cents."

Her mother's eyebrows shot up. "*Seventy* dollars?"

"And the tablecloth is one hundred percent linen. The prices are marked—the sewing machine alone is twenty dollars."

"Really, you can't even make buttonholes with a machine that old. Thirteen dollars, I think, is a fair price."

"It's an antique," the woman protested.

"A Singer from the fifties is not antique, it's just broken-down. Fourteen dollars."

"Can you do seventeen?"

"It's rusty by the bobbin and the pedal looks like it sticks. Fifteen. For something that's just sitting around the garage gathering dust, I'd say fifteen is a bargain."

"Okay, fine," the woman sighed. "Fifteen."

"Good. I'll use it to sew up the rip in this tablecloth—linen it may be, but it's still damaged. How about a dollar twenty-five?" She snapped the tablecloth open on the lawn. "There's a stain there at the right corner, see? See the brown splotch there?"

"That's a shadow."

"No, no, it looks like coffee to me."

"I don't drink coffee."

"Tea, then." Holding up the tablecloth, she studied the stain.

"Are we going to do this on everything?" the woman said wearily, leaning against the porch railing.

"A dollar fifty, that's all I can spend on a stained, ripped tablecloth."

Strands of hair had escaped from her mother's bun and settled in the corners of her mouth. She wiped them away. "Now, where were we? Fifteen and a dollar fifty for the tablecloth, that makes sixteen fifty. The bowls, you've got them marked at five dollars, one's chipped, and this one's got a hairline crack at the base, I'll give you two dollars. These saucepans don't have lids, you have them marked at three dollars apiece, I can give you one seventy-five each, let's call it three for both pans. I really can't pay more than a dollar fifty for a pair of used jeans, I don't care what the designer label says—"

Hannah couldn't help but marvel: this fierce fast-talker was her mother.

"—so that's what? Sixteen fifty plus two plus three plus a dollar fifty, which makes twenty-three."

Hannah stripped off a last piece of bark, then walked to her mother, who was already counting the money into the woman's hand.

In the parking lot, her mother opened the hatchback and unloaded the loot: a card table, ceramic bowls, the milky blue tablecloth, pans, jeans, and finally, the yard sale woman's dead mother's sewing machine. She had spent more than she wanted to and was upset, Hannah could tell, from the way she clunked everything down on the asphalt.

"I'll have to make curtains from this tablecloth," her mother said, wrapping it around the sewing machine. "The living room windows need them." Hannah grabbed the ceramic bowls.

"Wait, Hannah, let me load you up."

"I'll come back," she called out, but it was too late; her

mother was at her heels with a stack of pans.

"This way we won't have to make too many trips. Let's put these inside the pans." Her mother took the bowls from her. Hannah waited, feeling her face heat with an onrush of blood, knowing already what her mother had discovered.

"Hannah?"

She looked up. Her mother was wiggling the perfume bottle between her forefinger and thumb. "Didn't I tell you to put this back?"

"Yes."

"Didn't I?"

"Yes," Hannah repeated, softer.

"Then can you explain how it got here?"

"It was when you turned around," Hannah invented quickly. "The woman winked at me, like it was a secret."

After a tense moment, her mother said, "Well," and handed her the stack of pans and bowls, carefully laying the perfume bottle inside the top bowl. "That was nice of her. I guess she took pity on you, stuck with such a penny-pincher for a mother." She chuckled, smoothing the hair out of Hannah's eyes.

Hannah steadied herself against a dull, sickening weight, not just from the stack of pans and bowls, but from something more, something that bore down with her every blink. How easily she had deceived her mother. She didn't want the bottle, suddenly.

"My gawd, what's all this?" Tanya exclaimed, as Hannah handed her a plate of deviled eggs.

The eggs were arranged in concentric circles, topped with alternating sprinkles of paprika and chopped pickles and perfect little dollops of mayonnaise. At the last minute, Hannah's mother had let her put the sprigs of parsley on the sides of the plate. Even though it was Hannah's only contribution, she felt a swell of pride.

"You all shouldn't have gone to the trouble," Tanya scolded, picking up a deviled egg. She nibbled the edge. "Mmm, but I'm glad you did."

Tanya had curled the ends of her pigtails for the occasion. A white fringe ran along the plunging neckline of her blouse, forming a large V, and her skirt was hitched high enough that Hannah could see the jiggling of her thighs.

"Alma, try one of these, they're deelish."

A woman wearing a drapey dress and smelling of incense took a deviled egg from the plate. She gave Hannah a serene, sleepy smile. "I live in apartment two. You girls are sisters, I bet."

Daisy shyly edged behind Hannah. "Where'd Mommy go?" she murmured.

"Don't worry, honey," Tanya said. "She's over by the stereo, meeting the other neighbors. Alma's got a little boy, Trevor, I'll introduce you soon as I can catch him. Whoa, there, Sue-Sue." She tugged the back of a girl's T-shirt, dragging her back. She wore pigtails, too—like Tanya, Hannah saw, although her hair was stringy and brown, the color of the top inch of Tanya's bleached hair.

"Set these next to the cheese wieners," Tanya said, giving Sue-Sue the plate of deviled eggs. "Wait a sec. Meet Hannah and Daisy here before you run off."

Sue-Sue mumbled her hello. Then walked away with the plate, reaching behind to yank at her underwear with her free hand.

"That's one of my daughters," Tanya explained, "don't mind her manners. You'll meet my other kids soon enough, they're around here somewhere. Sandi, Davy, and Danny, they're good kids, you'll all get along." She turned toward the kitchen, a quick little twirl that made the fringe on her blouse fan out, then sway back and forth. "Now. Let's get you two something cool to drink."

In the kitchen, Tanya poured out two cups of cherry soda.

"I have to peeeee," Daisy cried.

She always has to pee, Hannah thought irritably. Tanya caught her eye and gave her a wink. "Make yourself at home, honey. I'm gonna go show Daisy here where the facilities are."

Hannah looked around at the room of adults, wondering what to do next. She spotted the deviled eggs next to the other snacks on top of a huge TV set with a crack running across the screen. The only man there was a skinny old black man standing by the TV, eating potato chips. Her mother was dancing with some of the other mothers to the country music on the radio, two women forming a bridge with their hands so others could pass under. A small boy ran past clutching a bag of barbecue corn nuts, his lips powdered with bright orange dust, and disappeared into a bedroom in back. The other kids, she figured, were in there too, hiding from the adults. But she didn't dare follow him. Instead, she made her way to the TV and ate most of the cheese wieners until the skinny old black man cleared his throat. Retreating, she plunked down on a plastic-covered armchair and drank her cherry soda down to the ice cubes.

Someone was pounding at the front door. Tanya yelled, "Come in!" but the pounding continued. The dancing mothers ignored the noise, forming a circle now, clapping as one of them twirled around in the center and snapped her fingers.

Hannah, glad to have something to do, leaped up from the chair and opened the door. When she saw who it was, she felt her throat catch.

"About time, Jesus! Fifteen minutes I've been knocking."

It was *her* again—the witch woman with the horsey nostrils, her long fingernails looking like the claws of a menacing bird. Her hair wasn't like Farrah Fawcett's like before, but short and black. Beside her stood Mim, bare stomach sticking out from under a T-shirt, eyes fixed on her dirty toenails.

Hannah inched herself behind the door, trying to hide. The woman didn't even give her a glance—she was scanning the room, searching for something, and when she scratched at her temple her whole head of hair moved. A wig, Hannah realized, shrinking back further.

"Hey! Anyone seen Bridget?"

The talking died down, making the music suddenly sound louder. The women stopped dancing.

"Let me check with my daughters, Joan," Tanya said. "Hang on." She turned away, fringe swishing, and disappeared into a room in back.

Joan. Joan. Hannah repeated the name, surprised that it sounded so normal. She had expected a witch name. But who was Bridget? She had seen all the girls in the building, except for one. The girl on the fence. That was her, Hannah realized. *Bridget.*

A moment later Sue-Sue emerged from a bedroom, followed by a slightly older version of her with bangs feathered at the side, stiff with hairspray. She wore a white long-sleeved T-shirt with a faded rainbow that stretched across the front and onto the sleeves.

Tanya looked at the rainbow-shirt girl. "Sandi, where's Bridget? Joan here is looking for her."

"Don't ask me, Mom."

"Aw, cut it out," Joan snapped. "I saw you and Sue-Sue with her an hour ago. Said you were going to Jan 'n Joe's."

Sandi coolly lifted her chin. "Last time I saw Bridget was when we left Jan 'n Joe's. We went one way and she went the other. I don't know where."

"She was running real fast," Sue-Sue cut in, "so we couldn't see where."

Sandi stomped on her younger sister's toe. Sue-Sue drew in a sharp breath, reddening.

Joan eyed the two of them. "You girls better hope a cop doesn't show up at my door with her tonight." Then she pointed her cigarette at Tanya. "And you better wake up or go back to Utah, sweetie. I hope you realize you're raising a couple of Mormon candy bar thieves."

Late that night, a steady clanging woke Hannah. She lay perfectly still in her sleeping bag in the dark, listening. The noise stopped. She waited for it to begin again, but there was nothing, just the grumbling of a passing bus. She slid out of her sleeping bag and tiptoed past Daisy, who was snoring softly, to the open window.

In the darkness, she saw Bridget. Sitting on the chain-link fence again, banging her heels against the metal fencepost. The fence rippled with each kick.

Then she realized that Bridget was looking straight up. At her.

"Hey," Bridget said. "C'mere!"

Hannah stood there, frozen, staring back. A shy flush

prickled her cheeks. Bridget was waiting for her to say something, do something. Could she just go outside? Now, in practically the middle of the night?

Bridget kicked her heels against the fencepost. "Come on!"

Hannah took one step back from the window, then another.

A thin sliver of light showed through the crack underneath her mother's bedroom door. She tiptoed past the door into the living room, and gently shut the front door behind her.

*Bridget*

Downstairs, ink black out, they were waiting for her, peeking: Bridget's wild eyes. Without a word, she reached for Hannah's hand—her skin dry and scratchy, nails gnawed down to the quick.

Holding hands now, she led Hannah to the garden out front, where the ice plants and dandelions grew under the telephone cables, crackling louder the closer they came. "Earthquakes can make them snap," Bridget whispered, "turn them into wild electric snakes that will burn you alive." She laughed. "You scared?"

Then the laugh again. A raspy *Haaaaaaaw*, followed by giggles that sounded like hiccups, Bridget's mouth opening so wide Hannah worried her chapped lips might bleed.

"No, I'm not scared," Hannah whispered, even though every inch of her was trembling.

Bridget stepped over the low stone wall encircling the garden and with a sideways jerk of her head motioned for Hannah to follow. The dirt was packed solid and felt damp through Hannah's socks; she hadn't bothered with shoes. In the faint glow of the streetlight, the ice plants, here and there in cabbagey clusters, looked other-worldly, plump green fingers waiting to grab your toes. But Bridget didn't seem to notice, crunching down on them in the black cloth shoes she called her Jap-Slaps as she made her way to the other side.

Seven tiptoes it took Hannah to catch up; Bridget was waiting in front of the chewed-up old cactus. She squinted. "What about graveyards—you scared of them?"

Hannah shook her head, feeling braver now.

"Good," Bridget said, "'cause you're standing in one. *Haaaaaaaw!*"

A chill knifed up Hannah's spine as Bridget let loose more of her hiccupy giggles. A scratchy hand touched Hannah's shoulder. She jumped. Then she realized it was Bridget's.

"Don't look so spooked, you dope. It's just a graveyard for my broken-necked guinea pig." Bridget jutted her chin at a small circle of rocks at their feet. "That's the grave right there. Wait— I gotta fix something."

Bridget knelt down. With her pinky, she nudged forward a rock that had been kicked aside, perfecting the circle. Then she wiggled her pinky at a dandelion. "Hey, pick that there."

Hannah obeyed, reaching for the dandelion. She pulled, bringing up a dark clod of little roots. Too hard.

"Hey wait a sec, watch me," Bridget said.

She jumped up and performed a spasmodic dance, jiggling her hips and shimmying her shoulders and finishing it off with a slow tongue-glide over her lips. She thrust her flat chest out. "Mmmmm, I'm gonna have the *big*gest boobs of *every*one one day."

Hannah clapped a few times, not knowing what else to do. She held up the dandelion with its hairy roots. "You still want this?"

Bridget snatched it from her and, kneeling down, placed it in the center of the circle of stones. "What was its name?" Hannah asked, squatting next to her. "Your dead guinea pig."

"Porky," Bridget answered. "Like the pig, not the movie. You seen it? *Porky's*?" She kissed the ground, then wiped the dirt from her lips with the back of her hand. "Poor Porky. At midnight, you can see the ghost. Hide behind the dumpster, spin around three times backward."

"When did you bury him?"

"Her," Bridget corrected. "A while ago. Sandi was the only one who was supposed to know. We put my mom's bracelet, real gold, around Porky's neck for good luck and so all the other dead animals would be jealous. But then like a week later I saw that the ground was all dug up and the bracelet was gone."

Hannah shuddered, picturing a guinea pig skeleton. "Sandi stole it?"

"No, Sandi's too chicken, you shoulda seen her that night, all freaked that we were gonna see Porky's ghost. It was Danny or Davy, I bet you a million bucks. That girl's a fuckin' loudmouth."

"I have a turtle," Hannah offered.

"Yeah? Whatddya call it?"

"Turtle."

Bridget rolled her eyes, and Hannah felt her face redden. Why hadn't she named it?

Bridget showed her a mashed pack of Virginia Slims in her shorts pocket and raised her eyebrows.

Hannah said she had never smoked before, and Bridget laughed so hard Hannah saw the pink splits in her chapped lips. When Bridget recovered, she said Hannah could be the Lookout. All she had to do was knock against the cabinets three times if anything was suspicious.

Bridget led Hannah along the chain-link fence to the parking lot in back, and showed her a row of storage cabinets high up, right underneath the building's overhang. There were three cabinets in all, the wood painted black, splintered at the edges. Except for the last one with the rusty padlock, Bridget told her, they were empty. The padlocked cabinet was Mrs. Grover's in number three, an old lady who put old newspapers inside it.

Bridget showed Hannah how to give her a boost, lacing her

fingers together to make a step. Hannah bent her knees, staring up at the dim speckled bulb dangling from the ceiling, and waited to bear Bridget's weight.

But Bridget, stepping onto Hannah's laced fingers with her muddy Jap-Slaps, was light as a bundle of sticks—her skin like bark, a twiggy calf rough against the inside of Hannah's arm.

"Eenie Meenie Des Aleenie," Bridget called out.

"Oo Ah Oo Ah Maleenie," came a voice from inside.

A cabinet door swung open, revealing Sandi and Sue-Sue hunched in there, wearing matching pink nightgowns, the air thick with smoke. Sandi grabbed Bridget's wrists and pulled her in, Bridget's legs bicycling the air until she got a foothold.

It was Bridget's secret hiding place. In the corner, Hannah could see, she had stashed a mountain of candy.

Bridget covered her legs with a nubby Mexican blanket and Sandi lit her cigarette, going through four matches before she got it right. Bridget sucked in, making her cheeks go hollow, then tipped her head back and blew the smoke out her puckered lips.

Sue-Sue nudged Bridget. "Hey hey, shut the door."

"In a sec." Bridget readjusted herself in the small space, ignoring Sandi's groaning, so her legs could dangle out.

Hannah rubbed her hands on her pajamas to get the mud from Bridget's Jap-Slaps off. Her feet felt damp and filthy; sharp pebbles from the garden had painfully lodged into the bottoms of her socks.

"Okay listen, listen up," Bridget said, and wiggled her hand to get Hannah's attention, ash landing on Hannah's forehead as she looked up.

"Listen up, I got"—and here Bridget took a huge breath and rolled her eyes up to the ceiling—"Butterfingers, Snickers, Red Vines, Milky Ways, Charleston Chews, M&M's—no nuts—Pop Rocks, Baby Ruths, Hersheys, Chunkys, Carmellos, Peppermint Patties, Nerds, Lemonheads, SweetTarts, Red-Hots, and for gum there's Hubba Bubba and Big League Chew and Fruit Stripe."

She checked the pile. "Oh and also Reeses, the crunchy kind only since pigface Sandi ate the smoothies, and some Hundred Thousand Dollar bars. You hungry?"

"Pop Rocks," Hannah said.

"Grape or cherry?"

"Grape."

"Catch." The small red packet hit Hannah's shoulder and fell to the ground. Embarrassed, Hannah bent down to pick it up.

Sandi leaned her head out, a cigarette in one hand and a half-eaten Hershey bar in the other. "Good going, klutz," she sneered.

"You should talk," Bridget said. "You're a fuckin' spaz."

Sandi's eyes flashed, but she said nothing back.

"Hey you, new girl, lookit," Sandi snapped, "here's the signal in case someone comes." With the Hershey hand, she rapped her knuckles three times on the cabinet door.

Sue-Sue's head appeared. "Even if you just hear footsteps, okay?"

"Tch," Sandi said, with a toss of her head. She ran a hand through her feathered bangs, then slammed the door shut.

Hannah listened to the lonely sputter of the automatic sprinklers on the playground grass. At the far end stood the school, looking strange and empty with its two doorless hallways, dark and open like mouths. That is my new school, she thought.

There were rules for everything, Hannah soon learned. First one to say "Shee Shee Wa Wa" gets to start hopscotch. Last one to touch the stop sign has to ring the doorbell if you're playing Ding Dong Ditch. Three quick, soft whistles at the Jan 'n Joe's candy display means that the tan old man behind the counter has turned his back and you could slip a candy bar into your pocket. If you hit someone, yelling "Slap Slap No Tag Backs" gives you an automatic force field, so they can't hit back.

Bridget taught her how to climb the chain-link fence: stick one foot in a hole in the chain-link, then push up and stick the other foot in another hole. When you reach the top, you swing your leg around so you're facing the other side, then jump down onto the playground grass.

Bridget could climb the fence in five seconds flat. Hannah practiced and practiced, trying to swing her leg around without her arms trembling. You weren't supposed to think about what could happen if you lost your balance at the top of the fence, but Hannah couldn't help it, imagining herself falling backwards, feeling the smack of the cement pathway on the back of her skull.

"Don't be such a chicken," Bridget said. "Pretend there's pillows everywhere."

Little by little, Hannah learned, and soon she could climb

the fence almost as fast as Bridget, her arms trembling only the tiniest bit.

One afternoon Bridget led Hannah to the empty lot across the street, where you could pick honeysuckle flowers. There was a chain-link fence around the lot, just like the one around the school, only it was wobbly and the metal was thinner, so it was harder to climb.

"Here's the shortcut," Bridget said, pointing to a long slit in the fence. "Mrs. Grover in number three told Danny to make a hole with wire-cutters."

"Why?" Hannah asked, climbing through the slit.

"So she could feed the cats. Mrs. Grover feeds them every morning. Hey look!"

A mangy gray cat shot past, jumping onto a trashcan turned over on its side. Hannah waded through the waist-high weeds, past piles of old torn tires and splintered wood planks, counting the flashes of fur and tips of tails. Ten cats, at least, made the scrappy lot their home.

"Let's catch one." Bridget lunged toward a kitten with white paws. But the kitten was too quick, and scrambled off the trashcan.

Bridget ran after another one, a fat black cat the size of a small dog. Yelping happily, she chased the cat through the weeds, leaping over tires, beer bottles, heaps of garbage. When she reached a cemented area, her hand got hold of its tail, but the cat slipped out of her grip. Bridget lost her balance and fell forward, landing smack on her knees. She rolled over on her back and clenched her teeth in pain.

"You okay?" Hannah ran to her. On the cement, there was broken glass everywhere. Bridget's knees had bloody dirt-caked scrape marks, little glinting shards stuck into her skin.

*Haaaaaw!* Bridget laughed, her face breaking into one of her wide grins.

Before Hannah could get a word out, Bridget leaped up and grabbed her hand. "Hey, lemme show you something."

The weeds scratched at Hannah's calves as she stumbled after Bridget. They ran until they reached the back of the lot, where the wild honeysuckle grew, tangled and twisted, on the chain-link fence.

Bridget told her you could taste the secret juice if you did it right. She demonstrated how to nip the bottom of the yellowish flower and pull out the silky green string until a single drop emerged. One day, she promised, they would fill an entire jar with honeysuckle juice.

*An entire jar!* Hannah marveled.

Late that night, Hannah crept down the stairs in her pajamas and met Bridget in the parking lot as planned. Sandi and Sue-Sue were there in their pink nightgowns, and Hannah was the Lookout again while they smoked Virginia Slims in the storage cabinets.

"Don't forget," Sandi ordered, "knock three times if you hear anything suspicious."

"I know," Hannah said.

"She remembers, she's not stupid," Bridget said. "Like you."

Sandi lifted her chin. "Shut up, I ain't stupid."

"Quit pushing!" Sue-Sue said, and slammed the cabinet door shut.

Hannah leaned against the VW bug and waited, alert to every noise. Near the laundry room, she heard a low rumbling, then a scratching sound. Just the dryer, she realized, someone's zipper or button or something scraping the metal inside.

The cabinet door swung open, letting out a cloud of smoke, and Bridget jumped down, followed by Sandi and Sue-Sue.

"Hey, hang on," Bridget said. "Don't go back yet. I got a secret." She huddled them all together. "I'm running away," she said in a low voice, her eyes gleaming.

"*Really?*" Sandi said, impressed.

Hannah felt her throat clench up. "When?"

"Right before school starts." She produced a safety pin. "Here's to make sure nobody tells." She stabbed at the tip of her forefinger with a safety pin until it oozed red, then passed the safety pin to Sandi.

Sandi pricked her finger, and they solemnly pressed their bloody fingertips together. Then Sue-Sue did it.

It was Hannah's turn now. Everything was happening too fast. *Don't run away, don't leave,* she wanted to say.

"Go on," Bridget said.

"What's your problem, Hannah?" Sandi snapped. "We don't have all day."

"Shut up, fuckin' loudmouth," Bridget said, glaring at her. Sue-Sue giggled. Sandi elbowed her younger sister in the ribs, which only made Sue-Sue laugh harder.

"Quit it," said Sandi and Sue-Sue said, "*You* quit it."

While they squabbled, Hannah felt Bridget's hot breath in her ear, smelling faintly of licorice. "Be my blood sister," she whispered. "Please?"

Hannah drove the safety pin into her fingertip. The pain was sharp, and tears came to her eyes. She pressed her fingertip against Bridget's and watched their blood mix into one glistening red smear.

"Good. We're all blood sisters now," Bridget said. "Now nobody tells."

"Eenie Meenie Des Aleenie," whispered Sue-Sue and Sandi, in unison.

"Oo Ah Oo Ah Maleenie," whispered Bridget.

\* \* \*

The next day, Bridget's kneecaps were lumpy with reddish-brown scabs where she'd fallen on the broken glass. She wore corduroy shorts and showed her knees to the rest of the kids in the building, proud of her injuries. The skin on Bridget's legs was strangely scaly and white, like the skin on her hands.

*What's wrong?* Hannah was about to ask, but stopped herself. She didn't want to hurt Bridget's feelings. Bridget's arms had that same scaly white skin. And her neck.

Bridget saw her staring. "I've got a skin thing. It's called a condition."

"Does it hurt?"

Bridget shook her head. "It's just that my skin's real dry. When I scratch, I can make marks that stay white a long time. I can write my name on my leg with my fingernail and you can still read it five minutes later."

Hannah resolved to find a cure. If she could make Bridget's skin better, she decided, then maybe Bridget would change her mind about running away.

After dinner, she snuck her mother's Keri lotion from the bathroom and ran down the stairs. She found Bridget perched on top of the chain-link fence, kicking her heels against the fencepost.

Hannah explained her idea for a cure, stumbling over the words she was so excited. She squirted half the bottle of lotion on Bridget's shins. Then she took off her knee-socks and gave them to Bridget. "Don't take these off until tomorrow morning," she instructed, helping Bridget tug on the socks. "This way your skin will soak."

At the crack of dawn, Hannah was awakened by a pattering sound on the half-open bedroom window. Looking down, she saw Bridget, still in her pajamas, with a handful of pebbles.

"Time to see!" Bridget called out. She lifted her leg to show Hannah that the knee-socks were still on.

"Meet you downstairs," Hannah said in a loud whisper.

Daisy, awake now, sat up. "What are you doing?"

"Shhh! Don't wake Mom."

"I'm telling."

Hannah realized that she would have to strike a bargain with her sister. "Okay, you can come, too."

Daisy scrambled out of her sleeping bag. Together, they tiptoed in their bare feet out the front door, still wearing their nightgowns.

The morning air was crisp and sweet-smelling, carrying a faint whiff of citrus. Bridget was waiting at the bottom of the stairs. Hannah hoped she wouldn't be mad that Daisy had come along, but Bridget was so excited she didn't seem to care. They sat down, all three in a row, with Bridget in the middle.

"What are we doing?" Daisy asked.

Bridget grinned. "Taking off my socks."

"Those are Hannah's socks."

"I gave them to her last night," Hannah explained. "Bridget's skin is so dry she can write her name with her fingernail and the white marks stay there."

"But Hannah found a cure. Watch." Bridget rolled up her pajamas to her knees. "I'll hold my breath and both of you count to three."

"*One two three.*"

Bridget yanked the knee-socks off like she was opening a present. She scribbled her fingernail up and down her shin.

At first, nothing happened. Then the zig-zags appeared like magic chalk.

II. JUNE

There she was at the front door, twisting a corner of a pillow, her hair a blonde scramble.

"Hi," Bridget said. "Can I spend the night?"

Elaine touched a hand to her chest. "Where's Joan?"

"In Culver City. Mim went with her. For a little bit Ned, that's my brother he's seventeen he goes to high school, he was home but then he left with his girlfriend." She scratched her arm vigorously, making elongated fingernail marks on her pale, chapped skin. "Joan's boyfriend doesn't like me or Ned, so she lets us stay home."

Elaine tried to recall what Tanya had told her about the girl. She was an infant when she was found, abandoned in a Von's parking lot in Del Mar, and had spent her life shuffling between group homes and foster homes. Joan was her latest foster mother—she'd taken Bridget a few years ago. For the money, said Tanya.

Elaine looked back at Daisy, who was napping on the living room floor with her head on a big pillow—she hadn't yet found a couch that was affordable, except for the dingy, threadbare ones at yard sales. As a compromise, she'd bought three big pillows on sale at Woolworth's.

"So can I?" Bridget asked. "Spend the night?" Her chapped

lips stretched into a pleading grin.

"Of course," she answered, feeling pity for the wayward girl. She took Bridget's pillow and laid a hand on her little bony shoulder, gently guiding her into the living room. Too bony, she thought—the poor thing must not be getting enough to eat. She found herself petting Bridget's shoulder, as if to warm her. "Are you hungry?" she ventured. "Do you want something to eat?"

"Okay!" Bridget made a beeline into the kitchen.

Pleased, Elaine turned back to Daisy, still curled in a ball but awake now. She leaned down and whispered, "We have a visitor, sweetie. Let's not sleep too long, you won't be tired at bedtime." Daisy blinked sleepily, her face beginning to pucker into a scowl.

Bridget hoisted herself onto the formica counter and kicked her heels against the cabinets below her feet, just like Hannah always did. "Why don't you sit here with Daisy," Elaine said. "It's more comfortable." She patted one of the pillows.

But Bridget stayed put, picking at a scab on her knee.

At the end of the hallway, Hannah peeked out her bedroom door.

"Hannah!" Bridget cried.

There was plenty of food for Elaine to offer, since she had just gone to Lucky's for groceries, but Bridget shook her head at toast and scrambled eggs, a tuna fish sandwich, a peanut butter and jelly sandwich, Rice-A-Roni, yogurt with strawberry jam mixed in, celery sticks with peanut butter and raisins, cereal, even at Elaine's idea of frying a banana with butter and brown sugar. Hannah had joined Bridget on the counter, both of them now gleefully kicking their heels against the kitchen cabinets. Daisy was in one of her shy, clutching moods, wrapping her arms tight around Elaine's thigh, refusing to let go. So Elaine limped, with Daisy still attached, from the cabinet to the refrigerator and back again, determined to find something that Bridget would eat.

"How about a cheese sandwich? Do you like cheddar?"

"Do you have American?"

"No, I'm afraid we don't."

"Joan has the kind with the plastic around each slice."

Elaine stifled the urge to tell her processed cheese was bad for you, and limped back to the cabinet. "Okay let's see, what about soup? Tomato?"

"I'm allergic," Bridget said.

"Cream of mushroom? Split pea?" she offered, but Bridget shuddered.

"All right, no soup. How about creamed corn?"

"Yes!" Bridget shouted.

Elaine made a whole new dinner for her, creamed corn and a fried chicken thigh and mashed potatoes, which Bridget swore was about the only food besides candy and cheeseburgers that she wasn't allergic to. Elaine's gentle probing brought out a queer little string of stories from Bridget, and she nodded encouragingly, trying hard to keep from wincing, while the girl rambled on.

"So then there was this man who came over and once he got mad and put Jennifer's hamster in a microwave and its eyes popped out and it got all red and mushy and then once at this other place a girl threw up on the baby hamsters in the cage and she got in trouble."

Elaine, lifting the chicken thigh out of the boiling oil, said "Mm *hm,*" unsure of what to believe. She set it on a paper towel and blotted the oil before putting it on a plate. Then she dished up the mashed potatoes and creamed corn and handed the plate to Bridget.

From then on, Elaine let Bridget stay over whenever Joan visited her boyfriend in Culver City, which was, as it turned out, nearly every Friday night.

How could she turn her away? How could she, with Bridget

standing there in the doorway with her blonde mangle of hair and her pillow and that chapped-lip grin, trying to endear herself, though the girl seemed to know already what would come next: Elaine would lead her in with a gentle hand on her shoulder, sometimes venture to wipe a dirt smear off her face or stroke a wisp of hair out of her eyes before Bridget yelled "Hannah!" and yanked herself away, rushing toward her daughter, who would come running out of the bedroom that she shut herself up in most days.

When Bridget stayed over, Elaine witnessed a trans-formation in Hannah. The dark, brooding cloud that settled around her would lift, and the two girls would chatter away during dinner, shoveling down their food—which Hannah usually ate without the slightest enthusiasm. There was Daisy, of course, with her tugging and clutching. Still, somehow with Bridget around she could tend to her younger daughter without the distraction of the glowering presence in the back bedroom; she could breathe easier, she didn't have to try to divide her attention in perfect, equal amounts between her two daughters or fret about why no matter how hard she tried all she had to give was never, ever enough—which is what her nine-year-old daughter, by her cold silence, would continually remind her.

When Elaine finally discovered her bottle of Keri lotion was half-empty, she surprised herself by not getting angry. How could she blame the child for taking what she wanted, when she grew up in such horrible circumstances, moving from foster home to foster home, and was no doubt accustomed to considering other people's property *her* property?

The next night Bridget stayed over, Elaine announced that she would show them how to play her favorite game when she was their age, Beauty Parlor. She let them use her nail file and boar's-bristle hairbrush and mixed up an oatmeal and egg-yolk mask for them to glop on their faces, and she even let them waste hot water for fifteen minutes to make a steam room, demonstrating how to wrap towels around their heads like turbans and running the shower with dish rags stuffed in the crack under the bathroom door to keep the steam in. She saved some of the mask to put on Daisy and herself, and while Hannah and Bridget giggled in the bathroom she and her younger daughter sat on the big pillows on the living room floor with towels on their laps, their faces lifted toward the ceiling so the eggy oatmeal wouldn't slide off.

When it was time for bed, Daisy whimpered until Elaine gave in and let Daisy sleep in her bed. The lights out, she sang Daisy a lullaby in a low, soft voice, *When you wake—you shall have—all the pretty little horses.* She was comforted by her daughter's small warm body nuzzled against hers, by the sound of Hannah and Bridget giggling and whispering in the other room, and she allowed herself the fantasy that she had three daughters instead of two.

Every morning Trevor's cartoons came up right through the ceiling of apartment two into the living room: *George of the Jungle* at six a.m., followed by *Tom Slick, Super Chicken, Loony Toons,* and *Wheel of Fortune*; then, at eleven, *The Dukes of Hazzard,* which was about the time Joan's son Ned started to play his records, making Elaine shut all the windows in the apartment until the music stopped later in the afternoon, when Ned took off for his girlfriend's apartment.

Elaine generally avoided confrontations if she could help it, and it wasn't until now, a scorching hot and unusually humid morning in the middle of June, when Ned had been playing the same Van Halen record over and over again, that she decided she could no longer stand to keep the windows shut. It was positively baking inside the apartment. She was going downstairs to have a talk with Joan.

"Baking," Elaine declared out loud, twisting her hair into a scraggly bun. She shoved the windows open, letting in some air, along with the thundering music—the male singer screaming "*Where have all the gooood times gone?*" Wincing, she slipped on her clogs and clomped out the door.

"One o'clock hell," Joan said, leaning out her window with

her Virginia Slim. "You should have been here last summer, when Ned didn't have a girlfriend to run off to. All day long he'd blast that thing. That Mormon bitch called Social Services on me, twice in fact. How do you like that?" She flicked an ash off her bare arm. "For a kid playing a stereo."

Elaine kept her distance from Joan, standing off to the side of the front door. "You mean Tanya? She called?"

"No, no, her sister Mary, the one who lived in the apartment you moved into. And *she* was the one with the dog howling day and night. Not to mention the goddamn babies." Joan shook her head, stubbing out her cigarette on the window ledge, then disappeared behind the curtains.

"*Ned!*" she screamed. "Turn it *down,* I said!"

Joan swiped open the curtains, for a moment revealing the ghostly blue flicker of a TV in the darkened apartment, and took her place at the window again.

"Anyway, so Mary and her husband, they did missionary work, that's how they met, preaching in some Mexican town. Then Mary gets tuberculosis from one of those Mexicans coughing in her face and calls Tanya, she's the older sister. Tanya convinces the landlord that Mary and her husband are good Christian folk, blah blah blah, and gets them the apartment next door to her, the one you're in now. You met Warren, right?"

"Just once, when he stopped by with the lease."

"That's all you'll see of him, if you're lucky. You know he acted with our President once in a Western?" She aimed an imaginary gun at Elaine. "Reach for the sky, Ronnie," she said in a cowboy drawl, then cackled until a hacking cough overcame her.

Elaine waited for her to recover, then said, "He told me he was just a stand-in."

"I never saw the movie myself, just heard about it from someone. Who the hell...was it..." She narrowed her eyes in concentration, making a thick black web out of her lashes. "Shit, I can't concentrate."

Her head disappeared behind the curtain again. "*Ned!*"

Joan took longer to come back this time, and when she did, she set down on the windowsill a Bloody Mary in a tall glass with a bruised stalk of celery. With a snort, she lit another cigarette and drew in a deep lungful before continuing her story.

"So Mary goes to the hospital and gets better and as a homecoming present her husband gives her a puppy—a goddamn German shepherd that never stops barking and they pop out three babies that never stop screaming and Mary has the nerve—the *goddamn nerve*—to call Social Services 'cause my teenage son plays a few records. They come in here with their clipboards asking me questions and poking around..." Her voice trailed off.

Elaine was slowly bobbing her chin—half nod, half shake— a noncommittal gesture she relied on when she wanted to keep the conversation going but was still sorting through her opinions on what was being said. She was a patient listener, a little like a nurse ministering to a lunatic, offering sympathetic, cautious hmms and uh-huhs, although Joan clearly needed no encouragement. She was surprised Joan was so talkative. Almost every morning she saw her, leaning on her windowsill, staring out at the playground while she smoked, saying nothing when Elaine passed by, not even glancing in her direction. She'd been meaning for some time to start a conversation with her about Bridget spending the night on Fridays, but somewhere between marching out her front door and down the stairs to Joan's front door, thinking *how could you leave that child alone all night don't you realize you're doing what her mother did abandoning her in a Von's parking lot yes Tanya told me I do know what I'm talking about,* she lost her resolve.

Joan stirred the celery stalk around her glass and took a gulp. She wiped off a little dribble of red down her chin with the back of her hand. "Then one fine day they pack up their station wagon with their babies and their dog and go back to Utah, thank fucking God, and that's the end of that. Wish her sister would go the hell back too—you better watch out, living next door to her. I'm in the same position, living underneath her."

"Who, Tanya?"

"Nosy," she said, pointing the cigarette at Elaine. "Won't mind her own business. Acts all sweet but don't let it fool you. And those kids of hers—I tell Mim to stay away from them. By the way, all I hear from her is Daisy this, Daisy that. She says your girl's got a whole collection of Barbies, thirty of 'em."

"Thirty? That's a bit of an exaggeration. More like four, I think. Or I guess five."

"She has it in her head you're loaded."

"I don't know where she got that idea."

Joan stubbed out her cigarette next to the others on the window ledge. "Well, getting back to Tanya's kids. I don't want Mim looking up to them. She's got enough bad influences from Bridget. A foster kid is a handful, I thought I knew that up front. But you don't know—there's no way to know what you're dealing with until you sign the papers and she's living under your roof. If I got her when she was just a baby, it would've been a lot easier. When you get 'em that young, they've got no memories, you can start fresh. But Bridget's a whole nother ball of wax."

Ned's music stopped. Elaine breathed a sigh of relief with Joan, almost in unison.

But it started up again—he was just changing records. *Come on feel the noise, girls rock your boys.*

The volume was even louder now, and Joan had to raise her voice as she went on about Butterfield Youth Home, where she said Bridget was diagnosed as having Conduct Disorder and a borderline personality ("It's not as bad as it sounds—all the kids there are that, standard psychiatrist bullshit," she said), then about the two other foster homes Bridget lived in before Joan got her, the first in the high desert, near Apple Valley, the second in Lancaster, with a foster mother who Joan said had a thing for retarded kids—there were three of them with Down's syndrome plus Bridget in the apartment. Bridget lived there a little over year, until she told a classmate she was getting molested. Joan shook her head and took another gulp of her drink, fished out a sliver of ice cube with her long fingernail and crunched it between her teeth.

"Wh-what?" Elaine stammered.

Joan blinked. "You want to know details?

"Well, I mean—"

"They found anal lacerations."

Elaine laid her hand on her chest. "*What*?"

"That's the word they used. Bridget's friend told a teacher at their school and the police took over from there, sent Bridget in for a medical exam, blah blah blah. They sent her to another one of those homes, you know, facilities, for kids. Westbrooke. Then I got her through an agency."

"Who was the man?"

"Her foster mother's brother or brother-in-law or something, I forget. I mean, the guy's in prison now. Goddamn perverted world we live in. Nothing you or I can do about it. Bridget's in God's hands. That's the one bit of Bible-thumping bullshit Tanya's said to me that's made any sense."

The music suddenly shut off. "Well, well," Joan said, as the front door opened.

Ned, a shaggy teenager with a glittery red motorcycle helmet bulging out from under his armpit, wordlessly shoved past them and loped down the pathway toward the parking lot in back.

"Good-bye," Joan called out, but got nothing in return. She leaned her elbows on the windowsill. Looking down into her glass, she fiddled with the celery stalk.

A few gingerly steps and Elaine was standing directly under the window. "Bridget is so—I mean, she's only a little girl…"

Joan didn't respond, just shut her eyes to the whiney sputter of Ned's mo-ped zooming down the driveway. "What did you want, anyway?"

"Oh, yes." Flustered, Elaine cleared her throat. "Well I just, I came down here—well, really, I wanted to talk with you about your son's music."

"Yeah? What do you want me to do?

"Maybe you could ask Ned to turn down the volume?"

"He doesn't listen to anyone, forget about *me*. He's seventeen, thinks he's got it all figured out. No one can tell him what to do."

"I'm sorry, it's just that I can't keep my windows closed all the time. It gets so hot and stuffy, with no air-conditioning, you know."

"What did I tell you about Warren. Cheap rent-control bastard. Forget about air-conditioning—you noticed the ants? You notice him doing anything about 'em?"

"There's just got to be...oh, I don't know. Some solution."

Joan snapped her fingers. "Wait. I got something for you." She disappeared behind the curtains. A clattering sound came from somewhere in the apartment.

The front door cracked open an inch, and Joan's foot appeared, kicking it open. She held a dusty square fan, a long cord trailing behind her. "Take it. Now you can shut your windows when the noise gets too loud and you won't get too hot."

"Are you sure...?"

"I don't need it, even in this heat—Ned calls me cold-blooded, maybe he's right. Now don't be calling Social Services on me after this, understand?"

Elaine accepted the fan into her arms. "Well. Thank you, Joan."

"Don't trip," Joan said, and she looped the dangling cord around Elaine's neck.

In the summer, it was no different: the school bells rang every day.

8:17 was the first—two quick clanging bursts that the people in the building set their watches to. Then again at 8:22—a single, long one. At 9:17, the two clangs repeated, again followed by the longer bell at 9:22. There were six more, staggered through the morning and early afternoon, until the final bell at 3:03.

Every time Elaine gave a little start and dropped whatever was in her hands, *JesusandMary* flying out her mouth in a furious whisper. Recovering, she'd take a long, slow breath, sucking in the air as if through a straw, then pick up whatever broken pieces were at her feet and send Hannah next door to borrow Tanya's mushed little tube of Super Glue. In one week alone Elaine broke a picture frame, three pottery mugs and a cereal bowl, not to mention smacking her head against the bottom of the mirrored bathroom cabinet when a bell went off as she was coming up from washing her face.

"Your ma's a little herky jerky, ain't she?" Tanya said the third day Hannah knocked on her door.

"She said to make you take this for reimbursement," Hannah said, offering her mother's dollar. Then she added, "It's because of the bells. They make her drop things."

"The bells? Oh the *bells*, at the school. Well now that explains it."

Tanya's impatient wave at the dollar sent it back in Hannah's pocket, where she had stuffed the two other dollars Tanya had previously refused. Tanya invited her to come in and take a load off. She needed to dig around a little, she said, for the Super Glue.

In the center of the living room there was a sun-lamp and a candy-cane-looking aluminum beach chair, with red and white plastic strips. The radio was tuned to a country music station. An empty can of Diet Shasta lay on its side next to a glass of melted ice cubes tinged brown.

"No time for the beach," Tanya said, taking a last sip before she folded up the beach chair and dragged the sun lamp to the corner. "I got work in an hour."

Standing on her tiptoes, the tiny woman reached for the volume knob on the stereo and turned it down, the backs of her thighs showing striped indentations from the beach chair. Through the stereo speakers, faintly, Hannah could still hear the twangy lilt of Dolly Parton singing *"In my Tennessee mountain home, life was as peaceful as a baby's sigh…"* In the corner of the room stood her huge TV set with the crack running across the screen, surrounded by stacks of *Reader's Digest*s and *TV Guide*s. On top of the TV was a clutter of plastic dolls with identical astonished expressions on their painted faces, but dressed in different ethnic clothing—blonde braids and wooden shoes for the Dutch girl, black braids and a feather for the Indian girl, red braids and a green skirt for the Irish girl. There were knick-knacks everywhere: a Magic 8 ball, *Star Wars* action figures, a paint-by-numbers *Charlie's Angels* painting, plastic ferns and flowers hanging from the ceiling in macramé plant holders, and a collection of souvenirs from Las Vegas—mugs and ashtrays and snow domes and silver teaspoons and a chorus line of dancing dolls with silver plumes sprouting from the tops of their heads.

"I hid most of my stuff when I threw my party," Tanya explained. "You never know who has sticky fingers."

Hannah plunked down in the raggedy armchair, causing the footrest to suddenly spring out from under it.

"What are you doing, honey, sittin' in that broken old thang? Go ahead, you can sit here." Tanya patted the seat of another armchair, the color of cream and still in its plastic cover.

Hannah rose from the raggedy armchair, jumping to the side when the footrest slammed back. Tanya bit the tip of her tongue, watching with twinkling eyes as Hannah sank into the plastic-covered chair. There was a slow, whistley sigh, like a tire leaking air. The thick plastic buckled and stuck like tape to the back of Hannah's legs.

"Comfy?"

Hannah nodded, lying.

"It's five years old! Can you bel*ieve* it? Still looks and feels brand-new, huh? The Hamiltons keep the plastic on all their furniture—smart, keeps off all the grunge. They're in number six, the blacks, you've seen 'em? That chair used to be theirs."

Then she said, "I gotta gear up for the story. You want some pop?"

Standing on a stepladder, she could just reach the cans of Shasta stacked on top of the refrigerator. "I got regular," she called out, "and diet—that's all my girls drink now, diet. Come on now, which?"

"Regular," Hannah said.

Tanya's fingers wiggled at the side of a can until it toppled down. She opened the can with a yelp, fizz spurting straight up.

"I'll have to tell my Sandi I found an exception—she told me all the girls were drinking diet." She positioned a small glass end table by Hannah's elbow, between the two armchairs, and set the dripping can and a tin of nuts on it. "Here, munch on some of these Beer Nuts, honey. I don't let a drop of alcohol in my house, you can be certain of that, but it sure tastes like they marinate these in *somethin'* sinful."

Tanya turned the raggedy armchair so it faced Hannah, and sat down. When the footrest sprang out, she lifted her legs just in time.

"So here's the chair story," she said, lowering her voice to a gossipy whisper. "Rich Hamilton Sr., that's the dad, gave me this chair as a sort of apology for his son Rich Jr. stealing checks out of my mailbox. Rich Jr. stole checks out of Mrs. Grover's mailbox, too—to make up for it, his dad gave her a couch. Rich Sr.'s a good-for-nothing drunk and it's no surprise that his son turned out the way he did, but that's besides the point.

"So while Rich Jr. is stealing my checks I'm thinking my ex had stopped paying child support for good—a month here and there he missed, not that I wasn't happy about that neither. But *five*?" She dug into the can of Beer Nuts and came out with a handful, which she tossed in her mouth. "Lord, these are good," she said, chewing.

Hannah reached for the can then.

"Good, honey, don't be shy. So I stick the authorities on him—my ex, that is. By the time they finally catch up with him he's living clear on the other side of the country, hitched up with some Florida floozy. Turns out Rich Jr. never got the nerve to cash the checks, he's just been stuffing them under his mattress along with the other mail he stole, *junk* mail he even saved—so my ex's got no record, no cancelled checks, nothing to show the authorities as proof. I didn't know this at the time, of course. So they lock up my ex in some Daytona jail and call me. I tell them I don't need him in jail, I need him out working so he can start making some of that money he owes me. Lucky for him, about this time Rich Sr. sobers up enough to realize his son's dropped outta school and doing drugs, so he goes through Rich Jr.'s room with a fine-tooth comb and finds my alimony checks under his mattress—along with a bunch of cassette tapes my Danny ordered from one of those mail-in-a-penny clubs, along with people's birthday cards, Easter cards, love letters. Must've been lumpy, sleeping on all that. Anyway, so Rich Jr. is in juvenile hall now."

Another bell went off. "School bells goin' off in the middle of summer," Tanya grumbled, "and the only ones to hear 'em are us." She checked her watch. "Darn, I gotta get dressed and get myself off to work. Wait. The *Super Glue!* I just about clean forgot. You know if I'd have used my head I would've kept it out for you, but I had to throw it back in my junk drawer. It'll just take a second. Then I gotta get going." She scurried into the kitchen. "What's your ma do? Where'd you move from?" she asked, her little hands rummaging through the drawer.

"She's a cook, she's cooked all over." Hannah recited the names of the places they'd lived: Spokane, Taos, Florence, Casper, Amarillo, Helena, Duluth, Aberdeen, Appleton, Yakima, Joplin, Odessa.

"Sounds like your ma's done a lotta cookin' and you all've done a lot of travelin'." Where's your daddy figure into all of this?"

"He's gone."

"Uh-huh, sounds like my ex."

"No, he's dead." Why she said it, she didn't know; she hadn't told anyone ever—hadn't even let herself say the word "dead" about anything.

"You say what? Your daddy's dead?"

Hannah nodded. Suddenly, she wanted to leave this cluttered apartment, flee from Tanya and her widening eyes, eyes that reminded her of Daisy's greedy look when she ate pancakes or popcorn or ice cream.

When Bridget knocked on the front door, looking for Hannah, Elaine steered her into the kitchen.

"How about a snack?" she said. She wanted Bridget to stay; she had so many questions she wanted to ask the child, about Butterfield Youth Home, about her foster parents in Lancaster.

"Where's Hannah?" Bridget asked, ready to bolt out the door.

"Outside, with her turtle, in the garden out front. But she'll be back soon." Elaine pulled out a chair and patted the seat. "Why don't you sit down, and I'll make you something to eat."

"Like what?"

"How about a nice apple and some hot vegetable soup with croutons on top?"

"Do you have Doritos?"

Junk food, Elaine mused, that was all the poor girl ate. "How about some Triscuits? That's one of my favorite snacks."

"Do you have Pop Tarts?"

"No, but I can spread some strawberry jam on the Triscuits."

Bridget shuddered.

"Or," Elaine thought desperately, "I can stir the jam into some yogurt and make strawberry yogurt. I have that for breakfast sometimes, it's almost like a dessert."

"Do you have ice cream?"

Defeated, Elaine opened the freezer and took out a carton of vanilla ice cream. She put two scoops into a bowl and sprinkled some almonds on top, sneaking in some vitamins. Then she decided to make a bowl for herself, too.

She brought the two bowls to the table and pulled up a chair. "Where did you live," she ventured tentatively, "before you came to Sunset Terrace?"

"Everywhere," Bridget replied, picking out the almonds.

Elaine dipped her spoon into the bowl. She had to be delicate—she didn't want to scare her off. "You used to live in Lancaster with another foster mother, is that right?"

"Uh-huh."

"What was that like?"

"There was a dog."

"A dog?"

Bridget whipped her ice cream around her bowl in a frenzy, making it into a soupy mess. "It barked all day and ate everybody's pets."

"What a mean dog."

"It was like the meeeanest. One day, I even saw rabbit fur in its mouth. And a guinea pig's fur, too."

"Really?"

"And there was a freeway exit by Anita's apartment—that was my foster mom's name—and there were cars and cars and cars zooming all the time, and all this oil and gasoline they left on the street that looked all swirley and rainbow-like, with all these colors."

"That sounds pretty," Elaine said. "Rainbows on the ground."

"Once I found a five-dollar bill right by the gutter where the gas station was," Bridget went on, no stopping her now. "And I showed it to Anita but she took it away and said she was going to put it in my savings account, but then I went to Butterfield and I never got it, she stole it, she stole it! I told the woman behind the desk—her name was Mrs. Nelly but all the kids called her Mrs. Smelly because she stank—I told her Anita stole my five dollars, but Mrs. Smelly didn't care. So once I spit in my hand when we were doing art and when Mrs. Smelly gave me the red crayon she touched my hand and she didn't even know, so I got back at her." Bridget brought the bowl up to her face and licked it clean.

"Do you want some more ice cream?"

Bridget nodded her head vigorously.

"Is that your favorite food?"

"No."

"What, then?" Elaine asked, thinking she'd prepare a special dinner for Bridget the next time she spent the night.

"Snickers," Bridget replied, "Milky Ways, Charleston Chews, mashed potatoes, tater tots, french fries, fried chicken, Butter-fingers."

As she babbled on ("...*Doritos, Fritos, Cheetos, Reeses, Red-Hots, cheeseburgers, Nerds, hot dogs, Hubba Bubba, Hundred Thousand Dollar Bars...*"), Elaine decided she would steer clear of the molestation issue. The story was locked up in Bridget somewhere—she knew it was. But Bridget didn't want to talk about it now, and it would be cruel to force the story out of her. The girl had suffered so much already, thrown into one bad home after another.

What mattered was that she was here, ready to feed Bridget. Ready to wrap her arms around the poor thing and let her cry into her breast.

* * *

"Green F 4," her mother said, pointing to the painted sign on the cement pylon of the parking garage. "Remember that, okay?"

"Okey-doke!" Bridget cried, and Hannah was surprised to hear her mother laugh out loud. Even more surprised when

Bridget slipped her chapped hand in her mother's as they walked to the parking lot elevator. She did not feel a deep stab of jealousy, witnessing Bridget's effect on her mother; that would come later, as the summer wore on. Today, on this sunny afternoon, all she felt was a bubbly joy that made her want to start skipping.

The elevator doors opened on the ground floor, and Bridget ran out onto the sidewalk with her arms open wide, spinning around, chanting, "Movies, movies, we're going to the movies!" Giggling, Daisy joined her; she'd warmed up to Bridget by now. Hannah skipped in a circle around Bridget and her little sister, who spun and spun until they got dizzy and collapsed on the sidewalk.

At the concessions stand her mother bought a large bucket of popcorn with melted butter. "This is a special occasion," she said, carefully counting out the money from her wallet. She gave the bucket to Bridget, who plunged a hand in.

"I wish they had *Porky's II*," Bridget said. "My brother Ned he saw it last week for the third time in a row. He said it's sooooo good."

Inside the theater, they found four seats together toward the front. Bridget showed Hannah a trick: put your feet up on the empty seat in front of you and then people still looking for seats won't sit there. It wasn't until Hannah started tossing popcorn kernels into Bridget's open mouth and accidentally hit a man in the next row that she got the stern look from her mother.

The movie was about a boy who makes everyone afraid he's going to blow up the world with his computer. During the part when he and his girlfriend escape to an island to find a man to help them, Bridget touched Hannah's bare shoulder with a scratchy finger and whispered, her breath smelling buttery, "I'm gonna run away just like her."

After the movie, they went across the street to Newberry's, where her mother bought them ice cream sodas. They sat at the counter and sipped the sodas from red-and-white-striped bendable straws, Hannah thinking *stay, stay.*

Danny and the boys ditched the girls as soon as they got off the bus. Bridget knew they would do it, whispering her prediction in Hannah's ear right when Tanya made him promise he'd be the adult at the beach and watch them.

The first on the bus, Danny passed the sleepy-eyed, beefy-lipped driver, jingling the quarters in his pocket as he led the way down the aisle to the back, away from the sorry-ass old ladies, which is what he called Sandi when she went for a front seat, "Shut up Danny Orphan Annie—" she began, but he already had her by the wrist, twisting it behind her back, "What'd you fuckin' call me what was that say it again say it," until she burst into soft, whiney sobs and the driver yelled for them to cut it out and sit down.

Smirking, Danny rolled his towel into a tight tube for a pillow, stretched himself out on the last row of seats, and laced his fingers over his chest.

"Reee-laaax-ation," he said.

At thirteen, Danny was the oldest of the group, followed by Sandi, who was eleven, and Sue-Sue, who was ten. Davy was nine, the same age as Bridget and Hannah. And Trevor was eight, the youngest of the boys in the building. Another kid used to go with them to the beach, Bridget told Hannah as they looked for a good seat in back—Rich Jr. in number six, the one who got sent to juvie, whose dad was also named Rich.

"Wouldn't that be weird?" Bridget said. "Having the same name?"

Hannah blinked, thinking this over, watching Davy and Trevor roll their towels tight like Danny's for a pillow and stretch out on the seats right in front of him. The three of them looked like twins, she thought, lying there, naked from the waist up, all wearing corduroy shorts with low-slung pockets and *Op* stitched at the bottom.

Sandi, still sniffling and rubbing her wrist, plopped down on the seat directly in front of Hannah and Bridget and ordered Sue-Sue to sit down and spread her towel like a blanket over their legs. Once they were settled, Sandi placed her arm on Sue-Sue's lap, wrist up.

"Do a Rose Garden," she ordered.

Sue-Sue complied, and scraped her nails up and down Sandi's arm, *now the farmer is raking the soil, now he's putting in fertilizer,* then pinched her skin in neat rows, *now he's planting the seeds,* while Sandi clenched her teeth.

"Now do the rain."

*Okay now it's raining and raining and raining,* Sue-Sue said, slapping Sandi's arm. *And the roses in the garden are growing and growing.*

Sandi leaned across the aisle and proudly showed Hannah and Bridget her reddened arm. "You guys want a Rose Garden?"

Hannah quickly shook her head. Bridget didn't answer, distracted by Danny, who was lying behind her in the last row, mumbling *Venice Free Clinic herpes si habla español ITT Technical Institute computer skills word processing data entry toll-free free brochure be a model or just look like one Barbazon arson burns everyone—*

"What are you doing?" Bridget demanded.

Danny squinted at her. "Reading," he replied, pointing to the strip of glossy posters above the bus's rectangular windows.

"Can't you read quiet?"

Danny ignored her question. He sat up and nudged his fingers under his Hawaiian slip-on Vans to scratch at his heel. "You know ITT Technical Institute is the wrong spelling?"

"So?" Bridget shrugged.

"It's supposed to be T-I-T. It's where you go to get titties." "So?"

"So," Danny said, "looks like you should go."

Davy and Trevor snorted. There was a narrowing and twitching to Bridget's face, but she said nothing. Hannah tried to catch her eye, to send her a silent message that Danny was mean and that she should just ignore him, but Bridget wouldn't look at her. Instead, Bridget stared straight ahead, fiercely, and Hannah was surprised to see on her friend's brave face what looked like a mortified flush.

Satisfied, Danny gazed up at the posters above the windows, and went on reading aloud, running all the words together from three separate posters. *Say nope to dope and ugh to drugs official city of the 1984 Olympics call Larry H. Parker,* he said, then jerked his foot up to scratch again at his heel, making the quarters in his pocket spill onto the floor in a dazzling clatter.

"Aw, *fuck!*" Danny cried.

In a moment, Davy and Trevor were on their hands and knees. They fumbled around with Danny for the coins, Trevor's head careening into an elderly woman's white stockinged shins as he chased a rolling quarter to the front of the bus. The cast on Davy's arm didn't stop him, and he scrambled on his knees, his cast thumping against the floor. Bridget and Sue-Sue joined in, giggling as they chased after the quarters underneath the seats.

"You *guys,*" Sandi said with disgust. "Don't *help* him."

Hannah was the only one who had remained seated, too shy to join in. Sandi turned and looked at her. Something in Sandi's expression awakened, as though recognizing an ally.

She sat down next to Hannah and draped her towel over their legs. She took Hannah's wrist in her hand. "You want one? A Rose Garden?"

"No!" Hannah cried, yanking her hand away.

Sandi's nose wrinkled up. "*Fine.*"

"Maybe later on though," Hannah offered, but it was too late—Sandi had pulled the towel away and was now arranging it to cover only her legs.

Hannah looked down, embarrassed by the tears that welled up in her eyes. Even though Sandi was bossy and she didn't really like her, she still felt the sting of rejection. Her eyes fixed on the floor of the bus, she spotted Bridget, who was crouched under a seat, slyly slip a few quarters in one of her Jap-Slaps before giving Danny the rest of the quarters she'd retrieved.

"I'm missing seventy-five cents," Danny announced at the curb, after the bus drove off.

He made everybody line up and turn out their pockets. Bridget beamed, looking victorious, with her secret stash of Danny's quarters in her shoe. And Hannah felt proud, seeing that Bridget had gotten her revenge.

Sandi and Sue-Sue each brought out a small handful of change. Danny squinted at them. "Gimme my money," he demanded.

"We didn't steal it," Sandi shot back. "And quit picking on us or I'm telling Ma."

"*Quit picking on us or I'm telling Ma,*" Danny mocked, in a high-pitched squeal.

"Shut up!" Sandi screamed.

"Make me," he hissed. He eyed Davy and Trevor.

"Ditch 'em," he said.

The three boys bolted off. They headed toward the pier, where the arcade was. Danny turned back and threw a quarter, missing Sandi and pelting Sue-Sue in the cheek.

Bridget picked up the quarter and scowled, watching the boys go. "Thinks he can boss us," she muttered. She reached into the Jap-Slap holding the stolen quarters and pocketed the money.

Sue-Sue cradled her cheek, tears filling her eyes. Bridget grabbed Sue-Sue's hand. "Don't cry, come on!" She tugged Sue-Sue down the sidewalk toward a narrow flight of splintery wood stairs that descended to the beach.

"Wait up!" Sandi shouted, chasing after them.

Bridget was always the leader, Hannah saw, even though Sandi was the oldest. She ran to catch up with them, skipping every other step down the splintery stairs.

At the bottom stair, Hannah tore off her sandals. The ocean stretched before her for miles and miles, blue and shimmering in the sunlight, millions of magic diamonds floating on its surface. If she were Daisy's age, she could almost make herself believe this—that the ocean was bejeweled. She'd been to the beach just once before, years ago, before Daisy was born. In the snapshots her mother had shown her of their Christmas trip to Florida, the ocean was just a fuzzy sliver in the background. The only memory she had of the day was of her father's hand holding hers as she waded into the chilly water, his fingers cold and clenching.

Bridget was doing one-handed cartwheels on the sand. Sue-Sue joined her, giggling, all tears gone. Sandi leaped into the air, spun around, and performed a series of back-flips. Hannah, sandals in her hand, watched them from the bottom stair, awed by their gymnastic feats. She couldn't even do a somersault on the ground without losing her balance.

"Hannah, c'mon!"

Bridget cartwheeled over to her and yanked her onto the sand. "Aaaa!" Hannah cried, dropping her sandals. The sand was scorching hot.

"You gotta keep moving," Bridget said. "Don't just stand there, stupid."

Cartwheels were impossible, so Hannah jumped up and down in place, feeling even stupider.

"Shade!" Bridget announced, and pointed to a trashcan orange with rust, ten feet ahead. Bridget dashed toward it, kicking up sand, yelping "Hot hot hot hot hot hot hot!"

They scuttled across the sand this way, soothing their burning feet in the scattered cool spots: on the thin curve of shadow around a trashcan, under the stairs of a lifeguard station, on a towel someone abandoned when they went swimming. Finally, Hannah found herself underneath the pier, where the water lapped at the rotting wooden pillars, bumpy with barnacles. She dug her toes into the slurpy mud and looked up at the fingers of sunlight shooting through the gaps between the planks. Above, a trio of seagulls hovered, screeching.

Sue-Sue put a gentle hand on Hannah's shoulder and told her about the big storm last March. The waves were almost as big as tidal waves and most of the pier had been destroyed, washed out to sea, she explained, including a whole restaurant, which was why everywhere on the shore there were still wood splinters that looked like toothpicks. Weird things washed up to the shore—doctors' needles with germs, and rusty nails that gave you diseases that could only be cured by getting twenty shots in your stomach.

"Really?" Hannah said, wondering if Sue-Sue was lying.

"The storm was God's punishment," Sandy insisted. "Ma said so."

Sue-Sue dug her fingers into the wet sand and came up with a dripping fistful. "Look," she said. "When the water gets sucked back after a wave the bubbles in the sand mean that a crab is hiding in there." She opened her hand and a grayish creature skittered out.

"There's another bubble," Sue-Sue said excitedly, pointing at the sand above Hannah's big toe.

Hannah scooped up the sand but came up with nothing,

just a chip of abalone shell, the underside like spilled gasoline, a runny purple-blue.

"This sucks, picking up crabs and stuff," Bridget said. She tore off her shorts and T-shirt. Underneath, she had on a lime green one-piece bathing suit. "Who's swimming with me?" Without waiting for an answer, she bolted off, tightening the bathing suit strings behind her neck as she splashed into the water.

Sandi stripped down to her bikini and ran in.

Sue-Sue flicked the crab off her palm. "Wait up!"

Alone now, Hannah looked out into the ocean and watched a small wave swell up to Bridget's shoulders. The wave broke gently before it reached Sandi and Sue-Sue, who were in past their knees. They raised their arms as the foamy water hit their waists.

It was low tide. A scallop of crusty foam edged along the sand, marking where the high tide had come to earlier. There, rubbery clumps of kelp dried in the sun, bronze, algae green, coffee-colored, with their bulbs and tentacles. Hannah lingered a while, watching her friends swim toward the waves. Just as a wave reached its peak, they flipped onto their backs and floated over it. When a wave crashed too soon, Sandi and Sue-Sue expertly dove under it, Bridget more or less let herself get tossed around and swallowed up, and one by one they surfaced, laughing, shouting, heads bobbing up through the foam.

Hannah kicked aside a shard of glass next to Bridget's balled-up clothes, listening to their distant shrieks and hoots. What Bridget and Sandi and Sue-Sue were doing in the ocean was trickier than doggy-paddling in the shallow end of a pool— which was all she knew how to do.

An enormous wave approached. Bridget swam toward it in a frenzy of kicking and splashing. The wave grew taller and taller, making Hannah think of the waves in the big storm Sue-Sue had told her about, almost the size of tidal waves. She gasped, hoping Bridget would reach the wave in time to float over it. But she didn't—Bridget raised her arms, as if surrendering, and it came crashing down on her.

Sandi and Sue-Sue dove under the surging foam, then resurfaced, whooping. Hannah waited for Bridget's blonde head to pop out of the water. Was she hurt? Didn't Sandi and Sue-Sue notice that Bridget was gone? Another wave swelled and crashed, and Sandi and Sue-Sue dove under, emerging from the foam moments later.

Finally, Bridget's head popped up, her mouth stretched wide in a triumphant grin. She shouted something and flung open her arms. Hannah couldn't hear her—Bridget was too far away—but Hannah understood what she meant. She wanted Hannah to come swim with her.

Hannah shook her head. Bridget waved and hollered something else, insistent that Hannah join her.

How she wanted to. How she wished she could dive and flip and skim along the water, her arms making swift, cutting arcs. Bridget would grab her hand and they would plunge down together, swimming side by side like mermaids, and when they grew tired they would float on their backs, faces tipped toward the sun.

Hannah felt her throat constrict. She was acting like a baby, frightened and shying away, just like Daisy would if she were here.

Taking a deep breath, she peeled off her T-shirt and shorts. Tentatively, she approached the ocean.

The water was warmer than she'd expected. She walked on tiptoe, hoping she wouldn't step on any needles or nails.

Her father, she remembered, had worn striped swimming trunks that day. Or was she just remembering the photograph? In Odessa, the night before they left for California, her mother sat between her and Daisy, balancing a slender photo album on her knees, turning the pages. Her mother lifted the thin, crinkly plastic so Hannah could hold the photograph. There he was, before he grew his beard: slim and pale, with wispy, windblown hair so blond it looked almost white. And there Hannah was, the water up to her knees, holding his hand and smiling. "No bigger than a button," her mother had said. The blurred tip of her mother's finger was there, too—she was the one who had taken the picture.

Bridget yelled, "Dive under!" Hannah looked up, saw the bottoms of Bridget's feet disappear into a towering wave.

Before she could take a breath the wave came crashing down, thrashing her around in a furious tumble. Hannah came up sputtering, just in time for another, and she was lost again in a seething brown mangle of seaweed and foam, tumbling, flailing, millions of little whirlpools sucking her under with their mouths. Somewhere above, there was Sandi's cruel laughter.

III. JULY

The man with the mustache asked Hannah if she knew who Bridget was, showed her a photograph of a squinty little girl with choppy blonde hair. She was posing for the camera, with one leg bent and the other stretched out to the side. The picture was out of focus, but Hannah could tell it was Bridget standing there, with that sassy hip jutting out. Hannah handed back the photograph to the mustache man, who stood next to a man in a police uniform. They were both standing in the doorway, the mustache man looking straight into her eyes, the one in the police uniform nosing his head through the half-open door, taking a quick survey of the apartment.

Hannah gripped the doorknob, rattled it. "I don't need a picture, I know Bridget. She's my best friend."

"She is, is she? Can you tell us where she is then?"

Hannah shook her head, and the mustache man said, "When was the last time you saw her?"

"Last night."

He took out a small notepad and a pen from his inside pocket. "Go on."

Hannah told him about lying in her sleeping bag and listening to the splashing sounds of Daisy taking a bath, then about hearing Bridget and looking out the bedroom window and seeing her, as usual, sitting on the fence down below. She watched him scribble what she said on his notepad.

When he finished, he looked up and said, "She was just sitting there?"

"She was yelling," Hannah said, "the same words over and over again."

"Yelling?"

"Sort of singing. She does it almost every night."

He ducked his head down so his eyes were closer to Hannah's. "So she seemed mad?"

"Sort of happy too," she told him.

"So happy and mad at the same time?"

Hannah nodded, although it seemed to be the wrong answer. She watched his mustache twitch. "What was she wearing?"

"Her jeans shorts, I think."

"Was she wearing a shirt?"

"Yes," Hannah said, wondering why he was asking her such a dumb question. The thought made her fear him less.

"What color was the shirt?"

"White."

"White?"

"It's her Diane shirt, Bridget wears it almost every day."

"Her Diane shirt?"

He gazed at her, waiting for an answer. Hannah straightened up, suddenly feeling important. "Bridget's brother Ned," she explained, "has a girlfriend named Diane. She gave it to Bridget. It has a stain right here"—she pointed to a spot on her own T-shirt right next to her belly button—"from the time Bridget's 50-50 bar dripped on it. It's a red spot, her favorite 50-50 bar flavor is cherry."

Just picturing Bridget wearing the T-shirt made Hannah want to tell the mustache man everything about her. Her mind raced—there was so much to say. "She's adopted, she lived in

Apple Valley and then at this apartment in Lancaster where her foster mother stole five dollars from her, and then she lived in Butterfield with all these other kids." Hannah tugged at the back of her tank top, below her shoulder blade. "Right here, there's another rip in Bridget's T-shirt where Bridget said a dog with rabies tried to bite her. But I know she was lying because another time we were climbing the fence and her sleeve got caught and Bridget said that's what happened to the back of her T-shirt, one of the wires from the fence was poking up and ripped it—she said she was climbing the fence and when she jumped down the shirt got caught on the wire and she flashed Danny by mistake and he called her Little Bitty Titty."

The mustache man winced, but she went on, breathlessly: "I think she forgot about telling me before that the rip was from the dog with rabies. I asked Sue-Sue later and Sue-Sue said that the first story was a lie, that she was there when Danny called her Little Bitty Titty."

He tapped his pen on his notepad. He'd stopped writing when she got to the part about the dog.

"Who did you say Diane was?"

"Ned's girlfriend."

"Ned, Bridget's brother you mean?"

"Sort of, but not really." Hannah said. "I mean, he's not adopted. Neither is Mim—Bridget's the only one who's adopted."

The mustache man nodded. He knew this already, she could tell—he didn't write anything down.

"Bridget hates being flat-chested," she added, confident this was a fact he didn't know—only best friends knew something like that. "She said Diane got developed last summer, after ninth grade. Diane gave Bridget the shirt because it was too small. It has iron-on glitter letters on the back, too."

"What do the letters on the back of the shirt spell out?"

"Diane," she said, thinking that Bridget would have added

"*Duh,*" so he would know he just asked another dumb question. She glanced at the policeman, who coughed and shifted his weight. His silver badge flashed, catching the light.

It was then that she realized Bridget was really gone. That these were really policemen who were really looking for her. She'd lost track of how many times Bridget told her she was running away, and she'd believed Bridget less and less. All Bridget meant was that she *wanted* the words to be true, like the story Bridget told about being born in France, where her real mom was a model—when everyone in the building knew Bridget was born in Del Mar, where her real mom abandoned her in a Von's parking lot.

The mustache man asked if Bridget was wearing anything else, and Hannah said "Her Jap-Slaps," hearing her voice go soft and trembly.

"Jap-Slaps?" He raised his eyebrows, deepening his forehead wrinkles.

"They're shoes," Hannah explained. "But maybe not."

"They're not shoes?"

"No-no," she stammered, frustrated. "I mean—"

He cleared his throat and glanced at the policeman. "Where did you say your mother was?"

"At Lucky's." She looked at the policeman, but his pale blue eyes said nothing. "I meant maybe Bridget wasn't wearing her Jap-Slaps. Maybe she was barefoot, I don't remember."

The mustache man nodded, and said, "Okay, okay, I see. So that's H-A-N-N-A-H? And your last name?"

"Kierson," Hannah said. "K-I-E-R-S-O-N." She watched his pen scribble her name on his notepad.

"You give this to your mother when she gets back," he said, handing her his card.

\* \* \*

Elaine came home hugging two Lucky's grocery bags, trailed by Daisy, who she'd put in charge of holding her purse. Walking into the kitchen, she set down the groceries on the kitchen counter and kicked off her clogs.

"Hannah?" she called out.

She found her daughter in her bedroom, crouched in the corner, holding her turtle to her throat. "Why don't you give him some fresh air, honey?"

"He doesn't feel like going outside."

"Well, then, why don't you go out yourself? Maybe Bridget can play with you."

"She's gone."

"Is there anyone else you can play with? What about Sue-Sue or Sandi? I don't think it's healthy for you to be cooped up inside when it's such a beautiful—"

"No-no, Bridget's *gone!*" she cried tearfully. "Bridget ran away, she told me before she was going to but I didn't think she would."

"Bridget did what?"

Hannah threw a business card on the floor. "If you know where she is, the policeman said you have to call him."

Elaine grabbed the card. Her eyes kept scanning over and over the black letters printed there, but she could not make them form words in her mind, it was racing so.

"You talked to the police? What did you tell them? Did you tell them where she is?"

"I don't *know* where she is."

"Hannah, this is serious, very very serious. Where is she?"

Hannah crawled into her sleeping bag, cupping her turtle against her throat, and stared at the ceiling. "I don't *know.*"

Elaine absorbed this. A thought occurred to her. "Before, you said? Bridget told you *before* that she was running away? When?"

"First time I met her," Hannah mumbled.

"You *knew* she was planning this? Why didn't you say something, Hannah? Why didn't you tell me?"

But Hannah said nothing, just pulled the sleeping bag over her head.

Exasperated, Elaine marched out of the room. In the kitchen, she grabbed the phone. She held the receiver in her trembling hands and gazed at the numbers. She didn't know who to call.

The kids in the building were all in a cluster out front, talking about Bridget's disappearance. Sue-Sue and Sandi were there, along with Danny and Davy. Trevor was there too, clutching a small bag of barbecue corn nuts, his lips powdered, as usual, with bright orange dust.

Danny balanced his foot on the tip of his skateboard and stepped down, making it pop up. Joan was faking the whole runaway story, he insisted. Trevor said he bet Bridget was blindfolded and tied up in the apartment right now. Davy swore he heard Bridget crying in her bedroom. Sue-Sue shook her head, pigtails swaying, saying "Nuh uh, nuh uh, nuh uh," and Sandi kept licking her lips, looking like she had a secret.

Hannah watched them from the garden, where she was playing with her turtle by the old cactus. She stood up, putting her turtle back in its shoebox, and stepped over the low stone wall to the sidewalk. "You heard her crying?"

Davy wiggled a finger under the cast on his arm to reach an itch. "Yuh huh, her apartment's underneath, you can hear everything."

"When was she crying?"

"I heard her lots of times. Last night, too."

Danny scowled. "You didn't hear nothin' last night."

Hannah felt a pinch on her thigh. She turned, and found herself staring into Sue-Sue's round face. Sue-Sue cupped a hand over her ear and whispered, "Bridget tell you anything?" Hannah shook her head. Sue-Sue leaned in again. "I know where—"

Sandi shot Sue-Sue a warning glance.

Sue-Sue, ignoring her, said, "—where Brid—"

Sandi swiftly clamped a hand over her sister's mouth. She swung her other arm around Sue-Sue's neck, fixing her in a headlock.

Sue-Sue turned around in a furious circle and waved her arms, trying to shake Sandi off. But Sandi held on—around and around she turned, keeping her hand pressed over Sue-Sue's mouth. Then Sandi's nose wrinkled, and she yanked her hand back with a horrified shriek. "She *licked* me, *nas*ty!"

The next morning, Danny said he'd tell Hannah where Bridget was, just as soon as he got high score.

They were at Jan 'n Joe's. Trevor and Davy were pressed against the Pac-Man machine on either side of Danny, breaths held, watching him expertly gobble up the little white dots on the screen. Sandi and Sue-Sue eyed a display of glitter pens on the counter by the candy rack. Hannah stood halfway between the Pac-Man machine and the pen display, caught between two sides, the boys and the girls, waiting for one of them to tell their secret about Bridget.

"How much is this one?" Sandi asked the tan old man at the register, holding up a purple pen. "How much?" She shook the pen, rattling the little ball-bearing inside.

"Don't do that," the tan old man said, scraping under his grimy fingernails with a stretched-out paperclip.

"It's just the *tester*. You got any paper?"

"It's $1.99, read the price tag," the old tan man said. "You have $1.99?"

"Banana!" cried Trevor.

"Get it!" Davy shouted.

"Yeah, yeah, you don't think I see it?" Danny said irritably. He whammed the joystick to the left, and there was a gulping sound. The two younger boys beamed, as if the victory were theirs.

"Okay, now tell where Bridget is," Trevor said.

Hannah inched toward the Pac-Man machine, not wanting to miss a word.

"C'mon," Trevor said, "*tell* her."

Danny sternly shook his head. "Lemme get high score first."

Davy scratched under his cast and peered up at Hannah. "You been to Rose Hill?"

"What's Rose Hill?"

"The graveyard," Trevor cut in. "There's a pile of dirt, and you can tell—"

"Quit it!" Danny whammed the joystick to the right. "Wait till I get high score."

"—that someone just dug it up," Trevor continued, " 'cause the dirt on top's wet. We saw last night."

"Joan buried her there," said Davy.

"Yeah," said Trevor. "She must've stabbed Bridget like fifty thousand times."

"Shut the fuck up!" Danny cried.

Alarmed, Hannah looked over at Sandi and Sue-Sue. Sue-Sue rolled her eyes. "Joan didn't kill Bridget."

"You guys lie," said Sandi. She'd given up looking for paper, and she drew a heart on the cardboard display card, admiring the glittery purple ink. Then she drew squiggly flames around the heart. "You didn't go to the graveyard last night."

"Did too," Trevor said. "Saw Bridget's grave, too."

"Prove it," Sandi said.

The Pac-Man machine made a sad dying noise. Danny smashed his palm against the glass screen. "You made me lose my *concentration*."

Dodging cars, they crossed Pico. Danny led the way through the tall, ivied iron gate, where the twisted bars on top spelled out *Rose Hill Cemetery*.

Hannah felt a spidery chill crawl up her spine, but she tried to pretend she wasn't scared, since no one else seemed to be. Sandi and Sue-Sue kept giggling. They knew that Bridget wasn't dead, she reassured herself. But were they just acting like they knew where Bridget was, to make the boys jealous that they knew something the boys didn't? If they did know, then why wouldn't they tell her? Were Sandi and Sue-Sue trying to make *her* jealous?

Everywhere she looked, there were gravestones, hundreds of them. They were neatly lined up, row after row of them, some decorated with a small, proud flag or wilting flowers. An old lady sitting on a nearby bench tossed sunflower seeds from a crumpled bag to a flock of tiny, hopping birds. She wore a dainty felt hat with netting that came down over her shriveled eyes. A light breeze made the netting and the ivy leaves around her flutter.

"That's Bird Lady," Sue-Sue whispered to Hannah.

Hannah studied the old lady's hat. The gray, motionless lumps tangled in the black netting were birds, too. "Are those real birds she's wearing?"

Sue-Sue nodded. "Dead ones."

"They're fake," Sandi said. "She's just trying to freak you out."

"Come *on*," Trevor pleaded.

Hannah reluctantly followed them, weaving around the gravestones, stepping over the small, flat ones that Sue-Sue told her were for dead babies. Davy and Trevor ran up ahead to a soap-white pillar on a platform surrounded by shallow steps. It was the tallest grave there. The richest dead man in the whole neighborhood was underneath, Davy told her. Four angels with frozen fat faces looked down at them, one at each corner. Danny picked up a small rock and threw it, hitting one of the angels square in the face.

Trevor scrambled up the marble steps to the top of the platform and pointed to the wood shed in the corner of the graveyard. "Bridget's ghost rose up exactly at midnight, right over there," he shouted excitedly. Sandi and Sue-Sue giggled.

"Yuh huh, it did too!" Trevor shot back. "Tell her," he said to Danny.

"Aw, this is stupid," Danny said. He spat on the ground and squinted wistfully in the direction of Jan 'n Joe's, jingling the loose change in the pocket of his shorts.

"Bridget's buried behind the shed," Trevor insisted, on the brink of tears. He tugged at Hannah's arm. "C'mere, look!"

Hannah yanked her arm back. "Bridget's not dead," she said, trying to make her voice hard with conviction.

Trevor looked past her, his eyes widening, fixed on something in the distance.

Hannah turned, and saw an elderly black man in a dirty blue uniform approach, his face drawn and withered, reminding her of raisins. He carried a rake and dragged a trash bag behind him.

"Hide!" Trevor screamed.

Everyone took cover. Hannah stood there, confused, until Sue-Sue grabbed the back of her T-shirt and tugged her behind a tree.

"That's Bones, he works here, he digs up graves," Sue-Sue whispered urgently. "There's bones in the bag. He gathers them and then he *burns* them."

Bones let go of the trash bag. "No horsin' around, understand? This is a place where people go to rest. You kids don't want to wake up the dead, now do you?"

When no one said anything, Bones coughed into his fist. "You think I'm foolin' huh? Let me tell you something. I worked here for thirty years, and I could tell you a thing or two about the things I seen. Kids get to horsin' around in here, thinkin' it's all fun and games. That is, until it gets dark. Then they're sorry they ever set foot in here. But," he sighed dramatically, "I guess you don't want to hear that story…" He started to walk away, dragging his trash bag and his rake behind him.

"What story?" Trevor called out to him.

"Hm?" Bones turned around. "You wanna hear it?"

Everyone came out from their hiding places, everyone except Danny, who hadn't bothered to hide and was sitting on top of a gravestone, smoking a cigarette and snickering. Hannah wondered what was in the trash bag at the old man's feet, whether there were really bones that he was gathering to burn.

"You see Bridget's ghost last night?" Trevor asked him. "Floating over the shed? Danny, tell him what you saw."

Danny smirked and exhaled a cloud of cigarette smoke.

So Trevor told the old man himself, blurting the story about sneaking out last night and spotting Bridget's ghost behind the shed at midnight. He might have even seen blood dripping from her mouth, he added, his eyes so wide they were nearly popping out of his skull.

Bones nodded solemnly, scratching at his stubbled chin. "Well I don't know about last night—it was my night off, you see, and I was home. But if this girl is anyone like the girl I knew a while back, oh, fifteen years or so ago, before you all were born, I wouldn't doubt it. Was this Bridget one of your friends? One of your friends who run around like you, stompin' over the graves and causin' a ruckus?"

"Yeah," Sue-Sue said, cautiously.

He leaned on the rake, as if preparing for a long story. "Well about fifteen years ago, like I said, there was a girl. Used to come in here and run all around, yellin' and makin' a menace of herself. Makes the dead uneasy, you see, all that noise. One night I heard a noise—I was workin' late, you understand, I have to keep this place clean, and this girl had made such a mess, tippin' over trashcans and throwin' rocks all around, that I had to stay past dark cleanin' it all up. So I hear this noise, sort of like…"

He paused, then stomped his foot on the ground, making everyone—even Danny—jump. Sue-Sue let out a scream.

"The noise—the noise was comin' from behind the shed, right where you said you saw your friend's ghost last night. Then all of a sudden I see a white thing, and I thought well get ahold of yourself, it's just your imagination. Workin' in a graveyard will give you these notions, you know. But then I see it's got these red glowin' eyes."

Sue-Sue screamed again.

"And then I see another, and another, there's ten, twenty of these ghosts with red eyes buggin' out, and they're all in a circle, and in the middle of the circle there's the little girl in her pajamas, and she opens her mouth and screams and right then—right then—"

Bones shook his head, like it was too much for him.

"What—what happened?" Trevor cried, breathing quick, almost panting.

"Right then," Bones lowered his voice to a hush, "one of the ghosts—he spits blood into her mouth. And the little girl—she's covered in blood now, all red and drippin' down her face—she opens her mouth to scream again but she can't make any noise this time, the ghost's blood burned like some kind of poisonous acid right through her tongue and vocal cords."

He gazed a good five seconds at Sue-Sue. "Open your mouth."

She did as she was told. He peered in. "You got a good tongue there. It'd be a shame to lose it, don't you think?"

Sue-Sue let out a terrified squeak and clapped her mouth shut.

"So all of you remember that little girl," he said, "next time you think about playin' in here, shoutin' and yellin' and carryin' on." He gave them all one last stern look before walking away, dragging the rake and the trash bag behind him.

Hannah held her breath until she saw that Bones was gone. Her heart was still pounding.

"Boooo!" Danny said, making Sue-Sue scream again.

"Quit it!" she yelled.

"Hey," Danny said to the other boys. "Ditch 'em!"

The three of them bolted off. At the gate, they ran through the flock of birds pecking away at Bird Lady's sunflower seeds.

* * *

Back at Jan 'n Joe's, Sandi commanded Hannah to be the Lookout while she and Sue-Sue went in.

Sandi was always bossy, and Hannah hated her for it, but she found herself following Sandi's orders anyway. She was used to being the Lookout—it was always her role when Sandi and Sue-Sue and Bridget smoked in the cabinets or stole candy—and she convinced herself she didn't mind.

Through the window, she watched them linger at the candy display. Sue-Sue slipped two Hersheys in her pocket and Sandi admired the purple glitter pen again, rattling the ball bearing inside until the tan old man shook his finger at her.

Sandi walked out first, followed by Sue-Sue. Then Sandi yelled "Run!"

Hannah raced after them. They tore down the block, then the next, then the next. When they got to the apartment building they stopped at the mailboxes to catch their breath.

Sandi glared at Sue-Sue. "Shut up about Bridget, okay? She said not to tell."

"Tell what?" said Hannah. She'd been taking it all in, getting more and more confused but trying to keep quiet, afraid of the quick turn things took: one minute someone acted like your friend, and the next they're laughing at you. Was Sandi lying? Why would Bridget tell Sandi and Sue-Sue and not her? Bridget was always talking nasty behind their backs, saying that Sandi was a CB and Sue-Sue was a BB, or sometimes the other way around—CB for Cry-Baby and BB for Blabbermouth Bitch—or sometimes Bridget would change the words, making them even meaner, *Pendejo* instead of Blabbermouth or *Cabrón* instead of Cry-Baby. Hannah didn't know what the Spanish meant, except that they were insults she heard the Mexican kids shout at each other on the other side of Pico.

"C'mon, why can't we tell her?" Sue-Sue asked.

Sandi bit her lip, considering. "First I wanna get one of those purple glitter pens. You got any money?"

"No," Hannah said.

"Liar!" Sandi lunged at her, and jabbed her hand down Hannah's pocket. Without thinking, Hannah shoved her back, so hard Sandi looked even more surprised than Hannah herself.

"Fine," Sandi said icily. "She talks trash about you, you know."

"Who?"

"Bridget."

"She does not."

"Does too."

"What does she say?" Hannah looked at Sue-Sue, who started giggling. "What? Tell me!"

Sandi crossed her arms. "You wanna know where Bridget is?"

"Yes."

Sandi was silent. "Yes!" Hannah repeated.

"I bet you do," Sandi spat back. Then she grabbed Sue-Sue's hand and stalked off.

Tanya had been going to the Parents Without Partners dinners for the past few months, and had started campaigning for PWP even more vigorously than she did for the Church of Latter-Day Saints. Though she declared she was soured on men ever since her ex left her high and dry, as she put it, she confided to the mothers in the building that she still held out for the possibility of there being a diamond in the rough at those dinners. The two things that were missing from the lives of these women were religion (or the right one, as Tanya saw it—the right one being Mormonism) and men (all of the mothers being single, except for Mrs. Hamilton in number six, who in Tanya's opinion was married to the wrong man, Rich Sr. being an alcoholic good-for-nothing).

As far as Tanya's recruiting efforts for the Church of Latter-Day Saints were concerned, they met with little success. The Hamiltons in number six didn't go to church anymore, since Sundays were the only days they could visit Rich Jr. in juvenile hall (to make up for it, Mrs. Hamilton woke up at six a.m. to watch the Holy Hour on TV, while Rich Sr. slept off his hangover). The widowed Mrs. Grover in number three had renounced God years ago when her husband and baby were killed in that awful auto accident; Joan in number one wasn't even worth asking (for all Tanya knew, she drew pentagrams on the Day of Rest); and Alma in number two was agnostic ("Or sort of Buddhist, anyway," as Alma put it). Finally, there was Elaine in number five, and even though she was non-practicing, Tanya knew better than to seek a convert in a Catholic.

But Tanya's recruiting efforts for PWP were much more successful: in the month she'd been going to the dinners she'd convinced Alma to go with her once already. She was bound to win over Elaine one of these days—she'd invited her to three dinners already, and the shaky resolve in her ever-so-polite refusals wouldn't hold out much longer.

*  *  *

"I can't," Elaine said when she opened the door to find Tanya standing there.

"I won't take no for an answer. How can we turn that can't into a can?"

"We can't. I'm sorry."

"It's just nerves," Tanya soothed. "You'll feel better, I promise. Wait till we get there. You'll find a nice man."

"How can you think about men," Elaine said, exasperated, "when a little girl is missing?"

"That's what's got you so upset? Bridget does this every six months or so. They'll find her, now don't you worry."

"Maybe the next time," Elaine said, hoping to put her off.

"You're scared, I know, it's an adjustment." She reached out to pat Elaine on the wrist. "I heard about what happened. To your husband, I mean."

Elaine drew back, stunned.

"I know, it's hard to move on. But it's time you got out there. Three years is long enough to mourn those who have passed from the earth to join God in His Kingdom."

Elaine hadn't told Tanya or anybody else in the building

about her life before California, about Roger or anything else. They were memories she hoped to bury. Hannah must have let the story get out to one of the children. And Tanya, as the eyes and the ears of the building—and, Elaine was learning, the wagging tongue—soon learned the truth. The idea struck Elaine as unseemly, Roger's death being reduced to gossip.

"It's not that bad, just a bunch of single people in a room together, eating food and talking. Tomorrow night I'll come by and see if you're up to it."

"Well, we'll see." She hoped Tanya would not think her unfriendly, but it was really out of the question.

"Let me know if all that thinking does you some good and you change your mind. You gotta start putting yourself out there again, honey. Your husband would give you the same advice if he was still here to give it to you."

Elaine nodded, clenching the doorknob, preparing to shut the door. It was an impossible hypothetical scenario to imagine—cheating time somehow to receive counsel from Roger who, if he were alive to give her advice, would never suggest she date other men, since if he were alive he would still be her husband and then why on earth would he advise her to betray him?

Later, while Elaine stood over the stove making dinner, she thought about her conversation with Tanya. She often mused about her day while she was cooking; the rhythm of her task released her thoughts, and as she moved her wooden spoon around the bubbling macaroni and cheese, she decided two things: either Tanya and the others did not know all of the facts about Roger's death, or Tanya's faith was flexible enough to forgive the fact that suicide was a mortal sin.

As for herself, Elaine hadn't been able to reconcile the Catholicism of her youth with her adult beliefs—or non-beliefs. Well, she didn't know what she believed, she conceded, dishing out the macaroni and cheese into three bowls. Try as she might, she could not purge herself completely of what Roger had insisted were the superstitions force-fed to her by her simple-minded parents.

"Dinner!" Elaine called out.

Hannah and Daisy clambered into the kitchen. She set out spoons and torn-up paper towels for napkins as her girls plopped down in their chairs.

As they ate, Elaine glanced away from the vaguely unsettling spectacle of her girls eating their macaroni and cheese—Daisy was devouring it, forgetting her manners, while Hannah listlessly picked out the onion bits—and looked down at her hands, which were, for the moment, folded in her lap. Her fingers, she was surprised to discover, were running through the imaginary beads of an imaginary rosary.

There wasn't a prayer in her head; it was the rhythms of her childhood faith that provided the comfort. She hadn't even been wholly aware that she was upset; it was her body that reminded her.

After putting Hannah and Daisy to bed, she decided to indulge herself with a warm, relaxing bubble bath to soothe her nerves.

Daisy's Mr. Bubble would have to do. She poured the cartoon-pink liquid into the running bath water. The bubbles foamed to the surface, releasing a sweet bubble gum scent. She undressed quickly, and stepped into the tub.

At last, she was alone.

Closing her eyes, Elaine tried to imagine what kind of man she'd like to meet. Tall, dark, and handsome was what came to mind. But this image did not belong to her. It was something she'd dredged up from some common reservoir, a silly romantic ideal women pictured when they didn't know what they wanted, exactly. Was it that they were merely dim, or unimaginative, or simply that they found comfort in a communal fantasy? She dismissed the thought; she didn't have the energy to pursue it. All she knew was that she wanted something of her own.

The water dripping from the faucet reminded her that time was passing, that she had not yet settled on the details of the man she longed for. And then it came to her: kind eyes and strong arms.

How long it had been since she'd been held.

She let her body sink deeper into the sweet-smelling, foamy water. Tanya was right, she thought.

It *was* time.

But what would she tell her girls? What would they say if she told them she was going out with Tanya and Alma to meet men?

She decided to make homemade pizza for her girls tomorrow night, hoping it would make her daughters more forgiving when she broke the news she'd be eating dinner out. Since moving to Sunset Terrace, she had only left them alone to make a quick trip to Lucky's, and although she knew she would soon have to start earning some money, she wanted to postpone getting a job as long as she possibly could. She knew how much her girls had missed her all those nights she had to work a late shift. When she returned to the hotel room, how Daisy threw her arms around her thighs. How Hannah hung back, moodily, with a pretense of indifference, though Elaine could detect something like relief in her daughter's eyes.

She turned on the hot water tap. The force of the water made the bubbles under the faucet enlarge again and pop. Pouring out the last of the bubble bath from the bottle, she made a mental note to buy more Mr. Bubble for Daisy when she went to Lucky's tomorrow. What else? Hannah would want pepperoni on the pizza. And she was running out of mozzarella—she will have to buy more of that, too. She wondered whether she had any dried yeast in the refrigerator, then decided to buy french bread and make pizza boats instead.

She will not go overboard, making crust from scratch; tomorrow, she will get through the day without running herself ragged. Yes, tomorrow, she will meet a man.

* * *

Tanya rapped on the front door at exactly six-thirty, wearing a short denim skirt and one of her fringed blouses.

Elaine found herself lagging behind as Tanya clip-clopped excitedly toward Alma's apartment. Tanya's high heels didn't slow her down, even though they put her feet at a painful-looking angle, the knuckles of her toes bulging out where the shoes came to a pointed tip. Gazing down at the cement pathway, Elaine walked past *SxMx* and *Danetta 1962* and *RD+JS=4-Ever* and *Hot Tuna Rocks!* When she reached the laundry room, her eyes settled on *Bridget '83*. She laid a hand against her chest, trying to press down the panicky feeling rising up in her.

"Excuse the mess," Tanya said, swiping aside an empty Diet Shasta can in the front seat of her station wagon. "Who wants to sit shotgun?"

"I'll sit in back," Elaine volunteered, wishing that she had insisted on going to the PWP dinner alone, in her Datsun. Her hand stuck to the vinyl seat as she climbed in—the drippings of a popsicle, or a melted lollipop—a reminder that children usually sat here.

Alma sat down in the passenger's seat, reaching behind her neck to fluff out the long, glossy, black hair that fell like a satin sheet down her back. She had draped herself in an Indian-print dress.

"Do you have enough leg room?" Alma asked, glancing back at Elaine. "I can move the seat up."

"No no, I'm fine."

Tanya had once called Alma a "hippie ma," and Elaine

looked at her now with this in mind. She had a wide, makeup-free face and a way of talking that made her seem far away: the words came out slow and easy, as if moving through a warm mist. Elaine knew Alma was Trevor's mother, but she didn't really know her, hadn't had a conversation with her—just the usual short, neighborly exchanges when they passed each other on the cement pathway. From Tanya's gossip Elaine had learned that Alma's ex-husband lived in Sherman Oaks and was waging a custody battle for Trevor, and that Alma worked as a court stenographer. Elaine tried to imagine Alma in a courtroom full of lawyers in expensive suits, with her long shiny hair and a drapey dress, typing away. It was difficult to picture.

"The engine needs to warm for a minute or so," Tanya announced.

They sat in the parked station wagon, waiting. Alma rubbed Vaseline on her lips and brushed her hair with a squarish, wooden-handled brush. She offered the jar of Vaseline to Tanya, who shook her head, saying she needed more color than clear, smearing on another coat of bright red lipstick.

"Vaseline, Elaine?" Alma said.

"Oh, no thank you," Elaine said, scraping her fingernail at the spot of tomato sauce she'd discovered on her sleeve.

There was a clanking sound above the engine's rumble. Tanya gave a good-natured sigh, patted the dashboard, and sang, *The ole gray mare, she ain't what she used to be.*

"We're in no hurry," Alma told her.

"Speak for yourself," Tanya said, her eyes twinkling. "I'm itchin' to meet some men."

Elaine gave up on the tomato sauce spot and closed her eyes, feeling frazzled. She'd gotten the pizza in the oven fifteen minutes later than she'd planned. By the time she'd found the tortoiseshell combs she used to keep her hair from bushing out on the sides she'd only had five minutes to decide on an outfit. And how difficult it had been to leave—Daisy wailed and threw her arms around Elaine's thighs when she kissed her good-bye, clinging so tightly that she had to literally peel her off. Keep the front door locked, she had cautioned. Don't let anyone in. Be good. They knew the rules, but she repeated them whenever she had to leave them alone for a quick trip to Lucky's, just to make sure.

Tanya revved the engine. "Okay, girls," she said, "fasten your seatbelts." The station wagon clattered down the driveway and out onto the street.

Elaine rested her head against the back windshield and let her thoughts drift. Thank goodness Hannah didn't fuss like her younger sister. At times like this, Hannah's dark moods almost felt like a blessing. She kept to herself, played with her turtle, requiring nothing. It was a relief, in a way. But when Elaine kissed Hannah good-bye and Hannah flinched, cupping her turtle against her throat, the relief shifted to the other, more persistent feeling she had around her daughter ever since Roger's death—a sort of melancholy helplessness, a wearying ache that ran through her like a cold fluid.

"Honey, open your eyes, this isn't a sleepover."

"Oh, sorry." Elaine straightened up. "I was just letting my mind wander."

"She's just teasing you, Elaine," Alma said. "You can rest if you want to."

"Rest?" Tanya said. "She can rest when she's got a man warming up the other side of the bed."

Tanya slid in a cassette tape and turned up the volume. "Dolly'll get you in the mood."

There was the strum of a guitar, then Dolly Parton's voice, singing *Sittin' on the front porch on a sum-mer afternoon.*

The car was heavy with a cloying scent of flowers and musk; Tanya had doused herself in perfume. Elaine coughed. Roger had hated the smell of perfume. He'd said—what was it?—that perfume was evidence of undisguised effort, that effort in matters of love was unappealing because it smacked of desperation, a force that did not attract but repelled. And although she had thought it was heartless and unromantic of him to cringe when she wore perfume on a special occasion, she could almost see his point, now.

How strange, that she could now concede to one of Roger's funny ideas—that she could look at Tanya as if through his eyes. A woman he did not even know—could not know.

No, not how strange—how cruel. He would never know it; she could never tell him this, could never whisper in his ear that one night on her way to a PWP dinner to meet single men she had found herself watching Tanya drive and thought, of all things, about what awful judgmental things he would say about this woman. The words he'd choose would be something like "irritatingly ebullient" and "prototypically Southern vapid charm."

She shuddered. Not how cruel. How morbid: she was looking at the living through a dead man's eyes.

Tanya glanced at her in the rearview mirror. "Bridget disappeared for a few days last year, too. I ever tell you the story?"

"No," Elaine managed to say.

"Well, the police came by, same as this morning, knocking on everyone's doors. No one knew anything about where she was. We were all worried out of our minds. Joan was running around in a bathrobe all day long, screaming Bridget's name every five minutes, screaming some other nasty things too if you know what I mean. If I was Bridget, I'd run away from her, too."

"Me too," Alma said sadly.

"Anyway, turned out Bridget was hiding out at her brother's girlfriend's garage. Ned didn't know Bridget had followed him. The girlfriend didn't know she was there, either. I bet you that's where Bridget is now. So don't you worry, they'll find her. She's probably in that garage right now, gettin' grease on her tushie."

Elaine realized, with a guilty pang, that Tanya was reassuring her. Tanya assumed she was feeling anxious about Bridget, when for the moment her mind was on Roger. It struck Elaine as a selfish act—she was indulging in feelings of regret for her dead husband, imagining conversations with him that she could never have.

All she could think to say was, "Do you think so?"

"I know so," Tanya said resolutely.

Elaine settled back into the seat and sighed. Regret, so much regret. Regret that she'd caused herself so much pain by picking the wrong man to fall in love with. Regret that she married him. Regret that she had not noticed his gloom was more than mere malaise. She'd been convinced that his mood swings—the fierce outbursts followed by stony silences—had to do with his disappointment in her. She was not bright enough for him, his insights about people and politics never occurred to her. You have no opinions, Roger often accused. She couldn't help but blame herself for failing to be what he wanted her to be.

At some point, looking back, she allowed herself the revelation that her shortcomings didn't have anything to do with his depression, with his suicide. She was not comforted by this thought: she'd missed the opportunity to help him when he needed her most. Instead, she had been consumed with herself, worried about the ways she didn't measure up—too wrapped up in herself to pay attention to him. And now he was dead, dead and gone.

But here was a little girl, full of life and vibrancy, who was out there, somewhere, waiting to be rescued. Someone who *could* be rescued.

Tanya turned up the volume. "Here's the best part," she said, as Dolly Parton started to yodel.

The truth was, even though Tanya had told Elaine about there being loads of men at PWP dinners, women outnumbered them nearly four to one. If you asked Tanya to explain the discrepancy between what she said she saw and what was the cold, hard truth, she wouldn't be able to account for it, but she'd fiercely deny that what she said was a falsification, as she fervently believed that lying is a sin. Maybe it's that people see what they want to see, or at least they believe if they hope for something badly enough, it will somehow materialize, placing their bets on the transformative magic of self-fulfilling prophecy.

She was right in telling Elaine that there were all kinds to choose from, though: there were a few businessmen in pinstriped suits carrying leather briefcases, just off work, mixing with what some might call members of the lesser professions. Not blue-collar men, exactly—construction workers and plumbers didn't frequent these sorts of social gatherings—just men whose positions made them feel as if their stature as men of the world was begrimed by the lowly tedium of their jobs: assistant managers of electronics stores and shoe outlets and chain drug stores, travel agents, postal workers, dental assistants, insurance brokers, public school teachers, accountants at second-tier firms, and the like.

But Elaine wasn't thinking about man-to-woman ratios or professional or social hierarchies as she stood in the back of the room during the cocktail hour, sipping now and then from a glass of house white as she surveyed the scene.

All that was on her mind was this: *Why am I here?*

People around her were filing into the smaller room in back, where the tables were set up. She felt a light hand on her shoulder and jumped.

"You okay?"

It was Alma, smiling her serene, drowsy smile.

"Oh, yes, yes. Sorry, I—"

"Come on, then. It's dinner time."

Elaine took a seat at the far end of one of the long tables, unfolded her checkered cloth napkin and spread it on her lap. A waitress came by and asked if she wanted another glass of white wine. Elaine ordered iced tea instead; the wine had given her a headache. When the waitress returned, Elaine saw that the glass was enormous, more iced tea than anyone could finish in one sitting.

There were free refills, the waitress said. Elaine wondered how she could ever manage to take advantage of such an offer.

"Leslie Smucker, hi."

Elaine turned toward the voice. It belonged to a man in a brown blazer, sitting at her right.

"And you are...?" His question ended with a jovial grin that revealed a poppyseed stuck between two lower teeth.

She had the curious impulse to make up a name, to disguise her identity from this messy man—and would have, if her eyes hadn't moved from the poppyseed in his teeth to the white sticker on the pocket of his jacket where, below the *Hi! My Name Is*, he'd scrawled LESLIE M. SMUCKER in cramped capital letters. She remembered then that she, too, had such a name tag stuck to her blouse, below the rounded collar. This Leslie Smucker didn't need to ask her name.

But she said "Elaine" anyway, selecting a sourdough roll from the bread basket.

"Nice to meet you, Elaine. Do you mind if I...?" Before waiting for an answer, he reached across her plate for the bread basket and snatched another poppyseed roll.

Elaine took a long gulp of her iced tea—too long—and started to cough.

"Went down the wrong pipe?" Leslie asked, patting her back.

She flinched and looked around the room, desperate for an excuse to move her chair a few inches away from Leslie without appearing too rude. She spotted Tanya across the table several chairs away, nibbling at a breadstick with a pinky daintily raised.

"Tanya," she said, and gestured toward Leslie. "This is—"

"We met already, he's a regular," Tanya said. "Hi, Leslie."

He gave her a stiff, courteous nod. It was clear he didn't like her either.

"Honey, you gotta get yourself a toothpick for that black thang in your teeth."

"I do?" He drank a glass of water and swished it around his mouth.

"I said a *toothpick!*" Tanya cried when he started jimmying a fingernail between his teeth. "Lord, didn't your momma teach you table manners?"

"Switch!"

The woman who had given them their name tags carved a circle in the air with her finger. It was time, Elaine was more than pleased to discover, to sit next to a new person.

A general confusion followed. It was a clumsy procedure, with everyone taking their silverware and glasses with them to their new seats. Elaine sat down in the first empty chair she could find. She didn't have an appetite, but she wanted to get her money's worth, so by the time dessert and coffee were brought to the tables, Elaine had drunk one and a half glasses of iced tea, and had eaten two plates of all-you-can-eat spaghetti. And she'd spoken to five men.

After Leslie, there was Rick, a twice-divorced gaffer with a handlebar moustache (Elaine half-listened to him explain what a gaffer did—something to do with movie crews); Sam, who taught at a small alternative high school and had a teenage son who lived with his remarried ex-wife; Philip, a defense attorney who lived with his son (his ex-wife, he said, couldn't handle the kid); and finally, Don, who didn't mention an ex-wife or a child, but instead talked her ear off about the success he was enjoying at Hughes Aircraft, now that the Defense Department had awarded $26.3 billion in contracts to the California aerospace industry.

Of the five of them, Elaine liked Sam the best. He'd also gone on and on about his job, but teaching interested her much more than military airplanes and movie crews. What a relief: she didn't have to muffle her yawns or nod her head with feigned curiosity.

"Troubled teens," Sam called his students, and the way he talked about them was positively moving. He was so passionate, so filled with vigor, his eyes lighting up as he went on about Jorge, who barely spoke English when he first came to the school and was now reading Hemingway—and about Christabell, who had gotten kicked out of her school and was now painting the whale mural on the wall outside the school library. Then he talked about his son, Mitchell, who was fifteen.

He felt as if he was losing him, Sam told her.

Elaine felt her breath catch. She was surprised by the naked admission.

"I am his enemy," he said simply, with a look of clarity in his eyes.

"Your...enemy?"

"Yes. It's only natural, I suppose, at Mitchell's age. I'm his father, he's fighting to define himself against me."

"But you're good with children," Elaine said, wanting to reassure him. "I mean, that's what it seems, from what you've said."

"Well, a teacher is different from a parent. Jeanine tells me that I should—that's my ex-wife—she says I should—" He cut himself off. "God. Sorry, never mind."

"No, go on," she said. She didn't mind him mentioning an ex-wife—in fact, it was endearing. Unlike the other men that night who'd rambled on about themselves, oblivious to her stifled yawns, he cared about what she thought.

"The world is different now. Meaner. And in some ways less mean, I suppose."

"How, would you say?" Elaine asked, intrigued.

"These kids have problems to worry about that we'd never dreamed of when we were their age. The meaner sort of problems, is what I'm trying to say. And as for the Less Mean— a misnomer, really—they're not faced with any wars, any ideological battles. Well, there's the Cold War, but that's a fiction, we'll soon find out, I'd bet on it. This 'Star Wars' nonsense is just a ploy for military expenditures."

Sam was beginning to sound like Roger. Elaine took another look at him now, and could not resist comparing them: bright, shining eyes (just like Roger's), thinning hair at his crown (Roger's hair was thinning at his temples), hands that seemed disconnected from his body, karate-chopping the air to emphasize an idea (Roger's stayed folded in his lap, except when he was enraged, when they'd fly around wildly).

"Switch!"

Sam looked startled. For a moment, he looked to her like a lost child.

"Well," Elaine said, picking up her silverware.

"Can I—?" he began.

"It was so nice talking with you. Really."

He looked wounded. But she wanted to leave him, just then, even though she'd enjoyed his company. His resemblance to Roger unnerved her.

After her mother left for the PWP dinner, Hannah ran down the stairs to Bridget's apartment.

Pressing her ear against the front door, she could hear the TV inside: the volume low, a sudden burst of tinny laughter. She tiptoed under the living room window—shut tight as it always was whenever Joan wasn't leaning out it smoking—and tried peeping through the thin opening in the curtains.

Who was in there? she wondered, half-hoping to see Bridget tied to a chair with a thick rope, a strip of silver tape over her mouth. She would rescue Bridget! Wait for Joan to leave for Culver City, then come crashing through the window in a magnificent shatter of glass. She'd use one of the shards to expertly cut the rope off, and the relief and admiration in Bridget's brimming eyes would never leave.

Hannah squinted, trying to make out in the shadows a chair, a girl, a rope. But she saw no one: the room was empty and dark, except for the blue flicker of the TV.

She tiptoed away from the window and ran around the building to the parking lot in back. Looking up at the row of storage cabinets, she remembered Bridget's hiding place. Hannah jumped up, trying to reach the cabinet's rusted handle to open the door, but it was too high.

"*Bridget!*"

No response. "*Bridget!*" she whispered once more.

Again, she pictured a chair, a rope. Maybe Bridget was in her bedroom. She ran up the asphalt driveway and stopped in front of Bridget's bedroom window. Here, just like the living room, the curtains were drawn, the room dark; no sign Bridget was in there.

Hannah tapped the glass anyway.

A meaty hand swooped the curtain back. A pair of glassy, bloodshot eyes appeared.

She jumped back, losing her balance on the loose gravel. Her palm hit the ground first, a sideways slap and skid that broke her fall but sent needles of pain up her arm. Behind the windowpane, he was laughing, looking down at her.

It was Ned, she saw. Only Ned.

The pain in her arm sharpened, coming on in full force now that her fear was gone. A rustle of curtains and a teenage girl's face appeared next to Ned's, her black eyeliner smudged, her eyes glassy and red-veined, too. The girl blew out a cloud of smoke and smiled down at Hannah, revealing the silver glint of a retainer.

Diane, she thought. Ned's girlfriend.

Then the faces disappeared. The curtain swung shut, but not before Hannah got a peep into the room: the bed in the wrong place, by the window, and a Van Halen poster on the wall. She realized her mistake: it was Ned's room, not Bridget's. She looked down the side of the building, where the windows of people's bedrooms—all sooty and small and covered with the same yellowish-white curtains—were lined up in a row. Bridget's was the next one over, the room also dark. She tapped on the window, but the curtain stayed motionless.

Hannah climbed the chain-link fence and straddled it, the way she'd seen Bridget do. Her scraped-up hand stung. She looked up and saw her own bedroom window. She was sitting right where Bridget perched herself on all those nights, singing her songs. The thought brought hot tears to her eyes, and she felt Bridget's absence carve inside her a deeper cavern.

She stayed on the fence for a long time, long enough to watch Ned and his girlfriend drive past on his mo-ped, and for Rich Sr. to come and go twice in his beat-up Buick. The streetlight by the dumpster came on, casting a faint, yellow glow over the Sunset Terrace sign and the chewed-up cactus in the garden out front. Someone was broiling hamburgers in a nearby apartment, and the smell made her stomach growl. Hannah listlessly banged her heel against the metal fencepost, remembering: *Mother-fuckin', titty-suckin' two-balled bitch, Momma's in the kitchen cookin' red hot shit, Daddy's in jail, sayin' go to hell.*

There was a hollow rumbling in the distance, the sound of roller skates on asphalt, growing louder. She heard a hoot— Danny's voice—and farther away shouts from Trevor and Sue-Sue.

She scrambled down the fence and ran out to the front of the building. Danny whizzed past on his roller skates. After a deft swivel he performed a smooth semicircle, turning his knees outward and bending down low. He skated back toward her, passing Trevor and Sue-Sue, who wove around him.

Davy was next, swinging his arm with the cast on it around and around like a propeller. There was a tennis ball in his hand.

Sandi, coming up from behind, screamed *Give it!*

Davy threw the tennis ball at the dumpster. It bounced off with a metallic thunk and rolled under a parked car. Danny scooped it up and zoomed past. Another quick pivot and he was skating backwards. He threw it back to Trevor, but Trevor tripped and the tennis ball hit the side of the building next door.

Hannah ran after the ball and grabbed it. Her scraped-up hand didn't hurt anymore, and she ran back, exhilarated.

Danny swiveled around and skated toward her, his hands cupped in front of him. "Give it here!"

"It's mine!" Sandi shouted. She gave Hannah a pleading look.

Hannah remembered Sandi's cruel refusal to tell her where Bridget was. She grit her teeth and threw the ball back to Danny.

Fuming, Sandi pivoted and chased after Danny. "Give it!"

"Monkey in the middle!" Danny shouted, and threw the ball to Hannah. She caught it, laughing now.

"Hannah, give it!" Sandi cried.

"Make me!"

"Fine!" Sandi skated toward her in a rage. Hannah clenched the ball in her fist, ready to throw it back to Danny, when Sandi's skate hit a rock and she fell face forward, landing at Hannah's feet.

Another second and Sandi was bawling.

"Fuckin' baby," Danny snorted, and skated off.

Sandi clutched her knee. "My bone's broke," she sobbed.

\* \* \*

The next morning, Elaine went to Lucky's with Hannah.

"Hello there," Tanya said flatly when they reached the head of her line. She plucked the coupons out of Elaine's hand, rang up four cans of tuna fish and slid them one after the other to the other side of the counter like hockey pucks. They hit the rim of the counter so hard Elaine wondered if she'd dented them.

"Where's my bag boy?" Tanya barked. "Tito? Miguel?"

"I told you, we're one short today," a checkout clerk two registers down wearily called out. "Tito's sick."

"Lazy's more like it. *Mexicans.*" She spit the word out like it tasted bad in her mouth.

*My my*, Elaine thought, inching back a step. She had never seen Tanya's streak of meanness before. Why was Tanya acting this way?

Then it dawned on her: here was a single woman with four children to raise all on her own. Stuck in a supermarket, ringing up groceries for a living. Tanya bore her burdens year in and year out, never letting on how much they weighed on her, the curled pigtails and Southern cheer poignant indications of her stoic refusal to let an empty purse and empty bed spoil an otherwise sunny California day.

"Here, let me help," Elaine said. She took a paper bag from the stack at the end of the counter and filled them with her groceries, careful to put the heavier items on the bottom. "You know, I noticed that the man with the beard was looking at you last night at the PWP dinner. Remember him? The one who sat across from you?"

Tanya's manner grew even chiller. "What's your point?"

"Well, maybe he'll be there next time."

"Hope not. The only one worth lookin' at was that teacher who gave you his number. At least someone got lucky. Thirty-five twenty-nine, please." Tanya snatched the money out of her hand.

"Why are—?" Elaine began, but Tanya cut her off.

"Listen here, don't act so innocent," she snapped, and looked Elaine dead in the eye. Then she glared at Hannah, who up until now had hoped to remain invisible, hiding behind the grocery cart. "I think your daughter over there has an apology to make to my daughter."

Hannah looked up to find both women staring at her, one with a frosty glare, the other with a look of fragile confusion.

On the ride home, Hannah did her best to explain what had happened the night before—that she was just standing there, throwing the tennis ball with everyone else, when Sandi lost her balance and fell down in front of her.

"You should say sorry anyway," her mother insisted. "Just to keep things peaceful. It's such a small building, and they're our neighbors, after all."

"But it wasn't my fault," Hannah cried.

"No one's blaming anyone."

"Sandi is! Tanya is!"

"Hannah," her mother said sharply. "I want you to apologize to Sandi."

Sandi sat on the bottom stair, the cast on her leg blinding white in the sun, with Sue-Sue by her side. Hannah walked toward them, moving as slowly as possible so she could think of something to say. She didn't want to apologize.

"Can I sign your cast?" she said at last.

Sandi coolly lifted her chin. "You got a pen?"

"No, but I can get one."

"Get the purple glitter one at Jan 'n Joe's."

"I told you before," Hannah insisted, "I don't have any money."

Sandi narrowed her eyes. "Well get some. My leg's broke because of you."

"It wasn't my fault," Hannah cried. "Danny threw the ball, and then I caught it, and then—"

"Tryin' to steal my ball."

"I was not!"

"You broke my leg!"

"I did not!"

"Tch," was all Sandi said.

Banished from their company, Hannah spent the rest of the afternoon alone, making a silent plea for Bridget to come back. Listless and hot, she dug in the sand by the swings (would she find someone's ring? a secret key?). But she came up with nothing, just glass and bottle caps mostly. Every hour or so a school bell would go off. Hearing one—the clanging jolt of it—she imagined the raucous scurry of children as they came back from recess or lunch and piled into the classrooms, tripping and skipping and shouting all around her. None of them would be like Bridget, she'd never find a friend like Bridget again, never ever.

Bridget ran away to find her real mother, a model in France—that was what Mim told Daisy. The two of them played Barbies in the living room for hours, pretending that Skipper was Bridget and the Cher doll with the long black hair was Bridget's real mother. *Mommy is that you?* Mim would say, making Skipper jump up and down. Daisy would make Cher jump up and down, too. *You can be a model like me now.* Hannah told them they were stupid, Bridget wasn't in France, and anyway how did they know her real mother was a model? Daisy and Mim would just glare at her and return to their game.

The front entrance of the school had a metal gate with a padlock, but anyone could enter it from the back through the two main halls—which didn't have doors and opened onto the playground—and wander around. The school was a series of bungalows and made Hannah think of a tic-tac-toe board, the two main halls crisscrossed by smaller horizontal halls, where the locked doors of the classrooms were. She wandered down the smaller halls, trying to guess which classroom would be hers when school started, peeking in a dusty window to see the rows of desks all facing the chalkboard, with their scuffed yellow varnish tops. The halls were long and cool and held on to sounds: the echo of her footsteps, the drip-drip of a leaky drinking fountain, the bell still resonating a full minute after it stopped, slowly receding, like the shiny ripple of a rising kite.

Hannah knew how it was done from watching Bridget. First, buy something that cost a quarter, and wait for the tan old man at the register to turn to the cash register. Then, quick as a wink, slip whatever you wanted to steal in your pocket. It looked easy enough. Stealing the purple glitter pen couldn't be any harder than stealing candy—she'd seen Bridget pocket three Butterfingers and a roll of Lifesavers before the tan old man looked up again. The hard part was leaving the store without drawing attention.

Running out the front door was a dead giveaway; no, she knew you had to calmly stroll out, even though your every muscle twitched with the knowledge that you might get caught. Walk five steps or so down the sidewalk, until you were out of sight. Only then could you take off.

Walking into Jan 'n Joe's, Hannah saw the problem right away: there were two people behind the counter, the tan old man and someone new—a teenage boy with a cluster of cherry red pimples on his cheeks that looked like a rash. And the pen display had been moved closer to the register. She spotted the purple one for $1.99.

She walked past the Pac-Man machine to the freezer at the back of the store, looking for something to buy for a quarter. She wiped the fogged glass with her palm and stared at the cardboard cartons of ice cream inside. Out of the corner of her eye, she saw the pimply teenager dusting the shelves with a ratty orange duster. The tan old man sat on a stool behind the register, picking underneath his fingernails as usual with a stretched-out paperclip.

Just ten more seconds, she thought.

She looked down at the ice cream and pressed her lips together like she'd seen her mother do when faced with a decision, putting on a show for him so he wouldn't suspect her of being a thief. The freezer door let out a gasp when she slid open the door, and the chilled air curled around her face like smoke. She grabbed a cherry 50-50 bar. Bridget's favorite. Sliding the freezer door shut, she peeked up. The tan old man and the pimply teenager weren't looking.

The walk to the cash register made her heart thump so loud she would have sworn they could hear. She reached into her shorts pocket and withdrew a quarter. The tan old man put down the stretched-out paperclip and punched a button on the register. The purple glitter pen was just two inches away, on the top row of the cardboard display. She had to be quick about it— another moment and his eyes would be on her again.

Out the door, the cherry 50-50 bar in her hand, she walked five slow steps, just like she'd seen Bridget do. Then she started running.

Sandi was sitting on the low stone wall out front with Sue-Sue. Hannah, panting, took the pen from her pocket. Sandi raised her eyebrows, impressed.

"You stole that, for me?"

Hanna nodded, trying to catch her breath.

Sandi rattled the ball bearing inside the pen and tested the ink on her cast right under her knee, drawing an eye in shimmery purple ink with long lashes and a single tear—Sandi's favorite thing to draw besides a heart with squiggly flames around it.

And Hannah was forgiven. She bit into the 50-50 bar and got a mouthful of cherry popsicle and vanilla ice cream. Swallowing, she tasted sweetness and victory.

Sandi didn't go as far as letting Hannah sign the cast wherever she wanted—she pointed out a far-off place behind her ankle—but this was good enough for Hannah. In the cramped space, she wrote her name. She had to mush the Ns together so they looked like an M, then had just enough room to add the year: *Hamah '83*.

Sandi stood up and positioned her crutches under her armpits. She walked as far as the mailboxes, moving in quick, smooth strides, like she'd been born with crutches, then turned around.

"C'mere," she said. "I wanna show you something."

Hannah followed them down the cement pathway to the storage cabinets in the parking lot. "Gimme a boost," commanded Sandi.

"But your leg…" Sue-Sue said.

"Shut up," Sandi snapped. Using her crutches and Hannah's shoulder for balance, she hoisted herself up to knock on the cabinet door.

"Eenie Meenie Des Aleenie."

"Oo Ah Oo Ah Maleenie," came a voice from inside.

The cabinet door swung open.

There, huddled in the dark, was Bridget. She looked down at Hannah, and her chapped lips stretched into a wide grin.

"Bridget!"

"Shhhh," Bridget warned.

"*Bridget!*" Hannah said again, this time in a whisper. "I looked here for you, I said your name but you didn't come out."

"Guess I was sleeping."

"You were here the whole time?"

"Yup."

Hannah leaped up to touch Bridget's scratchy hand and make it real: Here she was, not gone but here here here.

"Gimme a boost," Sandi said.

Hannah laced her fingers together and Sandi hoisted herself up on her good foot, letting the crutches fall to the ground. Then Hannah turned to Sue-Sue and said the words she'd wanted to say for so long.

"Gimme a boost too."

She stepped onto Sue-Sue's laced fingers and scrambled into the cabinet. Inside, she felt suspended above everything, looking over the parking lot, a bird's-eye view over the cars, over the fence into the playground, and beyond that—the two dark halls of the school. Bridget nestled next to her, clutching her pillowcase of candy against her chest like a teddy bear.

Hannah touched her hand again, feeling the rough, chapped skin, reminding herself that it was Bridget, that she was back. *Back!*

"Cut it out, that tickles," Bridget said, yanking her hand away.

"Hey guess what?" Sandi said. "Davy and Trevor still think your mom burned you and buried your ashes in the Rose Hill graveyard."

*Haaaaaaw!* Bridget laughed.

"There were policemen looking for you," Hannah said.

"Duh," Sandi said, "I already told her."

"Tell me again." Bridget's eyes grew wide and gleaming as Sandi described the policeman with the mustache putting a gun to her temple, swearing he almost locked her in jail. He was short and fat and mean, she said, and he wore a white suit and a cowboy hat.

Hannah listened, thinking that Sandi's description of him sounded like Boss Hogg from *The Dukes of Hazzard*. She would whisper the truth to Bridget, she decided, when Sandi and Sue-

Sue left. Then she would ask Bridget why she'd told them where she was hiding but had kept it a secret from her.

"Hey Bridget, guess what," Sandi said. "Hannah thought you were dead."

The two of them laughed, cruelly. Hannah, squished between them, fingered the cabinet's splintered wood by her heel. There was nothing she could say in protest.

Not dead, exactly, she wanted to say. But gone.

Same difference, she knew Bridget would respond. She felt embarrassed by her own gullible childishness, remembering the night she'd half-convinced herself that Joan had tied Bridget to a chair and imprisoned her in the apartment.

From down below, Sue-Sue called out, "Lemme up, Hannah, it's my turn. You be the Lookout now."

Glad to have an excuse to get away, Hannah jumped down. She laced her fingers together for Sue-Sue's foot and gave her a boost. After Sue-Sue scrambled in, Sandi reached out and slammed the cabinet door shut.

Sitting down on the dusty hood of the VW bug, Hannah stared at the glinting bits of glass scattered on the asphalt. She listened to the three of them giggling and kicking around in there, and wondered whether she should just walk away.

She heard footsteps. Tanya came around the corner, wearing her orange Lucky's uniform, heading for her station wagon.

Heart thumping, Hannah remembered the signal. *Knock three times on the cabinet door.*

She looked up at the cabinet and felt her throat catch. It was too high to knock on without a boost. And there was no one to give her one.

"What are you doing out here all by yourself, honey?" Tanya said.

"Nothing."

"Nothing? Where's Sandi and Sue-Sue?"

Hannah shrugged weakly, blood rushing to her face, her

ears. Sandi's crutches were on the ground, right behind the front tire of the VW bug, and she prayed Tanya wouldn't walk any closer and see them.

Tanya put her hands on her hips. "Hannah now. I'm late for work. You tell me where my girls are."

There was a thud followed by giggles and a *shhh*, and Tanya looked up.

Sue-Sue was the first to jump down, followed by Sandi.

"Good Lord, you wanna break the other one?" Tanya cried, gathering the crutches from the ground and shoving them at Sandi.

Sandi glared at Hannah. "You're a sucky Lookout."

"Sucky," Sue-Sue hissed.

"That's enough, girls." Tanya peered up at the cabinets. "Who else is hid up there? Davy? Trevor? Come on out, now. I don't got all day, I gotta go to work."

Tanya dug her keys out of her purse, then dropped them as Bridget, scowling, emerged from the cabinet and jumped down.

"Is *that* where you've been all this time?" Tanya gasped.

Bridget shoved her hands in the back pockets of her shorts and looked down at the ground. Out in the daylight, she looked more scraggly than she had in the cabinet. Her short scramble of hair was matted and greasy and sticking straight up in the back. And her Diane shirt was even dirtier than usual, with grubby smears of melted chocolate.

"Sandi, Sue-Sue, you girls are in a heap, and I mean a *heap*, of trouble. And Hannah, I don't know what's in store for you but your ma's not gonna be happy, that much I can say. I'm honestly surprised at you lately, the leg-breaking business and now this."

*Sandi broke her own leg*, Hannah was about to insist, *And no one told me about Bridget*.

Tanya checked her watch. "Oh, Lord, I'm late. Well, first things first. Sandi, Sue-Sue, you two go to your room and think long and hard about what you've done."

Sandi shot another mean glance at Hannah, settled her armpits over the tops of the crutches and made her way out of the parking lot. Sue-Sue lowered her head and followed. Bridget watched them go.

Tanya put her hand on Bridget's chin and swiveled it back. "We're going to have a little talk with your ma. Have you thought about what you put her through?"

Bridget narrowed her eyes, but said nothing. Tanya gripped Bridget's arm above the elbow and marched her up the cement pathway toward apartment one.

Hannah stood there for a moment, dizzied by all that had happened. Then she ran after Bridget. When she reached apartment one, she saw Tanya knocking on the front door. The door swung open.

Joan, standing in the doorway, dropped her Virginia Slim on the carpet. "Where did you find—" was all she got out before her face crumpled and the tears overtook her.

Then, Hannah was even more shocked to see, Bridget started crying too.

Joan lunged for Bridget and with both hands pressed Bridget's blonde mussy-haired head into her heaving chest— holding it down as they wept together on the doorstep.

"Don't you ever—*ever*—do that again."

Joan drew back and cradled Bridget's cheeks. Then she withdrew one hand and slapped Bridget's face. "You understand?"

She yanked Bridget into the dark apartment, slamming the door shut.

*Cheap Rent-Control Bastard*

With a frustrated stomp on the power switch, Elaine turned off the vacuum. The fringes on the area rug she'd bought on sale at Woolworth's had gotten swallowed by the machine. Dropping to her knees, she began untangling the fringes from the roller.

There were three sharp knocks on the front door. Elaine checked her watch and groaned. She'd asked Warren to come at two o'clock and look at the crack on the oven glass, but it wasn't even ten.

"Sorry I'm a wee bit early," Warren said when she opened the door. "You got yourself a tangle there I see. Mind if I take a shot at fixing it?"

Without waiting for her consent, he set down his battered briefcase and squatted to get a closer look at the vacuum, his knees making their popping sounds. He tugged at the fringes and frowned. "I got a call from the police a few days ago, heard that the little girl in apartment one was missing."

"They found Bridget," Elaine said. She'd alternated between relief and anger ever since. Bridget running away felt like a betrayal: all those dinners she'd made for her, all those nights she'd invited her to stay over. But maybe she'd misunderstood Bridget. When she hugged her, the girl's bony shoulders relaxed, but within seconds Bridget would squirm away, as if she couldn't bear to allow herself to be loved. Maybe Bridget felt undeserving of the affection she had shown her.

"So I heard," Warren responded. "That one's a troublemaker, you know."

"Bridget's just a little lost, that's all." She picked up the mug of tea she'd left sitting on the kitchen table. Her hand trembled as she took a sip, and some tea dribbled down her chin. She quickly wiped it away.

But her clumsiness didn't escape him, she was embarrassed to see. "You should relax more, if you don't mind my saying. You've got a good heart, Elaine. But you strike me as the type that's blinded by love." He cracked his pinky. "You got some scissors?"

"No, I'm afraid not," she lied. She didn't want him to ruin the brand-new rug. She'd bought it to cover a spot on the shag carpet that had become threadbare.

His frown deepening, he tugged at the rug, worrying the fringe. "Without scissors I'm afraid I can't be of much help. Sorry." And with a *Gaaaaaa*, knees popping again, he stood up. "Okay then. Well, let's take a look at that crack you told me about."

Elaine showed him the oven glass by the temperature dial. "I'm afraid the whole plate's going to fall out."

"I don't ah, remember this being here when you folks moved in."

"It was a hairline crack. It was bound to get bigger."

"Well, I'd be happy to replace the oven with a newer model, but you'll have to foot the bill."

This was not what Elaine had expected. "I can't afford to buy a new oven. You can't honestly expect me to pay for something I didn't break."

Warren shrugged. "Well then you'll have to live with it, I suppose. The oven still works, that's the important thing."

"What if I order replacement glass from the company?" she

ventured. "Would you pay for that?"

"Replacement glass can't be ordered on these ovens, they're too old. They don't make 'em anymore."

"I can't live here with broken glass. My children could cut themselves. The most I'll—the most I'll pay is fifty dollars." Why was she stammering? If she were at a yard sale, she could bargain with ease, but in Warren's presence she couldn't get past her feeling of smallness in his presence, of futility. She felt it all the more when he shook his head sadly and made for the door.

"I'm flat broke myself," Warren said. "I take a loss every month on this building, it's bleeding me dry. I'd buy a new oven for you if I could afford it, but I can't. I just can't. Best I can do is reimburse you for a roll of duct tape. You could tape a piece of cardboard over the broken glass so your children won't get cut."

"Wait!" Elaine ran to the door. "Before you go. The other thing I wanted to speak to you about is the ants."

"Ants?"

"Yes, ants. They've gotten into my sugar. I've been spraying them with Windex, but I really think—"

"I can't fumigate the building unless there's a problem in the whole building. So far, I haven't heard there's any sort of problem. Have you tried ant poison?"

"Well no, I—"

"Kills 'em like *that*," Warren said, smacking his hands together. "Save your Windex for your windows."

He picked up his battered briefcase. "I'm glad to see you're taking an interest in improving things around here. I'll see about carpets, one of these days, how about that? I've got a buddy owns a Carpeteria in Van Nuys, one of these days I'll see if he can cut us a good deal."

After Warren left, Elaine took another sip of tea, then slammed the mug down on the kitchen table.

"Cheap rent-control bastard!"

They were Joan's words. Joan, half-drunk on Bloody Marys, had slurred the phrase that afternoon she'd given her a fan. It didn't register then—she'd been so distracted by the unexpected generosity of Joan's gift. But now Joan's words returned to her, as if waiting for the perfect occasion to be summoned forth. As if they'd taken residence in her mind and had become by some strange alchemy her own. She caught sight of the rug clogging the vacuum cleaner.

How would Joan handle this situation?

Emboldened, she opened the silverware drawer and slammed a fistful of butter knives onto the formica counter. She rummaged through the drawer, throwing spoons and forks onto the counter, until she found what she'd been looking for.

"Aha!" She grabbed the scissors, slammed the drawer shut, and marched over to the rug. She felt the thrill of destruction as she cut a tassel free from the vacuum roller, then another, and another. The phone was ringing, but she ignored it, gritting her teeth and snipping away.

By the tenth ring, she threw down the scissors and picked up the receiver. "Yes?" she said irritably.

"I'm sorry, am I catching you at a bad time? It's Sam."

"Sam?"

"From the PWP dinner. I can call back later."

"No!" She took a deep breath, and tried again. "No," she said, softer. "Please don't hang up."

# IV. AUGUST

Sam lived in a two-bedroom bungalow in Venice, the house his ex-wife let him keep when she divorced him two years ago and married a wealthy city planning commissioner. The beach was just four blocks away, close enough that Sam could take his thirty-minute morning jog along the shore and still be back in time to complete the rest of his daily routine: hamstring stretches, three-minute shower, black coffee and oatmeal and the *L.A. Times*. On average, he could complete the crossword in twelve minutes flat, one of the many uses for his digital Seiko's built-in stopwatch. Sam was a punctual man. He drove his beat-up Tercel to the alternative high school where he taught American History and Government classes and coached the cross-country team, and not once in the nine years he'd worked there had he ever arrived a minute past eight. Sam felt a great passion for teaching and a great passion for living in Venice, one of the only remaining havens from what he called the razzle-dazzle of La-La Land. The neighborhood was quiet and peaceful, a regular sanctuary by the sea, except on weekends, when he along with the other locals grumbled about the beach traffic, car after car puttering up and down the neighborhood streets, polluting the air as their drivers looked in vain for parking spots, all heading for the one-and-a-half-mile stretch along the sand known as the Venice Boardwalk, a crazy circus of palm readers and breakdancers and sword-swallowers and bodybuilders and guitar-strumming, *ganja*-reeking Rastafarians on roller skates.

He'd lived in that house over a decade, long enough to see the tide turn: the hippies and artists and beach bums were slowly being outnumbered by yuppies with money to burn. Demolition crews knocked down an old house every week, it seemed—Craftsman bungalows like his, with low-pitched gabled roofs and eaves and sleeping porches. In their place three-story concrete fortresses were erected, whose expensive furnishings could be viewed through twenty-feet-high bulletproof windows, this architectural feature a testament to the paradoxical impulses of the nouveau riche, exhibitionism and paranoia, as Sam liked to note when his school lectures touched on class inequities and social stratification, as they often did. Even his cross-country team was treated to lectures on the subject.

The gentrification of Venice was one of Sam's favorite conversational topics outside of school as well. The night Elaine and her daughters came over for dinner, the subject came up within minutes of their arrival.

Sam set out on the porch table a wedge of Gouda, a steak knife and a box of Wheat Thins. Elaine sat to his left on the wicker loveseat; her daughters ran for the porch swing. He poured their drinks, Chablis for Elaine and him, milk for her daughters, into the jars he used for glasses. The jars, he informed them proudly, had previously held his favorite Dijon mustard.

"Fancy," Elaine said, admiring the jar's dimpled glass before she took a sip of her wine. She reached for the cheese.

"Allow me," Sam said. He unwrapped the Gouda from the plastic and cut four thin slices. With methodical gravity, he lined up the slices on his left thigh, then lined up four Wheat Thins on his right thigh. He moved the cheese slices, one by one, to the right thigh, carefully laying each one on top of a Wheat Thin. "Here you are," he said, offering Elaine the first one.

Elaine accepted her cracker-and-cheese with a smile, amused by his odd bachelor habits. Daisy and Hannah vigorously shook their heads when he offered them theirs. "Girls, you love appetizers," Elaine scolded. They both peered down at their jars of milk and said nothing.

"Well," she said, hoping to shift the focus away from their bad manners. She looked up at the sky. "What a beautiful evening."

"Yes," Sam said. And it was: the wind chimes hanging from a hook above the porch door tinkled as a soft ocean breeze blew by, and the setting sun gave their faces a tangerine glow. But after a few minutes Sam observed the sun dip down out of sight, obscured by the newly erected three-story house neighboring his one-story bungalow. He glumly shook his head, pointed at what he called the bourgeois monstrosity on the other side of his yard, and started talking about how development produces spatial apartheid.

It was almost dark when Sam's digital Seiko's built-in stopwatch beeped. "Time for dinner!" he announced.

With a clumsy flourish, he opened the screen door for Elaine. The dining room table was already set, she noted, touched by his considerate foresight. He jogged past her, saying that he'd take them on a tour of the neighborhood in his Tercel to show them more evidence of gentrification, and disappeared into the kitchen.

*Evidence of gentrification.* His teacherly tone resembled Roger's, but somehow it didn't put her on edge—while Sam clearly derived pleasure from explaining things, he had no intention of belittling his audience.

"How about a week after next Saturday? My son will be with me then, you can meet him," Sam called out from the kitchen. "We'll make an afternoon of it. I'll take you all to Nano's afterwards for a pizza lunch."

"Isn't that nice of Sam, to offer us a tour?" Elaine said, taking a seat at the table. Her girls did not respond. Daisy squirmed, and Hannah moved the wooden salad bowl away from her plate.

Sam strode out of the kitchen wearing purple oven mitts. "Here it is, my Sammy Specialty!"

It was a steamy, lumpy casserole with rice and beans and cheese and some kind of vegetable mixed in, with a heavy sprinkling of a mysterious multicolored spice mix. He set the casserole on a cutting board in the middle of the table and dished it out.

"Well, dig in," he said proudly.

Elaine glanced at her girls, and exclaimed, "Doesn't it look yummy, all those different spices?" She took a bite, and immediately regretted the question. It tasted awful.

As a distraction, she offered to toss the salad. When she caught her girls picking at their food, she shot them a disapproving glare. She had to be quick about it so Sam wouldn't see. His eyes moved around the table while he talked, boring into hers, then Hannah's, then Daisy's. He chopped at the air to emphasize certain words. He didn't let up until he had run out of breath or had to gather his thoughts, which seemed to happen at the same time.

Besides PWP, he was saying, he was involved in two other groups, not to mention the parent group at the school where he worked. There was the No Nukes group, FreezeNow!, which he'd been involved with for a long time—too many years to count. In addition, he served on its local steering committee, and now and then went to protests near the testing sites in Nevada, where he'd try to get himself arrested for civil disobedience. But what he was really putting his energy into lately, he said, was the other group that protested U.S. involvement in El Salvador. They had their biggest event in years last March in Washington, D.C. There were five thousand protesters from all over the country, and they brought their handmade signs and stood on the White House lawn and sang "Give Peace a Chance" and "We Shall Overcome," and aside from the usual handful of belligerent people who were really just after self-promotion it was a peaceful demonstration and he thought their message got across.

Sam reached across the table to spear a cherry tomato from the salad bowl. He paused just long enough to chew, then went on talking.

During dinner, Hannah watched her mother's eyes grow bright and proud, slowly twirling a frazzly strand of hair around her forefinger and once even reaching over to touch Sam's hand when he stopped talking and gazed at the floor to gather his thoughts. Hannah could see the pleasure her mother's attention gave him: he wiped his mouth with his napkin and looked at her with a mixture of surprise and affection, and at that moment the room held just the two of them, Sam and her mother, with Hannah left to mash the mush on her plate, waiting for the room to expand again.

He was talking about another activist group now. "Since 1979 we've committed over a billion dollars to their country. We're training their army, we're giving them weapons. Reagan's talking falling dominos—it's Vietnam all over again." He reached across the table for another cherry tomato and bit into it, sending a squirt onto Daisy's plate. Daisy looked down at the red seedy glob, and her face screwed up in disgust. Hannah saw the quick flash of her mother's widened eyes, warning them both not to let out a peep.

After dinner, Sam filled his and her mother's jars with more white wine. He led Hannah and Daisy into the living room, where a jigsaw puzzle lay on the floor, half-finished.

"I have an idea," he said. "Why don't you kids see how fast you can finish that puzzle?" He fiddled with the buttons on his watch. "I'll give you thirty minutes."

With a sly glance at her mother, he held the screen door open. "Would you like to join me on the porch?"

"Well, all right," she said, taking a gulp of wine before following him out.

Hannah looked down at the puzzle, knowing it was an adult ploy to keep her and Daisy occupied so Sam could be alone with her mother. The screen door slammed shut, and there was a tinkle of wind chimes. She was not going to touch a single puzzle piece.

It took some getting used to, going out on dates again. So much energy Elaine devoted to the preparation of her evenings with Sam, but not in the way a woman normally readied herself for a date—carefully considering an outfit, blotting and powdering her lipstick so it wouldn't smear all over his lips if they kissed, fixing her hair so not a strand was out of place. It was the dialogue part of the evening that she was more concerned with.

What would she say to this man?

She'd had a sort of superstition, ever since she first entered the world of courtship at the age of fifteen, that she had a limited well to draw from, as far as ideas and conversation were concerned. That one day she'd simply run out of stories to tell and observations to make, and she'd be left sitting there, mute, with nothing more to do but nod or shake her head.

To guard against this possibility, she had developed the habit of writing notes on a piece of paper she kept stowed away in her purse during dates. It amounted to a cheat sheet of conversation topics, usually three, just in case she was faced with an uncomfortable spell or two (or more, on a bad date) of silence. They were her salvation when she sat with a boy in a diner, or in the back seat of his car, racking her brain for something to say. These were the days after her father's death, when her mother had let her transfer from Holy Cross to the public high school at Salmon Creek. She kept her dates, and her cheat sheets, hidden—not much of a feat in the years after her mother's transformation from a vigilant guardian of virtue to an abstracted, barely-there woman in mourning.

*Miss Pim wears a red bra*, was a sample note on one of her cheat sheets. Elaine had made the thrilling discovery when her eleventh-grade English teacher, unaware that she was missing the top button of her blouse, leaned over Elaine's essay to point out the improper use of the word "infer." The note, Elaine knew, was a guaranteed conversation-starter on a date. A boy would certainly be interested enough to ask how she had happened upon the knowledge of Miss Pim's undergarments, which meant that Elaine could elaborate on the details for at least five good minutes. Also a proven hit was *Have you seen Deborah lately*—a question that she already knew the answer to ("No, not lately"), relying on the rumor that the girl was visiting "her aunt's farm" for a few months (meaning nine), and therefore was a topic that promised a lengthy discussion of the girl's sleazy conduct with other boys at their school. Finally, there was the ever-dependable (if dull) conversation-starter: *College?* It was a question she posed as a last resort. The boy would either shrug his shoulders or deliver a fifteen-minute expatiation on his first and second and third choices, and the relative merits of each.

At the University of New Hampshire, she found that the writing of her cheat sheets became a more difficult task. You weren't necessarily in the same class with the boy, so gossip about a particular teacher didn't mean much, and rumors about pregnancy, even abortion, didn't hold the same sting of scandal as it did in Salmon Creek. If you were scandalized, in fact, you were marked as provincial, a *square*. It was a contamination of sorts, as much of a *turn-off* as getting the *clap*; she learned the college lingo, but she couldn't quite master the slangy intonation, so the words always sounded overenunciated and awkward coming out of her mouth.

By her second year at UNH, she had given up on the cheat sheets altogether. She had renounced dating, deciding that she should not waste her time on college boys; it wasn't until her junior year, when she met Roger, that she went out on a date again. That sophomore year, her passion was reserved for anthropology and anthropology alone, largely due to a certain bespectacled, lanky professor on whom she, along with most of the other girls in his class, had developed a fierce crush. His impassioned lectures ignited something inside her, and transformed her into a serious student. And so she excised from her life every distraction, including boys—an irony, since she went off to college as a final rebellion against her mother's hopes for her to join a convent. Many hours were spent in the library, drinking paper cups of sour coffee from the hallway vending machine, poring over her notes, composing essays about Samoans or Inuits on yellow-lined paper that she would type up later in her dorm room, which contained observations she secretly hoped Professor Russell would gasp over (he didn't).

Elaine did compose a cheat sheet once, during that time, in preparation for an office hours appointment with him. Her intention was not to try to persuade him to reconsider the B-minus she received on her last essay but to understand where she had gone wrong. And since his mere presence had the effect of turning her into a silly, blushing featherhead, she thought it would be wise to have her thoughts sorted out on paper and tucked away in her purse just in case.

She wasn't exactly a blushing featherhead around Sam, even though he was a man of powerful opinions, but she still feared the embarrassment of a long spell of silence during a date. The only reliable tactic she could think of to guard against the possibility was to prepare herself as she had done as a teenager. A silly solution, she knew, but necessary nonetheless. She jotted down a few mundane questions on the back of an envelope, which she folded and hid under her checkbook at the bottom of her purse: *Did your FreezeNow! meeting go well? How is your son doing? Have you noticed the gladiolus blooming in your neighbor's yard? How was your morning jog?* The fact that he enjoyed talking so much meant that she could rely on him to expound at length on any given topic, even if the topics she'd introduced were not terribly original or thought-provoking.

She'd also begun to consult the *L.A. Times* for more rigorous topics. *Did you hear about what Mayor Bradley said about the HUD scandal?* she asked him on a recent lunch date at a coffee shop, and by the time the waitress brought the check they were still discussing government graft—or more accurately, he was doing the talking and she was doing the nodding.

The truth was, Sam had the ability to bore her to tears, especially when he went on and on about politics. But his eyes lit up with such gratitude when she asked him political questions, and he responded to them with such gusto, that she decided there were worse sacrifices a woman could make for a man's happiness.

She was looking forward to Saturday, when Sam planned to give her and her daughters a tour of his neighborhood and introduce them to his son. But he called to postpone the date, saying his ex-wife had made an appointment for Mitchell to see a therapist on Saturday.

"Next Saturday should be fine, though," Sam said. "In the meantime, would you like to come over for dinner again? I can cook up another 'Sammy Specialty.'"

Elaine hesitated, thinking of the almost inedible casserole he'd prepared the last time.

Well, she thought, eating it would be one more sacrifice.

Bridget was grounded for a week, not allowed to put even one foot outside.

The phone was off-limits too, but the next night when Joan went to Jan 'n Joe's for more Virginia Slims, Bridget called Hannah and blurted everything: how Joan yelled at her for a whole day, practically; how the social worker, Mrs. Pinsky, who spit when she talked, came over and interviewed Bridget for an hour, told her she was *this close* to being sent back to Butterfield; how Joan said, "One more chance is all she gets," and Mrs. Pinsky took a baggie of Nutter-Butter cookies out of her purse and started eating them and said, "I'm concerned about you, Bridget, this pattern of running away," and a speck of wet cookie landed in Bridget's eye when she said "pattern" and Bridget said "gross" and Joan grounded her for another week.

So it was fourteen days, then, that Hannah couldn't see Bridget. She spent most of her time in her bedroom, playing with her turtle. For Hannah, these days stretched on forever, a relentless tic-toc, tic-toc, the seconds and minutes and hours dragging on.

When the morning of Bridget's release came at last, Hannah dashed out of her bedroom.

"Where are you going?" her mother asked.

"To Bridget's!" She could almost see Bridget's chapped-lip grin, could almost feel her dry, scabby fingers closing around hers. Bridget would grab Hannah's hand and lead her to the second branch of the eucalyptus tree in the playground, or to the cabinets in the parking lot, or to the empty lot across the street, or to Jan 'n Joe's to steal popsicles—it didn't matter where. As long as it was far from the sad, stuffy apartment that felt like a jail, imprisoning her with her jittery mother and her crybaby sister. As long as it was away.

Her mother frowned. "We haven't even had breakfast yet. Then Sam's taking us on a tour of his neighborhood with his son, remember? He's buying us lunch at Nano's. Then we're going mattress shopping. I don't want you girls sleeping in sleeping bags anymore."

Hannah's hand was on the doorknob—she was almost free.

But her mother walked over and firmly shut the door. "You can see Bridget later, honey. We have a big day today."

* * *

Hannah was squished in the back of Sam's Tercel, with Sam's fifteen-year-old son on one side and Daisy on the other. There wasn't much of an introduction, just Sam saying "Mitchell, will you slide over and make room?" A hot seatbelt buckle pressed against her thigh.

"Fingers and toes in?" Sam said, and slammed the car door shut.

He jogged around the car and unlocked the door on the driver's side. Before sitting down, he adjusted the seat cover, made up of wooden beads strung together the size and color of walnuts. He reached back to pat Mitchell's knee. "Everyone, this is Mitchell. Mitchell, this is everyone."

Her mother was the only one in the car who laughed. Hannah waited until the car started before she snuck a peek at

Mitchell, whose long, bony teenage arm was pressed against hers. He glowered at her, his eyes ink-black, the loneliness in them and the long lashes somehow canceling out their meanness. She scooted an inch toward Daisy, who whined, "Stop pushing."

Sam adjusted the rearview mirror. "All set?"

"Did everyone pee?" her mother said. Hannah looked down at her lap and felt her cheeks burn with embarrassment.

"Well, then, off we go."

Sam drove at a crawl through his neighborhood, pointing at two construction crews that he said were signs of the big bucks moving in. Turning onto Brooks Avenue, he said that this was the only part of Venice that hadn't been gentrified. Impoverished black kids lived here, he explained, gang members most of them.

Hannah was fascinated, in spite of her efforts to ignore him. She looked out the car window at the single-story houses— much like Sam's, except that his house had a grass lawn and a pathway of little flat stones leading up to his front door, and most of these had dirt yards enclosed by low chain-link fences. Laundry hung from twine stretched between windows, some with frilled curtains, some with blinds drawn.

"Ghost Town is what they call this part of Venice, and unless you're a local it's difficult to determine its boundaries," Sam said. "But take a closer look. Look at the bars on the windows."

Daisy tapped his shoulder. "Where are the ghosts?"

"Ghosts," Mitchell groaned, making a face.

"It's just a local nickname," Sam answered in his teacher's voice, glancing at her in the rearview mirror. "'Ghost' is merely symbolic. Ghosts are things you can't see, they're the people who live here, the ones who slip through the cracks. Who most other people can't see, *refuse* to see—the only things in their field of vision are palm trees and movie stars. The squalor of the underclass spoils their vision, they want to bury it, put it out of their sight. But the phantoms remain here, to haunt, to remind us of what is—and will never be—dead."

Mitchell shifted his weight against Hannah. "Dad, can you put on the radio?"

"Not now," Sam said stiffly.

"What do you like to listen to, Mitchell?" her mother asked.

Mitchell shut his eyes, and his long lashes held still. "Music," he said.

They crossed a busy intersection and turned onto a side street. Sam slowed the car, and the traffic noises grew fainter. Then all was quiet. "These are the canals," he said. A soft mist descended, blurring the edges of things, and it seemed to Hannah that they had entered a fairyland. She gazed at a narrow stretch of water, forking off in the distance into another, at the enormous houses on either side that might as well have been castles, kings and queens tucked away inside. A lone swan drifted to the shore, beat its wings.

"Of course, you can't live in this part of Venice unless you're a multimillionaire," Sam said, pointing at a house that reminded Hannah of a gigantic sugar cube. Mitchell shifted his weight and unrolled the window. Hannah breathed in the warm, syrupy air.

They drove over a small wooden bridge that arched over the water. "Oh, let's stop right here, Sam," her mother said, unrolling her window, too. "Just for a moment. It's so beautiful."

"Absolutely. The history of this place is fascinating, you know. I'm trying to persuade the school to let me teach a class on the subject." He pulled up the emergency brake. "Abbot Kinney built the canals in the early 1900s to replicate Venice, Italy. He flew in gondoliers from Italy to make his Venetian fantasy complete, and people rode up and down these canals in gondolas. Now, of course, the water is polluted and ridden with bacteria."

"Shit, and I wanted to take a swim," Mitchell mumbled, and Sam glared at him.

Walking in to Nano's, Mitchell made Sam even madder when he scooped up a handful of the sawdust that covered the restaurant's floor.

"Mitchell," Sam said, "let's leave it on the floor where it belongs."

Mitchell let the sawdust fall through his fingers. "Let's not and say we did."

Sam stopped and faced his son. "One more smart comment, mister, and we're going home. Don't push me."

They sat at a booth in the back of the restaurant. Once more, Hannah had to squish herself between Mitchell and Daisy. When she saw her mother reach under the table and hold Sam's hand, she pinched Daisy, trying to get her sister to notice.

But Daisy didn't understand. "Ow!" she yelped, and her face puckered up. "Hannah pinched me, Mommy."

Hannah groaned. If Bridget were her sister, she'd understand.

"Let's try to behave, girls," her mother sighed. "You don't want to spoil everyone's fun."

Mitchell smirked. "The fun's begun? I hadn't noticed."

"Mitchell…" Sam warned.

*One, two, three, four, five, six, seven,* Hannah counted silently. Bridget said she once held her breath for one hundred ten seconds underwater and she wasn't even dizzy afterwards. She was going to reach one hundred eleven seconds—then, when she saw Bridget again, she could tell her that she'd beat her.

Her mother looked around at everyone. "You're all being so quiet."

"What the hell do you want us to say?" Mitchell slumped down in his seat. "That we're having a fabulous fucking time?"

"Okay, mister!" Sam boomed. He pounded his fist on the table. "That's the limit!"

"Gimme a break," Mitchell said. "Ooo I'm so scared."

"We're getting lunch to go," Sam announced, and he stormed over to the waitress.

In the parking lot, Sam headed toward the car, holding the cardboard pizza box. Hannah fixed her eyes on the back of her mother's clogs, the wooden heels making an angry smack each time her mother took a step.

He dropped them off at Sunset Terrace. At the curb, her mother watched his Tercel drive away with a firm set to her face, as if she were trying with all her might to keep it from crumbling.

Hannah turned away, heading for Bridget's apartment.

"Stop right there. We're going mattress shopping."

Hannah ignored her mother and kept walking, faster now. "I don't want a mattress, I want to see Bridget."

She heard the pizza box drop to the ground, the clogs stomping toward her. Her mother grabbed her arm above the elbow. Fury blazed in her eyes. "But first, we need to get one thing straight, young lady. Pinching your little sister in a restaurant is no way to make a good impression on Sam. He's very important to me."

"Daisy's a crybaby," said Hannah, shrinking back. "Bridget said so," she added, thinking that mentioning her mother's favorite—next to Daisy—would soften her anger.

"I don't care who said what. That's enough. Enough out of you!"

"A fuckin' crybaby," Hannah said, bravely, but soft, crying herself now. Feeling the hot tears slick down her cheeks, one by one.

Then, the sting of her mother's slap.

She touched her cheek and blinked at her mother, stunned. A garbage truck rumbled past, huffing a dirty cloud of smoke out its exhaust pipes. The cloud thinned as it rose, vanishing into the air.

She made her voice hard and husky like Bridget's. "Daisy is a mother fuckin' cry—"

Another slap, and another. She kept repeating the words, her eyes fierce through the tears, daring her mother to slap her again, feeling stronger each time she felt the sting on her cheek. Daisy, sounding scared, said "Mommy?" and started crying, too.

\* \* \*

Hannah lay on her new mattress, staring numbly at the ceiling. She'd been in her bedroom for hours, it seemed. The door flung open.

It was Bridget. "Scooch over," she demanded, leaping onto the mattress. Folding her arms behind her head, she told her about her new plan: she was running away for real this time. Right before school started.

Hannah turned to her and said, in a voice just above a whisper, "I'm coming too."

They climbed the fence together and crossed the playground, approaching the school. Bridget entered the first main hall and ran ahead of Hannah, leaping up to whack the little metal cages along the low ceiling, rattling the lightbulbs inside.

Hannah chased after her. She reached the end of the hall, where the sixth-grade classrooms were. In the corner was a splintery wooden shed, with peeling orange paint. A chain-link fence ran behind it, marking the far edge of the school.

"Over here!" Bridget shouted. She disappeared behind the shed, somehow squeezing her body between the shed's back wall and the chain-link fence.

Hannah held her breath and squeezed into the small space. Bridget was waiting for her there, squatting.

During school, Bridget explained, the shed was where you checked out softballs and baseballs during recess from Mrs. Thalometer—who was a fourth-grade teacher nicknamed Mrs.

Thermometer because she was always yelling *Cool down, people*
to kids.

"She sounds mean," Hannah said.

"You're lucky," Bridget said.

"Why?"

"You'll never meet her."

*I'm running away!* Hannah thought. *With Bridget!*

They stayed behind the shed for a long time, finishing off
the four melted Milky Ways Bridget had brought with her. If
someone asked Hannah later what they talked about, she would
probably have said "Nothing," which wouldn't have done it
justice, and if she changed it to "Everything," it wouldn't have
seemed like a large enough number. Some little girls talk about
the farmhouses they will buy next door to each other when they
grow up and get married and about the beautiful white flowing
dresses they will wear at their weddings. But Hannah just
listened to Bridget talk, savoring the sound of her hoarse, happy
voice running all the words together, talking about nothing and
everything, not even once mentioning farmhouses or dresses or
husbands.

* * *

The phone rang, and Elaine felt her heart quicken when she
heard Sam's voice on the other line. The fact that he hadn't
called in almost a week had been gnawing at her; she'd worried
that he was having doubts about their relationship ever since the
disastrous Nano's lunch.

"I've been tied up," he explained.

"That's all right," she said, though in truth she was relieved
to hear him say it.

"There's been some upheaval in the FreezeNow! steering
committee, some disagreements about our strategy in the next
demonstration, not to mention my summer school duties."

"Sounds like you've had your hands full," Elaine said, smiling. That he sounded exceedingly formal when discussing his activities was endearing: he took his work so seriously.

"And Mitchell…" he cleared his throat. "Jeanine and I haven't been seeing eye to eye on the custody arrangement. But I don't need to drag you into all that."

"You can drag me in, if you like." She kicked off her clogs and sat down at the kitchen table, ready to listen.

"No, it's really not that interesting. I'll spare you the details."

"Jeanine wants more time with him?" She hoped he wouldn't think she was prodding, but wanted him to share this part of his life with her, as a way of moving beyond his formality toward a more intimate connection.

"Of course," Sam said, and cleared his throat again.

At the PWP dinner, when she was an absolute stranger to him, Sam had been eager to share with her the details of his life, disclosing a great deal about Mitchell. Why was he holding back now?

Twisting the phone cord around her finger, she swallowed her resentment. After all, she hadn't been exactly forthcoming with him either—she hadn't told him, for example, that she had been unemployed for several months and now was desperately worried about running out of money. How could she, of all people, blame him for withholding the more personal aspects of his life?

"You know, I really need to get a job," she told him. Now was not the time for soul-digging disclosures, but she could offer him this, just this.

Every morning Elaine circled the "Help Wanted" ads in the *L.A. Times* and filled out applications at restaurants. At first, she took Hannah and Daisy with her and gave them tasks to keep them occupied in the car: Hannah was in charge of the newspaper, calling out the addresses and checking them off, and Daisy held her list of references. They waited in the parked car while she went into a restaurant and applied for a job, and often she would find them squabbling when she returned, so she decided to leave them at home.

At last, she found a job at Acappella, an Italian restaurant in Santa Monica three blocks from the ocean. The manager took one look at her and said she could start tomorrow. The Getty Museum had rented out the restaurant for a huge party, and one of their sous-chefs had just quit.

What luck! With her cooking experience at the Steak Shack and all the greasy spoons, her application would never pass muster in such an elegant restaurant. But her timing had been perfect. She had caught the manager in a moment of crisis.

Elated, she stopped at an ice cream parlor across the street from Acappella to celebrate her victory. Tubs of ice cream with exotic names were lined up behind a pane of glass—there were so many tempting choices. Chocolate Macadamia Nut, Chocolate Raspberry Truffle, Bavarian Cream, Vanilla Rose Petal, Savannah Key Lime, Pumpkin Pecan.

"Are those real rose petals in the vanilla?" she asked.

"Yes," the woman behind the counter responded. "Coated in sugar. They're delicious."

Balancing her cone of Vanilla Rose Petal ice cream in one hand as she steered, Elaine drove through the residential part of the neighborhood, deciding to take the long way home. She rolled her window down and gazed in wonder at the big, beautiful houses with their Spanish-tiled roofs. Here was where the orange trees grew, where bougainvillaea and Birds of Paradise flourished in exotic profusion, where the newspaper arrived in a warm, tight bundle on people's doorsteps and the ocean breeze was near enough to make their lips taste salty.

Her hair flew back in kinky wisps. Inhaling the breeze, she mused about the future: she'd work at Acappella long enough to save some money and meet a business partner, then open up a restaurant of her own.

\* \* \*

Elaine came home late from her first night at work, shiny-faced and exhausted.

Hannah and Daisy had fallen asleep on the big pillows on the living room floor, but they awoke as soon as she came through the front door. Elaine gave them each a miniature pastry swan filled with whipped cream; at Acappella she'd been responsible for filling them, hundreds of them, one after the other.

"Boy, what a night," she said, stretching out on the floor beside them.

She told them about the poor waitress who slipped on a grease spot on the tiled floor and dropped the three plates of gnocchi she was carrying, about the head waiter who yanked the waitress into the kitchen and yelled at her.

The night had resumed the pattern of the past three years: Elaine, back from her late shift, narrating the evening's dramas while her sleepy-eyed girls half-listened, wordlessly devouring the food she'd scavenged for them. It was a routine they all knew well.

The next morning, Elaine gave in to Daisy's pleading and made pancakes for breakfast, amazed she could muster the energy.

Squinting in the dazzle of sunlight, she drifted from cabinet to refrigerator and back again, setting out ingredients on the kitchen table. Even with the curtains drawn, the kitchen, facing east, was the brightest room in the apartment. Under her terrycloth robe, her cotton nightgown was damp against her skin. With the heel of her hand, she banged on the corroded metal latch of the kitchen window until it came unstuck.

But there was no breeze. The air outside was even hotter than it was inside.

Sighing, she reached above the stove to retrieve two bowls and returned to the kitchen table. She knew the pancake recipe by heart and didn't need to measure, judging the proportions of the dry ingredients by look and feel: three-and-a-half fistfuls of flour, large pinch of salt, two of baking powder, and enough sugar to fill her cupped palm. Sifting the mixture into the large bowl, she raised a floury cloud.

"Like an oven in here," she said aloud, coughing.

Joan's fan, she remembered.

The six steps it took her to amble from the kitchen to the living room were like advancing from the bright outdoors into a cave. She would keep an eye out at yard sales for lamps, she decided, maybe even track lighting.

She lifted the square fan and carried it into the kitchen. She flicked on the switch and cracked an egg into the smaller bowl. The swollen ache in her legs felt almost pleasant, a reminder of all that time on her feet last night, of a job well done.

Whisking in the melted butter and milk, she let her thoughts drift, smiling at her luck. The man who'd hired her turned out not to be the manager, but the head waiter filling in for the manager, who was out with the flu. Fabrizio, the head chef, had thrown a fit when the head waiter introduced her as the new sous-chef, shouting at him in Italian—curses, Elaine guessed, hearing the clipped, barking sound of the words. Luckily Fabrizio needed her: since the private party for the Getty Museum was an important occasion and he was behind schedule. She could stay until the end of the shift, he'd said.

Fabrizio had been impressed by her competence and efficiency, she could tell, figuring her at first for a novice, not knowing she'd worked in nine kitchens over the past three years. And though Acappella was surely more than a step up from the greasy spoons, all kitchens, she'd found, were pretty much the same: the cooks all at once high-strung and snappy and jovial, their moods as unpredictable as the weather, barking at you one minute, the next acting as if nothing could spoil their day. The rest of the kitchen crew was harder to pin down, but they usually fell into two categories, those who vied for the chef's attention, causing petty jealousies among them, and those who kept their distance from him, grumbling curses under their breaths when he was out of earshot.

Halfway through the shift last night, when she'd hit her stride, she caught Fabrizio watching her wield the pastry bag, deftly squeezing whipped cream into the bellies of four sheets of pastry swans in no time flat. At the end of the shift he said she could stay on for the next two weeks, maybe more. He frowned when he said it, as if he were disappointed to be the bearer of good news. When it was time to clock out, she was so distracted with excitement she put the wrong end of her time card in.

Elaine added the dry ingredients to the bowl, a little at a time. The mixture formed a thick, lumpy batter; she was careful not to overstir. She flicked a drop of water into the greased frying pan. It danced on the metal. Hot enough.

Working at a fancy restaurant wouldn't be much different from working at the greasy spoons, she reassured herself. She spooned four dollops of batter into the pan, thinking: He'll see. Soon, Fabrizio will be just like the other men she'd worked for, who after a few weeks grew to see her as a mother figure. Regardless of their ages, twenty-five or fifty, she seemed to have this effect on them. They treated her with a measure of respect, although they were quick to turn on her just the same, with their fickle demands, their childish fits. Hoity-toity restaurant or roadside diner, the trick was to keep that underwater sense at all times, muffle out the clattering sounds, let the rhythm of the task absorb you, swallow down and blink away the injustices.

Still, there were those days when the hours stacked up, blurred together, no distinguishing between them, just the heat of the grill and the sputter of grease stinging her forearms. How did she get here, she'd find herself wondering, how did it come to be that she ended up wearing this greasy apron, husband-less, in a smoky kitchen in a strange town with a strange man shouting at her to dice the onions smaller?

But they were in California now. This time, she knew, it would be different. This time, they were here to stay.

The tops of the pancakes were bubbling. She flipped them over, and waited another minute, then turned off the burner and piled the pancakes onto a plate.

"Breakfast!" she called out.

Driving to Acappella the next afternoon, Elaine found herself feeling less hopeful, preparing for the chaos she knew awaited her: the clanging of pots, the clattering of spoons, dishes, knives, the shouting—Fabrizio presiding over his crew, yelling alternately in Spanish and Italian, *An-dal-ay! Pronto!* She had an advantage over the pastry chef from Guadalajara, she knew, since Fabrizio yelled at the Mexicans the most, but the fact that she was not Italian put her in the second rank of his hierarchy: not quite as stupid as the Mexicans, in the bigoted man's eyes, but certainly stupider than the Italians.

She pictured herself standing behind the shiny metal counter in her white apron, her hair drawn back into a severe bun, squeezing dollops of whipped cream into the miniature pastry swans. This would be her job again, Fabrizio had told her—there was another private party tonight, this time for Paramount Pictures. One swan after another, baking sheet after baking sheet.

Her girlhood fantasies of her future chafed against the stark reality of these moments. She had imagined herself as a grown woman bathed in sunshine, sailing in and out of rooms, swathed in crisp white linen dresses. Her mother, of course, had cherished an altogether different vision, had wanted her to cover her body in black, become a nun. But Elaine wasn't a very good pupil at Holy Cross, and the Franciscan nuns punished her with ruler slaps across the back of her hand for daydreaming during class. She detested her drab uniform—dark blue woolen jumper and starched white blouse, the stiff collar scratching at her neck all day, making her feel strangled.

For ten years she submitted to the nuns' discipline, choked on the dry air, tasting of chalk and mothballs. Her release from Holy Cross came with her father's death. After two slow years of wasting away, his body yielded to the cancer that made a honeycomb of his brain, hollowed out the marrow of his bones. Her mother drifted into indifference, let the house fall into disrepair, let her hopes for Elaine fade. Elaine was fifteen when she transferred to the local public high school. Instead of nursing her grief, she threw herself into her new surroundings with frenetic abandon, sat on dance committees, joined the 4-H club, even became a cheerleader, spending as much time as possible away from the sad, quiet house where her mother sequestered herself behind drawn muslin curtains.

Elaine prided herself as someone who did not buckle under grief, who did not quit when things seemed unmanageable. Those growing-up years had prepared her for married life with Roger, when he slipped into the depths of his depression. She remembered the texture of their life together, how a pall stole over him, silent and suffocating, threatening to envelop her. How strange, she thought, that their little ramshackle house in Spokane soon took on the same dimensions as her mother's house in Farmington.

For two months after Roger's death, she clothed herself in the black dress of nuns and widows. The day she drove away from it all, when she ushered Hannah and Daisy into the Datsun, she wore a crisp white linen dress, transforming herself into the image of her girlhood fantasies. Then she traded the white dress for a cook's white apron, something she never dreamed of wearing. Moving from town to town, kitchen to kitchen, was a kind of liberation. There were no scenes, no confrontations, when she quit. She'd simply untie her apron and leave it on the counter, walk out the back door with her chin held high. Drive back to her girls, who she knew were waiting for her in the motel room, numbly thinking *Well then*, already mentally tracing the routes on her *Rand McNally's Road Atlas*, which she'd get out the moment she walked through the front door.

She pulled her car into the Acappella parking lot. Yanking up the emergency brake, she considered writing Thomas a letter, to plead once more for some money. Not much, just enough to take the edge off her desperation. How would she word it?

*I know that Roger was estranged from his family, but please, there must be something left over from—*

What could she say? From his father's will? But his father had cut Roger out of it, Thomas had said.

*Roger used to tear up the checks his mother sent him. There must be some way of finding out how much—*

No, Thomas would never go through his dead mother's old

bank records. Elaine considered offering to do the job herself, then dismissed the idea as foolish. He would be even less willing to relinquish family bank records. Thomas was a heartless man. He wouldn't give her a cent.

She glanced at her watch. Two minutes until her shift started. Grabbing her purse, she stumbled out of the car and headed for the back entrance to the kitchen, bracing herself for the clanging and clattering within.

Every morning Mrs. Grover in apartment three crossed the street to the vacant lot in her quilted robe and satin slippers with the fancy puff at the tips, holding a can of cat food and a spoon. She slipped her old, bony body through a slit cut into the chain-link fence, then waded through the waist-high weeds, holding the can and spoon high above her head, calling out *kitty kitty kitty kitty* and giving the air rapid kisses. Cats appeared from everywhere, yowling, pawing at her, rubbing their burred and matted fur against her legs, and in the middle of the lot she waited, a full minute almost, enjoying the attention, until at last she spooned out the food, setting off a frenzy of hissing and scratching and biting as the cats pounced on it—some barely getting any there were so many of them.

On her way back, Mrs. Grover picked two honeysuckle flowers, which she put in a brass bowl of water atop the L-shaped cinderblock wall halfway enclosing her little Astroturfed patio. The flowers from the day before she threw over the chain-link fence into the playground. Or tried to, at least; most times they fell short of their target and ended up on the apartment building side of the fence, on the cement pathway. Then she shut her door and no one would see her for the rest of the day—except when she emerged with her wicker basket of laundry.

Since the laundry room was just a few steps from her front door, even this appearance was easy to miss. But what you could count on seeing, walking past Mrs. Grover's apartment, were two fresh honeysuckle flowers in the brass bowl and a bunch of sad, smushed ones on the ground.

People made fun of Mrs. Grover, but they also felt sorry for her, which was why nobody stole her brass bowl, when most everything else left out on the downstairs patios sooner or later disappeared—a towel, an unlocked bike, flowerpots, a goldfish, even. When Mrs. Grover's empty five-gallon Sparklett's water bottle ended up in Trevor's bedroom as a penny bank, Alma, who pretty much let him run loose and do whatever he wanted, made him dump out the pennies and put the bottle back on Mrs. Grover's patio.

Once, city workmen came by and patched up the slit in the fence with a rectangle of new chain-link, but within an hour Mrs. Grover was marching across the street in her quilted robe and slippers with a pair of wire cutters. When Tanya, from her second-story window, saw the old woman struggling at the fence, she dragged Danny out so he could be a good Christian and do the job for her. Mrs. Grover angrily waved them off. But the beginnings of blisters on the papery skin of her palms stung, so after a minute or two, she let him.

* * *

Danny was out front, practicing his breakdancing to a thumping radio, when Elaine pulled the Datsun up to the curb. She had just returned from a yard sale, where she had bargained down the price on an almost-new TV. Danny's legs flailed in the air as he attempted a handstand. Then he lost his balance and fell to the pavement, cursing.

Elaine rolled down her window, racking her brain for something complimentary to say to Tanya's eldest son, who she hadn't ever really spoken to before.

Touching the top of his head to the pavement, Danny clumsily spun around, his body jerking wildly. "Well, look at you!" was all she could come up with.

Danny collapsed on the pavement. He brushed himself off, shooting an accusatory glance at her.

"Sorry!" Elaine offered. It was hardly her fault, his falling to the ground, but she didn't want to press the issue and make an enemy of Tanya's son, especially after the leg-breaking incident with Sandi.

"You got a nice TV there sticking outta your trunk, need any help?"

Elaine looked up, and saw Tanya leaning out her second-story window. "Oh, no thank you, that's all right," she called back, wishing Tanya wouldn't announce her new purchase to the world. She rolled up her window and accelerated into the parking lot.

The TV seemed heavier than it did at the yard sale. Grasping it in her arms, she slammed the trunk shut with her foot. Tanya appeared, with Danny following reluctantly at her heels.

"Lemme get Danny to help you with that. He'll show you how strong he is." With her two little hands on the small of Danny's back, she pushed her reluctant son toward the car.

"Well thank you," Elaine said, touched by the offer. "I can take one side of it, Danny."

"He can handle it." She playfully pinched her son's bicep.

"*Mom*, quit it."

"Touchy," Tanya said, with a wink at Elaine.

Scowling, Danny lugged the TV up the pathway. "That's a nice set," Tanya said, watching him go.

Elaine heard the touch of envy in her voice. "No really, it's not," she said apologetically. "It's two, three years old. Maybe four. I got it for fifteen dollars." But Tanya ignored her, or didn't hear her—Mrs. Grover, who had just come out of the laundry room, had caught her attention.

"Hi there, Mrs. Grover," Tanya called out.

"Tanya," the old woman said levelly. "If you refuse to speak with those girls of yours about that rude game of theirs I will. Twice this week my doorbell rang and not a soul was there when I opened the door."

"You sure it was them?"

Mrs. Grover's penciled-in eyebrows arched in disdain. "It's none of my business," she began, setting down her wicker basket of laundry. "And I know you don't have a husband around to assist you. But I think you should know you're doing a terrible job of disciplining your children. They'll be thieves and drug addicts before you know it, they'll get thrown in juvenile hall like Rich Jr. Danny is already behaving like him, playing that awful music, twirling around idiotically on his head."

"Mrs. Grover, now, he's just havin' a little fun. Breakdancin', it's called."

"Well he'll break his neck one of these days, it's a wonder that Rich Jr. didn't. Running around setting off fire alarms in the school, stealing people's belongings off their patios—I tried to warn his father, just like I'm warning you now, but evidently it was too late. A week later Mr. and Mrs. Hamilton are treated to the spectacle of the authorities carting their son away in handcuffs. Stealing checks right out of my mailbox. For months, I find out."

"Mr. Hamilton gave you a couch as compensation, didn't he?"

"I don't need a couch," Mrs. Grover snapped. "I have a perfectly good one, what I needed were those government checks."

"You have an extra couch?" Elaine interjected, hoping the women wouldn't be angry with her for changing the subject.

Mrs. Grover eyed her shrewdly. "Why, do you need one?"

"We've just been sitting on pillows. I've been looking for one at yard sales, but—"

"Take it, by all means—it's a few years old but the plastic's still on. I can't tell you how many times I've banged into it walking through my living room."

"We'll have matching furniture now, Elaine," Tanya said. "I got the Hamiltons' armchair, you know. Rich Jr. stole my mail, too."

"Well thank you so much," Elaine said. "How kind of you."

Mrs. Grover waved her hand dismissively. "Nonsense, it's just taking up room. I've got the leg bruises to prove it." She turned back to Tanya. "Now, I mind my own business, but when Danny and his hoodlum friends are doing that crazy dancing out front in what used to be"—she drew in a ragged breath—"a respectable neighborhood, when your daughters are playing tricks with my doorbell every five minutes, throwing my honeysuckle flowers around and filling up the vase on my porch with milk and gasoline and eggs and dishwashing soap and paint thinner and all kinds of rubbish, *your* business becomes *my* business. I waited too long to tell the Hamiltons and witness the outcome."

"I didn't know anything about this gasoline and eggs business," Tanya protested.

"There's a great deal," Mrs. Grover said sternly, "that you don't know about."

"I don't deny that they get mixed up in a little trouble now and then, but they're good kids, when it comes down to it. They don't mean no harm."

"When they're carted away in handcuffs perhaps you'll think otherwise." She leaned down and heaved the laundry basket into her withered arms.

Elaine moved to help, but Mrs. Grover waved her off. The old woman's fierce energy both impressed and intimidated her. She took a small step back and decided to let the two women resolve the conflict on their own.

"It's not against the law," Tanya said, "to play a few pranks."

"Are you telling me you refuse to discipline your children?"

"Now hold on, there's other kids in the building besides mine. Bridget, for instance. I talked with Sandi and Sue-Sue about ringing your doorbell already and they told me it wasn't them."

"They were *lying* to you, Tanya, lying to their own mother. Disgraceful, dis-graceful." Mrs. Grover disappeared into her apartment, shutting the door firmly behind her.

Tanya scratched at her scalp below a curled pigtail and glanced at Elaine. "Mrs. Grover's got a lot of pain in her life," she said, "with all she's been through."

As they walked up the stairs to their apartments, Tanya told Elaine the story about Mrs. Grover. The old woman had lived alone in the apartment for thirty-five years, longer than anyone else had lived at Sunset Terrace. Everybody knew about the husband and newborn baby Mrs. Grover lost years back. It was a hit-and-run that did it, and when Mrs. Grover came out of the coma and learned of their deaths, the trauma knocked a few screws loose. The two honeysuckle flowers she put in her brass bowl every morning were in honor of them. Tanya once had a rare peek inside the old woman's apartment when she helped Mrs. Grover mop up the water from a busted pipe. Framed photographs of Mrs. Grover's husband and her baby cluttered every wall, and one room was piled from the floor to the ceiling with newspapers.

Tanya made a cuckoo sign at her temple. "So just keep all that in mind when you're dealing with Mrs. Grover."

Elaine, still taking it all in, asked, "This happened when?"

"Oh, thirty-four, thirty-five years ago, like I said. It was right when they first moved in, you know, when they were still getting started."

"How does everybody know, then?"

"People talk."

"It was such a long time ago, though."

"Well," Tanya said. "Talk travels."

* * *

Motel Time.

That was how Daisy referred to it — a six-year-old's name for the time she and her sister spent alone in the apartment, without their mother, whenever Elaine left for work or went on a date with Sam.

After kissing her daughters good-bye, Daisy would mumble, "Motel Time," her lower lip trembling.

How the words wrenched Elaine's heart. The transient days of living in motels were behind them, but they had certainly left their mark. What could she do now? Taking Hannah and Daisy with her to work and out with Sam every time was clearly not an option. They knew how to behave in her absence, but still— she wished she had a babysitter who could care for them. She wondered if Mrs. Grover might be willing to do the job.

There were plenty of others in the building she could ask, but for some reason Elaine felt she could trust her the most, even if the old woman was a little on the eccentric side. She had an air of stability about her, a sense that her feet were firmly planted on the ground. This, Elaine felt, in spite of the general impression among the mothers in the building that Mrs. Grover was a hermit with too much time on her hands, carrying on a crazy morning ritual with cats and honeysuckle flowers. And though the mothers all had their good qualities, Alma seemed like too much of a hippie, and had a full-time job, too; Mrs. Hamilton, well, she didn't really know her, since Mrs. Hamilton rarely left her apartment; then there was Joan, who was simply out of the question. The only one left was Tanya, but she worked full-time, too.

As for Mrs. Grover's shortcomings, age was the only one, and though Elaine guessed that she must be well into her seventies, the old woman was sharp. She knew deep down that

Mrs. Grover, with her grumbly sweetness, could be relied upon, as a grandmother among grandchildren.

Mrs. Grover picked up the phone after the fifth ring.

"This is Elaine, in number five. I hope I'm not disturbing you." Asking a lonely old woman to babysit now and then wouldn't be too much of an imposition, she hoped. It might even cheer her up to be in the company of young children, to feel useful.

She gently asked Mrs. Grover for the favor. "They're very responsible," she added quickly.

Mrs. Grover said, "Hmph," unconvinced.

"And they'll just be watching TV—they're not permitted to leave the apartment."

"I am not a babysitter," Mrs. Grover said sharply. "But in my experience, children left unattended in this building leads to mayhem and destruction of property. Usually mine. I suppose I could drop by your apartment to make sure your girls are behaving themselves, but I certainly won't stay and look after them the entire time you're gone."

"Oh, thank you so much," Elaine said, but Mrs. Grover had already hung up. She decided to bake cookies for Mrs. Grover as a gesture of gratitude. There were so many errands to run before her date, which included picking up an *L.A. Times* so she could compose a cheat sheet to prepare for her date and offer something in the way of conversation.

She started her To-Do list, putting *Chocolate chips* at the top of the list. Next she scribbled *L.A. Times,* and *Ant poison,* since Warren refused to address the problem. She kept writing— *Aquarium for Hannah's turtle, Ficus for living room*—until the phone rang.

It was Sam, calling to say that he'd miscalculated the time when the sun set. She'd have to arrive at his house a half-hour earlier than they'd planned if they wanted to catch it.

Elaine put her hand over the receiver to muffle a raggedy sigh. "Okay," she said at last.

"You don't sound too enthusiastic," Sam said.

"Oh, I am, really. I'm just a little frazzled, that's all."

After hanging up, she immediately amended her To-Do list. She crossed out *Ficus for living room*. Then she crossed out *L.A. Times*. No cheat sheets, she thought grimly, I'll just have to wing it.

And, as it turned out, it went better than she'd expected.

Sam and Elaine, side by side, walked along the shore, pants cuffs rolled high, shoes and socks in hand—past tangled, tea-colored clumps of kelp fetid and alive with skittering flies, broken shells and bits of glass worn smooth by the water, and the wet, lumpy remains of a child's sand castle. The rise and ebb of the tide lent a rhythm to their steps, and though they did not hold hands or think of matching strides they walked as one, right foot, left foot, splish-splash through the water. At the horizon, the descending sun cut a glorious, glistening swath through the ocean. A lone surfer paddled to shore, a sleeping sunbather woke with goosebumps on her burnt skin: it was a time of shaking the sand out of towels and heading home, of packing it up and calling it a day.

But for Sam and Elaine, it was a time of arrival, of shared silence that gave way soon enough to confessions.

Sam stopped, picked up a stone ribboned with white, turned it over in his palm before letting it drop. "After Jeanine left me, I walked along this beach every night, all the way to the pier and back again."

"It's a beautiful walk," Elaine said. "Peaceful."

"For two years straight, every evening for two years." He squinted down at his feet. "Getting up in the morning was the hardest part. Waking up without her. I had to force myself out of bed."

"I know. When Roger died I felt that way, too."

"Then one morning I woke up and decided, Enough. What's done is done. Life goes on. I started jogging then. Switched one routine for the other."

Elaine smiled. "I'll never forget, one of Roger's old friends from school showed up at the wake with his wife. I had never met them. The wife took me aside and told me she made birdfeeders, ever since her father died the year before. There were eleven of them in her garage, she didn't know what to do with them. Just gathering dust. I was so distracted, I guess, I didn't understand the point of her story. I thought she was trying to sell me a birdfeeder."

"What *was* the point?"

"Well, that the best medicine in the world for grief is a hobby. In your case walking and jogging."

"Ah, a routine, yes," Sam replied. "So did you start making birdfeeders?" He gave her a playful jab in the ribs.

"Ooo." Elaine jumped, laughing, surprised that such a gesture could come from him, Mr. Serious.

"No birdfeeders?"

"No, no."

"Jogging?"

"No, nothing like that. I guess I didn't have much interest in doing anything." She breathed in the brackish air, feeling invigorated, released. "But one day after I dropped off Hannah at school, the brakes in the Datsun gave out and I had to take it to the mechanic. They told me it would be two hours and Daisy—she was just a toddler then—was getting fussy, and so instead of waiting in their little office I decided to walk around town. I passed a pottery shop that had just opened up, and there was a sign on the door that said they were giving pottery classes. So I just went in and signed up."

"Pottery?" Sam said.

"I made a set of mugs." Elaine found herself giggling. "A whole set."

She met his eyes and he smiled. "You think that's funny? I've broken them all. Well, all except one mug. The school bells next door, you can't imagine how startling they are. I don't notice them much anymore, but the first few weeks…"

Sam laughed.

"Oh, you think that's funny too?"

"Let's sit down," he suggested. He pointed to a line of craggy rocks that jutted out into the ocean.

They picked their way over the rocks, Sam pointing out the dry spots where it was safe to step, until they reached the outer tip. Elaine winced as her toe scraped a barnacle. He offered her his hand and they sat down, their pants soaked through now up to their knees. She dangled her foot into the water and said, "Ooo, ahh, sting."

"The hazards of adventure," Sam said, and he surprised Elaine by kissing the tip of his finger and touching her toe.

The waves crashed on the rocks below. She let her eyes rest on the horizon and filled her lungs with the briny mist and found herself overwhelmed by a desire to unburden herself, to tell this man who kissed his fingertip to soothe her scraped toe everything—about loving another man, a brilliant man, too brilliant, maybe, about the three months of happiness they shared and his sudden slide into a deep, dark depression, about suffering through his suffering, about living day after day with someone you loved but couldn't help, no matter how hard you tried, who locked himself in his study morning through night, hour after hour reading books he bought with money that should have gone toward bills and toddler's clothes, about the checks his mother secretly sent him after his father had given up on him—bribe money, Roger called it—about the horrible fights they'd have after he'd torn up the checks and sent them back in a sealed envelope, about the frigid hush that finally wrapped itself around their house after Daisy was born, his silence louder than if he screamed and yelled—screaming and yelling, in fact, was what she ended up wishing for, even tried to provoke, though it wasn't her way, but when he would drift away and shut himself up in his study that's what in the end she started doing—about the day that was *really* the end, when she came home from grocery shopping and stepped into the house and she knew that something was terribly, terribly wrong, even before she opened the door to his study and found him lying there—

She burrowed her face into Sam's chest. A crashing wave sent its mist showering down on them and she felt the words dig their way back inside her. He laid a hand on her head and stroked her hair, which she knew was a perfect mess now. She shivered.

"Are you cold?"

"No, it's all right."

He caressed her arm. His touch was gentle, tentative. "I see goosebumps."

"All right, maybe I am, a little."

He took off his windbreaker and draped it over her shoulders. They stayed there on the outer tip of the rock, watching the darkening waves swell toward them, until the last rays of the sun sank below the horizon.

\* \* \*

When Mrs. Grover came by the apartment, as promised, she was pleased to see that the girls were lying on the couch she had given Elaine, peacefully watching TV. Not that TV-watching was particularly healthy for young children, but at least they weren't causing a ruckus in their mother's absence. A melée was what she always expected to find, but Elaine was right: Hannah and

Daisy were, for the most part, well-behaved. And given her knowledge of the other children in the building, these girls gave her a glimmer of hope for the future generation, which she had come to see as hopelessly degenerate.

Hannah and Daisy were so mesmerized by the TV show they barely acknowledged her arrival. After greeting them, she sat down on a folding chair in the kitchen and stayed for a while, watching them watch TV. They continued to ignore her, but Mrs. Grover saw through their feigned indifference. Every so often, they would sneak a glance back at her, as if to reassure themselves that she was still there.

Surprisingly, Hannah entwined her legs around her younger sister's, and the sleeping bag Hannah ferociously clutched like a beloved teddy bear was draped over Daisy's body as well. Mrs. Grover suspected that her presence had a calming effect on them—that the sisters would otherwise fight with the zeal of army generals over the incursion of a toe or a fingertip in the other's territory.

The girls remained motionless during the commercial break. The show came on again: there was a car chase, followed by an explosion when a Cadillac rammed into a wall. A man tumbled out of the Cadillac, screaming in agony as the flames consumed him.

"What absurdity are you watching?" Mrs. Grover cried, unable to restrain herself.

But Hannah and Daisy, their heads laid against the armrests on opposite sides of the couch, did not make a sound. She got up and strode into the living room, intending to deliver a gentle but firm lecture on the dangers of television. Their eyes, she saw, were closed; they hadn't seen the horrid explosion.

Relieved, Mrs. Grover nudged them awake. "Time for bed, you two," she said firmly. "Hop to it."

Surprisingly, they obeyed. As she ushered them into their bedroom, she thought Yes, they are good—docile, as children should be.

After turning out the light, she lingered in the bedroom doorway. Soon, she would return home and climb into bed herself, coaxing her old bones under her quilt for a welcome rest. But for now, she would stay here, just a wee bit longer, and gaze at their sweet young faces. Life had robbed her of this pleasure, of children. Nothing wrong with a little make-believe.

*Warren,* Elaine thought, when she heard the three sharp knocks at the front door.

At Alma's suggestion, she had called the Housing Authority about the broken oven glass, and learned that her landlord was required, after all, to foot the bill for its repair. Alma had even typed up the letter to him on her behalf, informing him of his responsibilities. She knew the legal lingo, she'd assured Elaine, from listening to lawyers all day while she typed the transcripts.

Elaine hadn't heard from Warren since she sent the letter several weeks ago, in July, but she was certain he would drop by any day now to bully her into paying for it herself. Squeezing out the soapy water from the sponge she was using to scrub the grimy grouting in the formica counter, Elaine went to answer the door. She was so convinced her landlord would be standing there that she jumped when she saw instead an overweight, middle-aged woman clutching a clipboard.

"Elaine Kierson?"

"Yes?"

"Someone has registered a complaint with us. I'm from Social Services."

Confused, Elaine whisked aside a stray hair that had come loose from her bun. She thought back to her conversation with

Joan—Joan had mentioned that she had received several visits from Social Services, prompted by Tanya's sister's phone calls to the agency. Maybe Tanya registered another complaint against Joan, Elaine concluded. Ever since her sister had moved back to Utah, Tanya must have assumed the role as the watchdog of the building.

"Oh, no, apartment one is downstairs. You're looking for Joan?"

"No, I'm looking for you, Mrs. Kierson." The woman tapped her pen against the clipboard.

Elaine took a step back. She saw at once all that she hadn't yet managed to attend to: the soot on the windowpanes, the unwashed kitchen floors, the spare furnishings, the greasy child's handprints on the TV screen. And here she was, hardly presentable, in her raggedy terrycloth bathrobe.

"May I come in?"

Stay calm, Elaine thought, feeling a tremor in her hands. She opened the door wider and gestured to Rich Sr.'s old cream-colored couch that Mrs. Grover had given her, relieved that she had a couch for the woman to sit on, and that she'd scrubbed the spot of dirt from the armrest earlier that morning. No wonder the Hamiltons left the plastic on; no matter how many times she warned her girls to wash their hands and remove their shoes before sitting on the couch, the dirt showed up.

Her relief quickly turned to embarrassment as the woman paused to pick up Daisy's Skipper—*nude! and filthy, besides!*—from a cushion before sitting down. The couch springs groaned under the woman's ample weight.

Elaine pulled the ties on her bathrobe tight, moving to sit down next to the woman. But the generous folds of the woman's navy skirt had spread over to the other half of the couch, claiming it. She left the woman and quickly retrieved a chair from the kitchen. Returning, she positioned the chair by the couch and sat down.

"Well," Elaine said. She tried to produce a confident smile, hoping it would compensate for the shabby surroundings.

"Are your daughters here?" the woman inquired.

"No. I mean, they're out playing. With the neighbors' children."

The woman consulted the clipboard on her lap. "What do you do, Mrs. Kierson, for a living?"

"I'm a—I'm a cook."

The woman nodded, examining Daisy's grubby Skipper. The naked doll looked suddenly lewd in the woman's fat hands. Elaine fought back the urge to grab it from her.

"According to the complaint we received," the woman said, "your children are left unattended and neglected. How many hours are you away from your home?"

"Who—?"

"How many hours," the woman repeated mechanically, "do you spend away from your home?"

"I have a babysitter, she comes by to check on them, she won't—I mean my children are well-behaved, they don't—" Elaine winced, hearing the shrill note in her voice.

After the woman left, Elaine returned to her scrubbing. She shook a container of Comet with haphazard rage over the formica counter, blanketing the surface with bluish-white grains. A little Comet goes a long way, her mother used to chide her, when as a girl Elaine dutifully performed her chores—her mother always hovering over her, criticizing her incessantly for using too much cleanser, too little elbow grease. It would take ten spongefuls of water at the very least to rinse away the soapy foam from the counter now. But she didn't care. Whatever she did, it was too much or not enough, it seemed, and there was always someone hovering nearby to tell her so.

This is a just a routine visit, the woman from Social Services had informed her before leaving, adding that she'd be back with a more thorough inspection if they received another complaint.

Furiously, Elaine scrubbed the counter, wondering who had called Social Services to tattle on her. Yes, there were the times she worked, and the dates with Sam, but her arrangement with Mrs. Grover seemed to be working out well. In a few months, she might be able to save enough money to afford a babysitter who could stay all night, but in the meantime, what more could she do? And why was she, of all people, singled out, of all the mothers in the building? She was, beyond a shadow of a doubt, more attentive to her children than Tanya, or Alma, or certainly Joan. It was brutally unjust.

She moved to the stove, where she scrubbed until the aluminum gleamed, wondering what meddling hypocrite had the gall to tell Social Services she was an unfit mother.

\* \* \*

"How's your man?" Tanya asked. "Is he marriageable material?"

Unloading her groceries from the shopping cart, Elaine handed Tanya a styrofoam package of ground beef. At Sunset Terrace, there were plenty of opportunities to talk, since they were, after all, neighbors—but she found that Tanya did her deepest probing while standing behind the Lucky's checkout counter, ringing up groceries.

"Darn ink's blurred," Tanya said, squinting at the white sticker. "Can't read the price. Let's call it two-fifty."

"Thank you," Elaine said. It was over a pound and a half of beef, and both of them knew Tanya was giving her a deal. She wondered if Tanya was the one who had called Social Services. But would she really have done such a thing? Tanya, of all people? Maybe she regretted the phone call, and was now trying to undo the damage.

"Well? How is he?"

"Sam? He's fine," she said guardedly.

"Uh-huh." She gave Elaine a wink. "You're leaving out the good stuff."

"Yes, well, he's very sweet, very involved in things." It had seemed like the right way to describe Sam, but she could tell that Tanya wanted more. "Politically," she added. She left it at that, remembering then what she'd learned at Roger's wake. Telling anybody about anything that mattered always left her feeling silly and exposed. You could never find the right words, and the eyes of the person listening always glazed over while you struggled to express the inexpressible. People never had the interest or the attention, it seemed, to wait for you to unravel the complexities.

"I guess your lips are sealed." Tanya rang up a jar of mayonnaise. "All right, then. We'll talk about something else. Your girls excited about school starting?"

"Yes, I suppose," Elaine said, glad that Tanya had given up the other line of inquiry. "I wonder when we'll hear about their teacher assignments."

"Oh, they'll post it by the principal's office a week beforehand. I can't believe it. Sandi'll be in junior high."

"They just keep growing."

"Shore do." Tanya shook her pigtails amiably.

Tanya couldn't have been the one, she decided. Tanya was too nice to do anything that cruel.

Joan, she thought. Joan was the one.

"Turn off that TV!" Mrs. Grover ordered, striding through the front door. She produced a deck of cards. "Your mother should be coming home soon. We've got just enough time for a good game of poker."

At the kitchen table, Hannah watched the dizzying blur of cards in Mrs. Grover's hands as she dealt them out, snapping and flicking and slapping them around. She was filled with respect and awe.

Mrs. Grover tapped the deck twice on the table. Then, faster than Hannah could count to ten, Mrs. Grover dealt out four piles. "Well don't just stand there gaping, sit down and pick up your hand. Daisy, you're on my team."

"Goody!" Daisy said, and scooted her chair right up next to Mrs. Grover's.

Hannah picked up her cards, one by one. They felt slippery, and it was hard to arrange them in a neat fan, the way Mrs. Grover had them, with even spaces between each card.

"First things first. There are different ways you can arrange the cards in your hands. Let's put all the twos together, then the threes, and so on."

When Hannah had completed this task, Mrs. Grover instructed her to group the cards according to suit—clubs, diamonds, hearts, and spades. Then she told her to combine the two ways of arranging, with each suit grouped together and in numerical order.

"Now for the rules. It's an easy game, but you have to pay attention."

For twenty minutes Mrs. Grover patiently explained and re-explained rules and strategies. Daisy laid her head on the old woman's shoulder and let out a contented sigh. Mrs. Grover didn't stop talking, but for a moment she did seem to lose her train of thought. Looking down at Daisy, her expression was no less baffled than if she'd discovered a radish had sprouted up there.

Then she told a story that no one in the building knew, not even Tanya.

"A long time ago," she began, "my father owned a speakeasy on Hill Street downtown. It was upscale, don't misunderstand. My father's customers were in the upper echelons of society."

Hannah said, "What's a—?"

"High class. Upper echelon means high class, people with money. I'm sorry, I'm not accustomed to the company of youngsters."

Then Daisy said that *she* knew what echelon meant and Hannah told her she was lying. Mrs. Grover's face grimaced, looking like she'd just sucked on a lemon. "My blood pressure, girls," she warned. "No bickering." Gazing up, she drew a deep breath and laid her right hand across her chest, as if she were about to say the Pledge of Allegiance.

Once Mrs. Grover had collected herself, she continued her story. "Now, we lived upstairs, my mother and father and me, in the apartment above the speakeasy. I had two older brothers, but I never knew them. Both were killed building the Panama Canal." And she went on, telling about how her mother had received two telegrams within a month of each other, each informing her that one of her sons was dead. She shook her head sorrowfully. "My mother was so heartbroken she swore she'd never have another child. Life was too uncertain in those days, and the possibility of losing another one was just too painful for her. Illness and death among children back then was much more common. But in May of 1913 something happened."

She waited until Hannah burst out with "What?"

"Well, I was born, despite my mother's precautions. My father always said that when I was born, he was reborn. You should have seen him, so handsome, with a thick black mustache and skin so tan he looked bronzed. He was a gentleman, indeed, with gentlemanly manners. All the ladies were after him, but he only had eyes for my mother. He taught me everything, or nearly everything, that he would have taught his sons.

"Including," she said, her eyes twinkling, "how to play poker. By the time I was fourteen I could have beaten most of the men who came in there to play. He never let me play with them, of course, no matter how much I begged. But once in a while, on Sunday mornings, the bartender would come upstairs for a cup of my mother's coffee—he was an old friend of my father's—and the four of us would play a hand of poker, right there in the kitchen, just like we're doing. I was your age when I learned how, so don't think you're too young. Nonsense, is what I say."

Before they started the game, Mrs. Grover told Hannah to rummage through the kitchen to find something to gamble with. "Your mother seems like the type of woman," she said, "who would keep dried beans on hand."

Sure enough, Hannah reached into one of the orange Tupperware canisters lined up on the kitchen counter and came out with a handful of black beans.

Pleased, Mrs. Grover counted out ten for Hannah and ten for herself. "We'll use these for money. Remember, Daisy, it's you and me against your sister. Are you ready?"

Mrs. Grover was careful to lose on purpose enough times to let Hannah experience the thrill of winning at poker, which to Mrs. Grover was one of the rarest and finest pleasures this earth has to offer you—even if a few dried beans were the only bounty you received. When Hannah called out "Straight Flush!" or "Three Ladies!" it was utter joy to see the look of triumph on the young girl's face. Not once did Hannah and Daisy bicker, and Mrs. Grover didn't have to mention her blood pressure again.

Toward the end of the dinner shift at Acappella, Elaine dropped a bottle of Grand Marnier while making tiramisu. All night she'd been preoccupied, filled with shame that Social Services had a complaint about bad mothering with her name on it.

Her two-week probation at Acappella was up a week and a half ago, but Fabrizio hadn't mentioned it. She hadn't dared to remind him, figuring she'd keep on working and cashing her paychecks and behaving like a regular employee until he said otherwise. But now he certainly would remember, she thought grimly, looking down at the mess she'd made.

She dropped to the floor to pick up the broken glass. There was a sudden drop in voices and she flushed, feeling the eyes of the other kitchen staff on her. She would have refused to let anyone assist in the cleaning-up, wanting to bear the full responsibility for her mistake, but no one, as it turned out, offered to help. Her hands trembling, she made a neat pile of the broken glass and dropped the pieces one by one into the trashcan.

Out of the corner of her eye, she spotted Fabrizio. Panicked, she mopped up the spill with a rag someone had tossed at her feet. As he stormed toward her, the kitchen staff resumed chopping and mixing and sautéing. The rag was almost soaked through with the alcohol, and she refolded it to the drier side so she could mop up the rest of the spill. She saw red splotches on the rag, and realized her hand was cut. It was then that she felt a smart of pain. Pressing her lips together, she quickly brushed off the bits of glass from her palm and stumbled to her feet, wrapping her hand in the Grand Marnier-soaked towel to stop the bleeding. Fabrizio stopped before her, face beet-red and veins popping out at the temples.

The more she apologized the more enraged he became, shaking his head, barking "Stupid stupid stupid!"

And she was fired.

Instead of surface streets Elaine took the freeway home to get there faster, though it only shaved off five minutes. Changing lanes in a frenzy, she would have side-swiped a motorcyclist if he hadn't swerved in the nick of time. Without turning around, he thrust his leather-gloved fist in the air and raised his middle finger as he sped ahead.

Once she reached the fast lane, she rolled her window down. The night air, warm and bone dry, came thundering into the car. That man almost died, she thought with sudden, sickening clarity—I almost killed him. The words replayed themselves in her head, until she could almost hear the dull thud of his motorcycle against her car. Her teeth began to chatter. She turned on the heater.

The off-ramp fed her onto Pico. At the stoplight, a car jam-packed with teenage girls pulled up in the next lane, a song blasting on the radio and all of them singing the words—*White Liiiines*—at the top of their lungs. They honked the horn, quick insistent bleats that stripped what was left of Elaine's nerves raw.

Rolling up her window to block out the noise, she realized they were trying to get her attention. "Headlights!" the girls were yelling over the music, gleefully pantomiming with splayed-out fingers.

Embarrassed, Elaine turned on her headlights.

\* \* \*

Her daughters were in their usual place, waiting for her on the couch, watching late-night TV.

And here was Daisy now, running up to greet her, throwing her arms around her thighs, crying, "Mommy! We played poker tonight with Mrs. Grover!"

"Oh, good," she said, feeling the tears well up. Unable to stop them, she dropped her keys and found herself on the floor, sobbing. When she could get the words out, she said, "Don't worry about Mommy. Let's go to bed."

She managed to get them into their room without any fussing. She pulled their bedspreads up to their chins. They lay there peering at her, studying her face, swallowing down whatever they wanted to ask.

Not now, she decided. Tomorrow morning, she would tell them she'd lost her job.

Walking to her bedroom, she saw that the filthy Grand Marnier–soaked rag was still wrapped around her injured hand. She tore it off and hurried to the kitchen, where she threw the rag away in the trash, then tied up the bag and left it outside the front door to take to the dumpster in the morning. At the sink, she soaped the cuts on her palm and held it under a scorching hot stream of water that brought fresh tears to her eyes.

\* \* \*

On Monday, Elaine was surprised to receive—from Mrs. Hamilton of all people—a bag of clothes that Rich Jr. had grown out of. Mrs. Hamilton was so shy she couldn't even look Elaine in the eye when she spoke to her.

"I don't know what to do with them, I know they're boys' clothes, but I thought you might be able to use them," she blurted in a soft little-girl voice.

"Thank you," Elaine said, mystified.

Mrs. Hamilton ducked her head and was halfway down the stairs before Elaine could say anything else.

An hour or so later, Tanya showed up with a cardboard box filled with sliced bread and hamburger buns that "were just a few days past their prime." They were perfectly fine—the Lucky's manager was just going to throw them away, she explained. "Just pop 'em in the freezer and they'll last a lifetime." When Elaine unpacked the box, she found some dented cans of soup and a six-pack of Diet Shasta hidden underneath the hamburger buns.

Why was she being showered with all of these gifts? Later, as she walked down the cement pathway to the laundry room, she passed Alma, who was on her way to work at the downtown civil court.

"I was just thinking of you," Alma said. "I heard you lost your job."

Elaine caught on, then, and wondered if there was anything Tanya learned from the children's gossip that didn't end up in the ears of everyone else in the building.

"Listen to this," Alma said. "So there was a civil case the other day, this restaurant owner was suing the landlord for breach of contract. The landlord refused to pave the parking lot, and since nobody could park, the restaurant was losing business. Anyway, the landlord lost. The restaurant might be needing some extra help soon, since there's going to be a new parking lot. I usually go on automatic pilot, you know, but I heard the owner say that the restaurant was close by, and…well, I thought you might be interested. So I took down the information for you, just in case." Alma handed her a scrap of notepaper.

"Thank you," Elaine said.

"Hey, good luck." Turning away, her flowing dress billowed, releasing a whiff of sandlewood incense.

"Wait, wait just a moment. Can I ask you something?"

"Sure."

"Do people in the building think...?" After a brief hesitation, she decided to be blunt. "Do people think I'm a bad mother?"

"Jeez, what makes you say that?"

"It's really very...generous of everyone. But really, I'm fine. I can find a job, I've always been able to. My children won't go hungry. They have clothing."

"We look out for each other here, you know."

"Yes, but—"

"Don't worry so much about what other people think," Alma gently interrupted. "We're all in the same boat."

Elaine climbed the stairs to her apartment, wondering if she should call the restaurant to inquire about openings. Alma was so sweet to think of her, but it was such a far-fetched idea.

At the top of the stairs, she wondered if she should knock on Tanya's door and thank her for—what exactly? For telling everyone in the building that she'd been fired from Acappella? She remembered Sandi's broken leg, how Tanya had blamed Hannah for the injury. How Tanya had seemed jealous that she had managed to find an eligible man at the PWP dinner. Maybe Joan wasn't the one who called Social Services. Maybe Tanya had done it, after all. No—not maybe. She was sure of it.

Tanya, spreading rumors about her being a bad mother. Tanya, who left her children alone for half the day while she worked at Lucky's. The injustice of the accusation stung her again. Tanya, of all people.

She heard the phone ringing. She dug into her purse for her keys and made it through the front door by the third ring. It was Sam, asking her to dinner.

"Oh, I can't," she sighed.

"Okay, some other time then?" She heard the strain in his voice, the formal tone that she now recognized as a sign of his discomfort. She had never turned him down for a date before.

"Yes, of course. Sometime soon," she offered vaguely, wondering when that later would be. Telling him about the Social Services incident was out of the question. Not only was it embarrassing—but if Tanya, who was supposedly her friend, could accuse her of being an unfit mother, then Sam could easily draw the same conclusion.

She struggled to think of an explanation that would sound reasonable. Now that she was fired, she couldn't use work as an excuse. Or could she? No, lying to him now about work obligations would only complicate things. She racked her brain for a solution to her dilemma. Finally, she came up with one.

"Why don't you come over for dinner tomorrow night. I'll cook."

After hanging up, she immediately regretted her invitation. So far, he hadn't set foot in her apartment; whenever they had a date, she'd meet him at his house. She felt ashamed by her shabby apartment, imagining what he'd say, or at least think. He was a man with such convictions, such *opinions*.

He would disapprove.

Yes, Sam, who seemed so open-minded, so willing to embrace the downtrodden, would see her in a different light. She recalled Sam's criticisms of his ex-wife. Jeanine was *unstable*, he'd said. He'd married someone he thought was a free-thinking individual, like him.

A free-thinking individual who turned out to have no *ideological infrastructure*.

These were Roger's words against her—Elaine—not Sam's against Jeanine. Sam's words against Jeanine were something like *She had no backbone*.

She tried to remember the precise circumstances of Sam's

disclosure. At the Mexican restaurant with photos of customers Scotch-taped all over the walls? ("To the right of the hanging sombrero," he'd said, pointing out where the snapshot of Jeanine and him was once displayed, which started him off on a tangent about Jeanine's vanity.) In his car, when he told her about Jeanine leaving him for the city planning commissioner, whose politics he claimed were too trickle-down? Or had it been the time she sat in his living room, holding the Indian pillow with the little round mirrors against her chest as she listened to him enumerate all the startling examples of Jeanine's hypocrisy? (*"If Gallo gets in the way we're gonna roll right over them / We're gonna roll this union on,"* he sang. "I mean I was there, I heard the words come out of her mouth. Do you see what I'm getting at? Here is a woman who once marched with Cesar Chavez. The same woman who now pays a Mexican maid two bucks an hour to keep her Brentwood condo spotless").

Yes, she was not Jeanine. Sam had not voiced any complaints against her. Not yet. But he wasn't one to give many compliments, either. Recently, though, he said something nice about her hair. He reached over, in the middle of dinner, to stroke it in that tentative, gentle way of his.

"Oh, don't, it's so frizzy tonight," she protested.

"No, it's nice," he said.

(*Medusa, look not on me with thine eyes!* Roger used to say.)

*Hippie hair* were the words she feared Sam was thinking, what others had called it in the past. Others, who had similarly been misled by her physical appearance. Who had thought she meant something by the way she dressed and made herself up— or didn't make herself up, more accurately. Others, who had misinterpreted her hair and her clogs and her general avoidance of makeup, except for maybe a little powder and a quick swipe of lipstick, as a political statement.

The truth was, she had no politics.

The truth was, physical appearance for her wasn't political.

She liked her hair long. She had nothing against makeup, really, except that it was expensive, and the one time she had allowed a saleswoman at a cosmetics counter to give her a free makeover, the black liner and purple shadow the saleswoman had insisted would accentuate her blue irises made her look like the woman had punched her in the eyes.

And her clogs were practical, that's all; she'd discovered them when she started working in kitchens, and found that most of the employees there—including the men—wore them, since they were the most comfortable shoes available for people who had to be on their feet for hours on end. Even when she was off work, she found that she preferred wearing them. People who did not work in kitchens didn't know that clogs were part of a uniform, and often assumed her choice of footwear, combined with her no-frills appearance, meant she was a hippie. Or a feminist.

But she was not a feminist, or a hippie. She was not an anything. Which Sam would see as a character flaw: *No backbone.*

As for Sam's other criticisms of Jeanine, inviting him to dinner at her apartment might lead him to associate her with his ex-wife. *Unstable,* he might think, noting the yard-sale furniture, the broken oven glass, the threadbare patch on the shag carpet only partially disguised by the rag rug—with a hunk of the fringes snipped off after the vacuum cleaner incident.

It all came down to this: *The fatuous assumption that appearance bears some relationship to interior truth.*

Roger's words, not hers.

Most of what he had said when they were married had flown in one ear and out the other. He'd said so, in fact, during one of their later arguments, and it was the first time she could readily agree with one of his criticisms of her. She'd felt victorious at the time, shouting *Yes, that's exactly true, yes, it flies in one ear and out the other.* It wasn't until the hint of a sneer revealed itself on Roger's face—the slightest twist of his mouth was all it took—that the rage inside her was snuffed out, smothered by a familiar feeling of defeat. She knew what Roger had meant.

*The fatuous assumption that appearance bears some relationship to interior truth*—these words did *not* fly out of her ear. She knew Roger had thought she was someone else when he married her. She knew about looks, about what Roger had meant by *interior truth*. She knew he'd been disappointed.

Would Sam see her for who she feared, deep down, she really was? A hopeless, unemployed single mother living in a run-down apartment building with a rag rug. Unstable and foolish. If Roger were alive, he would say so.

Here he was again, whispering in her ear.

*Bad Mother*

Cooking for Sam was something Elaine yearned to do. And not simply because his "Sammy Specialties" were practically inedible.

It was more than that.

It was a way of showing her true feelings, of bypassing silly words of endearment. The look she imagined on his face when he swallowed a forkful of a meal she'd prepared especially for him: that would feed *her*.

For the menu Elaine decided on roast chicken, scalloped potatoes and brussels sprouts tossed with sautéed shaved almonds: something a little different, but not too adventurous. If the way to a man's heart was through his stomach, then maybe the meal would soften his judgment of her shabby surroundings.

After breakfast, she sent her girls outside to play in the schoolyard. With the apartment to herself, she devoted four uninterrupted hours to a thorough cleaning. She swept and dusted and mopped, and went through half a can of Comet scouring every surface in sight. No matter how much she did, though, the apartment never looked clean, never seemed to belong to her—an accumulation of dirt and grime remained in the cracks and crevices, a stubborn reminder of all the lives lived before her in the apartment.

Before vacuuming, she remembered this time to remove the area rug. She took the rug down to the laundry room and threw it in the machine with enough soap for three loads; the fringes were snipped off on one side of the rug now, but it was better than exposing the threadbare carpet underneath. Back in the kitchen, she nearly panicked when she spotted a line of ants coming through the widening seam between the wall and the floor. With a hot, wet sponge she smashed as many of the filthy things as she could, when it occurred to her that she'd bought a can of ant poison, which was now in the cabinet under the kitchen sink. At least she could put one worry out of her mind, she thought, sprinkling the white powder into every visible crack.

Sam arrived promptly, knocking on the front door at seven o'clock on the dot. Elaine made a final quick appraisal of the apartment, stopping to fluff the couch cushions and pick off a long, frizzy hair—hers—from the armrest.

"Be right there!" she called out.

Dashing to the kitchen sink, she wet her hands and smoothed down her hair—a tried-and-true remedy for the frizzies—before opening the door.

"Girl Scouts," Sam announced with a wry grin. He was holding a small, white bag. Over his usual sports shirt he wore a brown blazer, and instead of the tennis shoes, he had on what looked to be a new pair of brown loafers. She caught a whiff of cologne.

"You're supposed to say 'You're not a Girl Scout.'"

"Oh-oh, sorry," she stammered. "You're not a Girl Scout."

"Yes, but I have cookies," he said, handing her the bag. "I know, corny. That's why I don't tell jokes."

"No, I like it. I like your jokes."

"I don't tell them, really."

"But I want you to tell them, is what I mean." Already she

was off to an awkward start. "Well," she said, "don't just stand there, come in."

As he walked into the living room, she watched for a hint of disapproval to show itself in his expression, but there was none.

She poured out two glasses of wine, and sparkling apple juice for her girls, a special treat that she hoped would encourage good behavior. "Dinner's almost ready, just a few final touches. Let me just run to the bedroom and check on Hannah and Daisy."

He caught her by the arm. "Wait. Before you do." He drew her to him. It was an urgent kiss, and as his grip tightened a pleasant shudder passed through her. She breathed in the citrusy tang of his cologne, savored the hard scratch of stubble against her skin. Something was thrillingly different in him tonight: the hesitancy was gone, and with it the chaste gentleness of his touch.

There was a thud in the girls' bedroom, followed by Daisy's cry. "*Mommy!*" Alarmed, Elaine glanced in the direction of the bedroom.

"Don't you dare," Sam said, and before she could utter a word he kissed her again.

The girls picked off the almonds from their brussels sprouts, but they were otherwise on their best behavior. And Sam, Elaine was pleased to see, ate with gusto, and when his plate was clean he even sucked the marrow from the chicken bones. Hannah wrinkled her nose and turned to Daisy, who started to giggle, but after Elaine shot them a stern glance they managed to compose themselves.

"Delicious," Sam said, dropping the chicken wing he'd sucked dry. "Best meal I've had in years."

There was a knock at the door, and Daisy jumped up from the table to answer it. Bridget bounded into the living room, clutching her pillow.

"I'm spending the night, okay?"

Elaine stood up from the table and walked over to her. As usual, Bridget had arrived unannounced, which wouldn't have been a problem if Sam weren't here. Still, she couldn't see herself telling Bridget that she wasn't welcome. She gently took the pillow away from her and placed it on the couch. "Is Joan in Culver City, sweetie?"

"No, but I want to anyway."

Laying a hand on Bridget's head, she stroked her tousled hair and glanced at Sam. "This is Bridget, she lives downstairs in apartment one."

He stood up from the table, holding out his hand. "Hello, I'm Sam." Bridget shook it vigorously, looking up at him with bright, gleaming eyes.

He chuckled. "That's quite a strong grip you've got there."

"Watch I can make it more," Bridget said, and squeezed tighter, gritting her teeth, and her face flushed a deep red.

"Well well, very impressive."

"I can do it, too," Hannah insisted, and held out her hand. Sam played along, and soon all three girls were crowded around him, daring him to shake their hands one more time.

Elaine stood back and watched, laughing. It was so unlike Sam to play with her girls. He had always seemed a little reserved around them, lapsing into the formal tone that she recognized as his teacher's voice, which he used whenever he spoke of his students or of his political activities. But Bridget had managed to break through all that. What a wonderful ability she had of brightening everything up.

"Okay, that's enough," she warned, on the third round of handshakes. "Sam is our dinner guest, let's not wear him out."

"Can I have dinner, too?" Bridget said, racing into the kitchen.

"I'm afraid there's nothing left. Would you like a cheese sandwich?"

Bridget peeked into the pots and fished out of the roasting

pan a lone shred of chicken. "No," she said, chewing.

"How about peanut butter and jelly?"

"Blecch."

"I have a can of chicken noodle soup," she offered, but Bridget clutched her throat and made a gagging noise.

Elaine smiled; she knew this game well.

"I have an idea," Sam said, grabbing the bag of cookies he'd brought. "Who likes chocolate chip?"

"Me!" Bridget shouted, and Hannah and Daisy joined in, "Cookies!"

"Slowly, no gobbling," Elaine cautioned them, but it was too late: they devoured the cookies, dropping crumbs everywhere. She moved to clean them up, when Sam came up behind her and put hands under her armpits. Before she could turn around, he lifted her into the air.

"Put me down!" she screamed, and waved her arms. The girls giggled, clapping their hands.

At nine-thirty, Elaine announced that it was time to get ready for bed. The girls pleaded, as usual, to stay up later, but they gave in at last and shuffled into the bathroom to brush their teeth.

"Bridget stays over here several times a week," she explained to Sam, once they were alone. "Usually when her mother's away, but lately she's been coming over even when Joan's home." She recounted the details of Bridget's troubled past while Sam filled their wine glasses.

"Doesn't she mind that her daughter stays over here so much?"

"I don't know," she admitted. "Maybe. But she hasn't said anything yet. Wait, let me just go and put the girls to bed. I'll be right back."

They were already in bed, waiting for her. She kissed Daisy goodnight, then moved to the other bed, where Hannah and

Bridget lay side by side.

"Sleep tight," she whispered, and gave them each a light kiss on the forehead.

When she returned, she found Sam in the kitchen, pacing. He looked up, and Elaine was surprised to see his brow creased in an expression of deep concern. "I'm sorry," she said, "I didn't mean to leave you alone, I just had to say goodnight."

"I don't know how to say this," he said, and cleared his throat. "I had a seventh grader last year who had a similar situation as this girl Bridget, his mother left him home alone for days at a time, and I had to report it. It was my duty as his teacher. I know you mean well, don't get me wrong. But I'm not sure you're helping her in the way she should be helped. You're not the person who can really help her, is what I'm saying."

A bolt of anger shot through her. "What's wrong with me? What am I doing wrong?"

"Maybe there's another way of handling this. I just thought I should tell you what was on my mind."

"Is that your duty too?"

"Please, Elaine, I don't want you to take this the wrong way."

"How else can I take it?" She poured the last of the wine into her glass, her hands trembling.

"As some helpful feedback. I'm not telling you what to do—frankly, I don't know what I'd do in your situation. I hope I'm not overstepping the bounds here, but there are agencies that can help with this sort of situation."

"What kind of agencies? Social Services, you mean? They'd come and whisk her away, put her in a group home. Would that be the right thing to do? Is that the best environment for a little girl? Some kind of institution?"

"No, it's not the best. But maybe she'll be better off than she is now."

"You don't know that. How can you know that?"

"How do you see this playing out, then? Will this continue until she's in junior high? In high school?"

"Maybe," she said, hearing her voice catch.

"Even if this seems like the right thing to do now, what about the future, have you thought about that? I'm just asking."

She felt tears welling up, but she swallowed, steeling herself against them. "I lost my job, Sam. I got fired actually. I don't know what's in the future. In a couple months I'll have run through all my savings." It didn't matter now, she didn't care what he thought about her. "And speaking of Social Services, what do you think of this? Someone in the building—Tanya, I'm pretty sure of it—called them and accused me of being an unfit mother. A woman with a clipboard showed up at my door asking questions. Don't look at me like that, don't look so astonished. I can't even leave the apartment now for longer than a shopping trip without worrying that they'll come and whisk *my* children away."

"Elaine…" He moved to touch her shoulder, but she shook him off.

"Hey, listen, I'm not—" he began sharply. "Why the hell didn't you tell me about all this?"

"It doesn't matter, I'm telling you now, I—" She stopped, realizing that she was shouting. She glanced back at the girls' bedroom.

"Don't worry for godsakes," he said impatiently. "They're sleeping."

"They're awake now," she said flatly.

He walked away from her and stared at the refrigerator door, clearly trying to control his temper. After a moment, he returned. "I'm going to help you work through this, all right? You obviously take good care of your kids, no social worker could possibly question that. You've told me that you have a good, workable arrangement with Mrs. Grover."

Elaine heard the rhetorical lift in his voice, and hoped he

wasn't going to launch into a speech on social injustice and class stratification. When he looked down at the floor and blinked rapidly, she braced herself. But when he lifted his head, she could see that he wasn't thinking about politics.

Gently, he cupped her chin in his hands. "You're doing the best you can. So don't worry. Nobody's going to come and whisk your kids away."

\* \* \*

"That's fake fire," Hannah said.

"Real People" was the show on TV, and the stunt was playing back in slow motion—a man exploding into flames as he fell from the balcony of a wooden house.

"No duh," said Bridget.

Sighing, Hannah picked up Skipper, which lay on the couch where Daisy had left it.

"Gimme that," Bridget said, and grabbed it from her. She swung the doll around in a circle by its hair. "I'm bored," she said. Each time it went around, she said Bored.

Daisy ran over. "Stop!"

But Bridget ignored her. "Bored bored bored bored bored bored bored."

"That's *mine*, give it!"

"Bored bored bored bored bored bored bored."

Daisy's face crumpled, and Hannah could tell her little sister was two seconds away from bursting into tears. She snatched the doll from Bridget's hand—she didn't know why she did it, except that she saw Daisy was helpless and she suddenly felt sorry for her.

Bridget's eyes became two glaring slits. She tried to grab it back, but Hannah held on tight. A tug-of-war began.

Mrs. Grover marched through the front door, saving Hannah and Bridget from what was about to be their first real fight. "What on earth is going on here?"

"Nothing," Hannah said softly, loosening her grip from the doll. Bridget snatched it back.

"Nonsense." Drawing a deep breath, Mrs. Grover laid her right hand on her chest, reminding Hannah again of the Pledge of Allegiance. "My blood pressure," she said, "is elevated by squabbling children. Your mothers will be very upset to hear about this incident."

Bridget tilted her head and put on her sweetest smile. "Don't tell them, pleeeeese?"

Mrs. Grover was unmoved. "You may be able to manipulate Elaine with that performance, but I can't be fooled."

Daisy stuck her tongue out at Bridget, newly courageous in Mrs. Grover's presence, then took cover behind the old woman, clinging to her thighs. Mrs. Grover looked down at her with a mixture of amusement and discomfort, as if she were a muddy puppy. "Daisy, I have to move."

"Noooo."

"Yes, oh yes. Bridget and I have to go downstairs and speak with Joan."

Bridget's eyes clouded over then, looking so sad that Hannah's anger drained out of her. "You can't talk to Joan," Hannah told Mrs. Grover. "She's not home."

"Oh? Where is she?"

"In Culver City."

Mrs. Grover pursed her lips. "Culver City, I see. Of course. So we've got *two* missing mothers."

Bridget threw Skipper across the room. Daisy let out a shriek and ran to pick up the doll, then scurried back and hid behind Mrs. Grover's thighs.

Alma was the one who found Mrs. Grover, sprawled on the cement laundry room floor in her quilted robe, her arms still embracing a mush of cold, dripping towels.

Alma had been on her way to work, heading toward her VW bug in the parking lot. Anyone else might have walked right by, their thoughts consumed with work grievances—traffic and bosses and late paychecks—not even noticing that the unpainted laundry room door was wide open, where an old woman's pale leg jutted out. Alma was the type, though, who liked to look at things, who took in the brightening blue sky and a passing bee as she walked to her destination.

It could be argued that she was also the type to miss a lot of things, too, gazing around with her dreamy eyes as her Indian-print dress billowed and swished, trailing a scent of sandlewood incense. But on this particular morning there was a yellow honeysuckle flower on the cement pathway. Bending down to pick up the flower, she thought she might tuck it behind her ear, when out of the corner of her eye she spotted the pink, feathery puff of Mrs. Grover's satin slipper.

After calling 9-1-1, Alma called Tanya, and the news spread quickly.

The mothers raced out of their apartments—Tanya, in her

Lucky's uniform with her pigtails still in sponge curlers, Joan in skin-tight jeans and her Farrah Fawcett wig, smoking a Virginia Slim, and Elaine, drying her hands on a dish towel. They huddled in the doorway of the laundry room, looking down with worried faces at Mrs. Grover sprawled on the cement. Trevor and Danny and Davy ran up behind them, breathless with excitement.

"She got bit by a rattlesnake," Trevor said.

"She got stabbed," Davy said.

"She's dead!" Danny said.

"I wanna see," said Trevor.

"Let's wait until the paramedics arrive," Elaine gently suggested.

"No, move!" Trevor shoved his cast against Elaine's stomach, trying to get past her into the laundry room. Elaine stumbled backwards and peered down at him, astonished.

"Trevor!" Alma exclaimed. "Apologize to Elaine, that wasn't very nice."

Trevor stuck out his tongue at his mother. Danny and Davy whooped with laughter.

"Now that's enough, boys," Tanya scolded. Her stature didn't give her much advantage over her sons—Davy was just about her height, and Danny was a full two heads taller—but they backed away from her anyway. Their cheeks puffed out as they tried to keep from laughing, making choking sounds.

"Apologize," Alma repeated.

"Make me!" Trevor shouted back.

Joan stepped forward and slapped his face. "That's for talking smart to Elaine." She drew her hand back and slapped him again—"That's for shoving her"—and a third time—"And *that's* for talking smart to your mother."

Stunned, Trevor shrunk back, blinking back tears.

Alma looked at Joan, horrified. Then lurched forward and shielded him from Joan with her arms. Her voice came out low and thick: "How dare you, how *dare* you touch my son."

"Aw, get off it, Alma. He needs discipline."

"Joan, please…" Elaine stood in the doorway of the laundry room, wanting to diffuse the situation while at the same time maintain a safe distance, shocked and embarrassed that Joan had slapped Trevor on her behalf.

"How I discipline my son," Alma shouted at Joan, "is none of your business!"

"Oh, come off it, if you weren't such a goddamn pussy-footing hippie-dip you'd thank me."

"How *dare* you," Alma gasped.

What happened then is hard to recapture, but if you thought of the sound of one of Trevor's firecracker-in-a-beer-bottle explosions you'd get the general idea, the mothers' shrill voices all rising up at once—Tanya screaming that if Joan so much as laid a finger on any of her kids she'd kill her with her own two hands, even if it meant burning in hell for all eternity, while Joan shouted *Listen, you Bible-thumping bitch, don't you threaten me* and Alma screeched *Who do you think you are how dare you*, the tears running down her face in quick, slick streams, while Elaine cried *Please everyone calm down everyone everyone calm down please.*

The boys were torn between looking with open-mouthed astonishment at their mothers and looking to see if Mrs. Grover—now that their mothers were no longer huddled around the laundry room doorway—was really dead.

"Mrs. Grover's waking up, look!" said Davy.

There was a sudden hush. Everyone turned and saw the old woman's eyes blinking. She groaned, and her leg twitched.

Then, the far-off whine of a siren.

"Ambulance!" Davy cried.

In a split-second, the boys took off, scrambling up the cement pathway. Out front, the ambulance neared, with its red, flashing lights, the siren growing so thrillingly loud they had to put their hands over their ears. They huddled around the ambulance as two paramedics popped out of the back bearing a stretcher.

The mothers' faces were marked with the shame of what had just happened between them, which changed to concern as the paramedics bent over Mrs. Grover and attended to her with their instruments. A clear mask attached to a tube was placed over her mouth. It fogged up, and Joan said, "Well, she's breathing," and lit another cigarette.

"One, two, three," one of the men said, and they lifted her onto the stretcher.

"Will she be all right?" Elaine asked worriedly. "Where are you taking her?"

"U.C. General."

Elaine and the other mothers followed the paramedics up the cement pathway to the ambulance out front. Everyone watched the ambulance drive away, growing smaller and smaller, until it finally disappeared, turning onto Pico Boulevard.

A subarachnoid hemorrhage, the doctor said, was what Mrs. Grover had. Multi-infarct dementia was likely. Elaine paced in the kitchen and twisted the phone cord around her finger, waiting for the translation into layman's terms.

After she hung up the phone, she heaved a deep sigh, then picked up the phone again and dialed Tanya's number. Somehow, it was too much energy to walk next door.

"It was a stroke," she told Tanya.

"A stroke? She gonna be all right?"

"Well, the doctor at the hospital said she suffered partial paralysis, which may or may not wear off. She'll be under observation for a few days."

"Lord have mercy. Do you want me to call the others?"

"Would you?" Elaine said, relieved, for once, that Tanya would spread the news.

Hannah burst through the front door, crying "What happened to Mrs. Grover?"

Elaine set down her mug of tea and hugged Hannah into her chest. "Shhh, it's all right, she's at the hospital now. She'll be better soon," she added, trying to convince herself as much as Hannah that this would be true.

Hannah crumpled the candy bar wrapper in her hand. "But what *happened*?"

Elaine heard a clamor of footsteps up the stairs, and in another moment Bridget rushed through the front door, followed by Sue-Sue, both of them clutching candy bars, their faces flushed.

"Danny said she's dead!" Bridget shouted, mouth half-full of chocolate.

"Davy said her head was busted open!" Sue-Sue cringed. "Like totally *open*."

Sandi appeared, moving swiftly into the room with her crutches. "We came back from Jan 'n Joe's and everyone said we just missed the ambulance," she said breathlessly. "Was there really an ambulance?"

"Girls, calm down, all of you." Elaine shut the door and faced them, hands on her hips. "Mrs. Grover is not dead, she had a stroke, that's all. Bridget, please be careful where you put your hands, with all that chocolate on them. Sue-Sue, you, too." Bridget rolled her eyes and plopped down on the couch, stretching her arms high above her head and keeping them up there, absurdly. Sue-Sue giggled, and did the same.

Hannah blinked. "What's a stroke?"

"People have them all the time, sweetie. Old people especially."

"But what *is* it?"

"It's just a—" she faltered, wondering how exactly to put it. "Just a broken blood vessel in your brain."

Bridget squinted. "In your *brain*?"

"Ewww, gross," Sandi said, wrinkling her nose.

"Nasty," said Sue-Sue.

Hannah left her friends and ambled into the kitchen, where she plopped down on a chair and moodily stared at the wall. Once more, Elaine made an attempt to hug her, but it was no use; Hannah shook her off.

Bridget jumped up from the couch and whispered something in Sandi's ear. Sandi brightened, and they disappeared out the door. Sue-Sue ran out after them. "You gonna be the Lookout, Hannah?"

Bridget popped her head back in. "C'*mon*, Hannah!"

Elaine drew her chair up closer. "Do you think you might feel better if you went and played with them, got some fresh air? Or you can stay here with me—we can make pizza dough for dinner tonight."

Hannah backed her chair away from the table, noisily skidding it against the linoleum floor. She shuffled out the front door, eyes fixed on the floor, not even glancing at Bridget as she walked past her.

Sighing, Elaine picked up her mug of tea, feeling helpless; trying to comfort Hannah just drove her farther away. She walked over to the living room window and gazed out at the school playground. In a far corner, where the patchy grass gave way to asphalt, she spotted Daisy and Mim playing hopscotch. Telling Daisy about what happened to Mrs. Grover would not be easy. Just this morning, Daisy practically begged her to go on a date with Sam this weekend, insisting that she wanted to see Gramma Grover again—*Gramma!*

She pictured Mrs. Grover sitting at the kitchen table at night with just a single light on, slapping cards into different piles. "You're home," Mrs. Grover would say, without looking up. *Finally*, was the word Elaine always expected her to add; there was something in the firm set of the old woman's mouth that hinted at this reproof, but it never came. Mrs. Grover would report that Hannah and Daisy were sleeping soundly in their beds, then march out the door, as if she had some pressing business to attend to.

She pictured the poor old woman now, lying on a hospital cot, surrounded by tubes and machines, slapping cards into different piles with the hand that wasn't paralyzed.

Solitaire, the game for lonely people.

Elaine had played it herself, in various motel rooms across the country. Sometimes after a late shift she was so wound-up that she couldn't fall asleep; sitting at a table or sometimes on a musty carpet, she had dealt out the cards, waiting for her fatigue to reach its breaking point.

She would never play Solitaire again, she decided now. The game seemed to put her in an uncomfortably similar parallel line with the old woman, as if repeating Mrs. Grover's actions would lead to the same outcome, would tempt fate. Not a subarachnoid hemorrhage, precisely, with possible multi-infarct dementia. Not that precise fate.

But a fate in more general terms: of living, and dying, alone.

She shook off the thought. What silliness. Her girls were still in the thick of girlhood, their pimples and periods comfortably in the dim future. And she was certainly not one of those lonely single women who waited all week to receive a phone call from a grown-up child on a Sunday evening, who sat in a lonely kitchen holding the receiver to her ear, listening to the grown-up child's voice report to her the details of a life that no longer included her, enjoying a few minutes of bliss before hanging up and returning once more to a life of dinners for one, TV for one, and finally a bed for one.

No, she was not one of those women.

But still, the possibility was there for her, lurking, like an ominous taunt. One day, she could be her. One of those women. She could be.

But would she?

And her thoughts turned to Sam. With Mrs. Grover babysitting, she had seen him without worrying that she was abandoning her girls. But what now? The possibility that she could still babysit her girls after her release from the hospital was unlikely.

Well, one thing was certain: she must not lose Sam.

When Bridget swung open the door, a gust of stagnant air hit Hannah's face, smelling of ashes and warm bologna. It was dark inside the apartment, with all the curtains drawn.

"Where's your sleeping bag?"

Confused, Hannah said, "Why? I can't spend the night."

Bridget rolled her eyes. "Just bring it for an hour, dummy, it's for Lifesavers."

Lifesavers was one of her favorite games with Bridget. Hannah raced up the stairs and grabbed the sleeping bag out of her bedroom, wondering what the inside of Bridget's apartment looked like. It was against the rules for Bridget to invite anyone in.

She returned with her sleeping bag. "Wait, what about Joan?"

"She won't find out—she's spending the night again with her boyfriend in Culver City and Mim's with her as always. C'mon, come in!" Bridget yanked her into the apartment, slamming the door after her.

Hannah stepped carefully through the dark room and sank into a spongy couch, setting the sleeping bag at her feet. Bridget ran around plugging in purple nightlights shaped like seashells that she said she'd stolen from Lucky's that morning. When she finished, she sat next to Hannah on the couch and they said nothing for a while, sitting in the dark, staring at the glowing seashells on the walls.

"Where's Ned?"

"At Diane's," Bridget said. "Hey and guess what—she gets her period."

"How do you know?"

"I saw. There was a cotton thingie in the garbage in the bathroom with blood. Here," she said, giving Hannah a roll of Wint-O-Green Lifesavers.

They giggled in Hannah's zipped-up sleeping bag, chewing the Lifesavers and watching their teeth spark. When Bridget would spend the night at Hannah's, they'd wait for the sliver of light to go out under her mother's bedroom door, make sure Daisy was asleep, then tiptoe into the living room with the sleeping bag and burrow deep down into it and eat the Lifesavers and giggle about their sparking teeth until they finished off the roll. Sweaty and mouths thrillingly numb, they'd squirm out of the sleeping bag and Bridget would whisper the next game, *Matches* or *Truth or Dare* or *Beaner* or *Psychic*. Hours later, they'd creep back into Hannah's bedroom and slipped into bed. In the morning no one would know what secret games they'd played deep into the night.

Tonight Bridget announced that they were going to play a new game, *Stripper*.

"But first," she whispered, "I have a secret." Her breath on Hannah's face was warm and minty.

"What?"

Bridget grabbed her hand and pulled her down the small hallway into Joan's bedroom. She flicked on the light switch.

Wigs on hooks hung on the wall around a circular mirror— black and orange and fiery red, streaked, speckled—like a collection of strange, sleeping insects. When Hannah saw the Farrah Fawcett one hanging limply, she felt a shiver up her spine.

"What's she wearing now?"

"I dunno. Maybe the blonde one with bangs—she always wears it to her boyfriend's."

"What does her real hair look like?"

"It's like, really thin and short and red. Like she's almost bald. *Haaaaaaaw!*"

Bridget collapsed into a giggling fit and fell on the bed, a king-sized mattress covered with a leopard-spotted comforter, the only furniture in the room besides the white wicker vanity table. Hannah stood there, watching her, wanting to laugh with her but unable to suddenly—thinking of Joan with a bald head, cackling in that witchy way of hers.

When Bridget recovered from her giggling fit, she looked up at Hannah, her arms and legs splayed over the bed. "Don't look so spooked," she said. Then she jumped up and snatched a frizzy brown wig from the wall. "Here. Put it on."

Hannah took the wig. Inside, there was a brown cobwebby net, which all the fake hair was sewn onto. She thrust her head into it.

Bridget grabbed a black curly wig from one of the hooks on the wall and put it on.

"You look weird," Hannah told her.

"So do *you!*"

They ran into the bathroom and took turns in front of the smudged mirror, pretending they were actresses in a commercial. Bridget held what remained of the roll of Wint-o-Green mints by her face, grinned at the mirror, and sang out, "Certs! With Retsyn!" Hannah couldn't remember anything else about the Certs commercial, so she just rested her head against Bridget's and smiled at her reflection.

"Okay let's play Stripper now."

Before Hannah could answer, Bridget pulled her back into the living room. She leaped onto the couch and struck a pose, one hand on her hip, the other behind her head. All around her in the dark room, the seashell nightlights glowed on the walls.

"Come on, we're starting Stripper now! You have to take a picture!"

"How?"

"Like *this*," Bridget said, exasperated. She mimed taking a picture with an imaginary camera. "Click click click."

Hannah held up her hands in front of her face like Bridget was doing and curled her forefinger. *Click click click* she said.

"Wait we need music, *music*," Bridget cried. "Okay, pretend the record man's putting on a record, and I'm the model, and you're taking pictures." She tore off her T-shirt and performed a spazzy dance on the couch, shaking her hips and flailing her arms above her. "Blet's blance!" she sang out, goofily rolling her eyes. "Blut on your bled bless and blance the blues!"

Hannah giggled in spite of herself and joined in, "Let's sway, sway to the sound of the lady-oh."

"It's *on the radio*, you dope, not the *lady-oh*."

"I know," Hannah said, in a small voice.

"Take another picture!" Bridget jumped up and down on the couch and patted the small pink nipples on her flat chest. "Take it of my boobies."

Hannah weakly kicked the sleeping bag aside. "What if Ned comes home?"

Bridget, her hands on her hips, glared down at her. "He *won't*," she snapped. "Take a close-up!"

Hannah looked desperately at the front door. "I have to go. Mrs. Grover is coming by soon to check up on me and Daisy."

"Take a picture, I said."

"Can't we play Psychic?"

"Take a *picture!*" A fierce rage blazed in Bridget's eyes.

Bridget had transformed into someone else, a strange cruel girl. Hannah felt her knees wobble as the room closed in on her. Hot tears came to her eyes, and the glowing seashell nightlights on the walls grew brighter, became blurry.

"How come you're always such a fuckin' baby?"

"I'm not."

"Waaaa waaaa!"

"I'm not!"

"Then take a *picture!*"

Hannah lifted her trembling hands and held up her imaginary camera, murmuring *Click click*. Bridget stripped off her shorts, then her underwear. Hannah saw four thin blonde hairs there, right where the slit was, and squinched her eyes shut.

"Picture!" Bridget screamed.

# V. SEPTEMBER

Soon enough, it was September. Men came in coveralls to mow the playground grass, readying it for a new crop of students, driving banged-up orange mowers that spat the clippings out the back. They started at opposite corners of the playground, driving up and down its length in neat rows, until they reached the center. Afterwards, the kids in the building climbed the chain-link fence and jumped down onto the playground and scooped the fresh clippings, smelling faintly of gasoline, into mounds.

They played until it was dark, then a little bit longer. Mim and Daisy decided that the mounds of grass clippings were giant pizzas to pretend-eat or beds to pretend-sleep in. Trevor and Danny and Davy threw fistfuls at each other in games they invented with territorial lines and safe zones. Sandi and Sue-Sue took turns burying each other with the clippings. Bridget lay on the ground and demanded that they cover her with the clippings, too. Hannah joined in, scooping up the grass and throwing it on top of Bridget until her body and face disappeared under the mound. She remained there for over a minute, motionless.

"Let's go to the halls," Sue-Sue said, and Bridget leaped up, resurrected, grass flying every which way.

They ran down the darkened hallways and peeped through the dusty windows into the empty classrooms with their empty desks, trying to guess which room would be theirs and which desk they would sit in when school started—just two weeks away.

They played this game every day now. Sue-Sue would be in fifth grade, in the fifth hall, and Bridget and Hannah in the fourth hall, with the fourth-graders. Since Sandi was going to junior high, she pretended she was bored and told them they were acting like babies, but she'd peek through the classroom windows and offer her predictions just the same.

Sue-Sue pointed out a desk. "I bet that's gonna be yours."

"Which one?" Hannah said.

Sue-Sue licked her palm and rubbed the dirt off the glass. "That desk there."

Bridget glared at Hannah. *Don't tell Sue-Sue we're running away*, her eyes said.

*I won't*, Hannah mouthed.

Secretly, though, she wanted to. Maybe Sue-Sue would try to convince her to stay, repeating what Sandi had said once, *Bridget talks trash about you, you know*. Ever since the night they played Stripper, Hannah couldn't help wondering whether this was true.

When it was time for dinner Bridget told Hannah she was coming over. At the table, she chattered away, telling her mother jokes Hannah thought were stupid ("What did the dog say when he walked across the sandpaper? Ruff ruff!"). Her mother laughed and laughed, dabbing at her eyes every now and then with the corner of a paper towel.

*I'm running away!* Hannah had to stuff spaghetti in her mouth to keep the words from spilling out.

Bridget ate noisily, leaning over her plate and sucking a single noodle in, then another, then another. "Hey, what did the grape say when the elephant sat on him?"

"Hmm, let's see…" Her mother twirled a forkful of spaghetti until it became a neat, circular clump. "Oh, I give up. What?"

"Nothing, he just gave out a little wine. Get it? Whine? *Hawwwww!*"

Daisy giggled, even though she didn't understand Bridget's stupid joke. She leaned over her plate and sucked the noodles into her mouth one by one, imitating Bridget.

"Oh, Daisy."

Her mother grabbed a yellow sponge from the sink and rubbed a spot on the tablecloth where Daisy had splattered spaghetti sauce from her last suck. She worked at it, pressing her lips into a grim, straight line, until the red smear by the lily pads on the tablecloth became a wet smudge.

"Let's not make a mess, spaghetti sauce can stain. Everybody gets an extra paper towel." She brought the roll to the table and ripped off four more sheets.

"Mom?" Hannah said.

"Mmhm?"

"When do we know what teacher we're going to get?" Hannah felt Bridget's kick under the table, but ignored her.

"Well," her mother said, "Tanya told me they would be posted a week before school starts. Maybe we should go over to the office together tomorrow. They should have the class assignments up by now, so we—Daisy, can't you drink without dribbling?"

She crumpled a paper towel and dabbed the milk running down Daisy's chin. "You're going to be in kindergarten, let's try to act like it, okay sweetie?"

Bridget took a gulp of milk and let some drip out of the corner of her mouth. "Oops, I spilled some, too!"

Hannah watched with resentment as her mother dabbed at Bridget's mouth, then tucked a paper towel under the collar of her T-shirt.

The next afternoon, Hannah crouched down among the ice plants in the garden out front, playing with her turtle. She avoided

the circle of rocks by the old cactus, where Bridget's dead guinea
pig lay buried. Out of the corner of her eye, she saw Bridget
creeping toward her, tiptoeing around the cactus.

"Blaaaaaa!"

Hannah jumped, in spite of herself.

"Scared you! *Haaaaaaaaaaaaaw!*" Bridget clutched her
stomach and collapsed onto the dirt, laughing.

"Stop, it's not funny."

"Scaredy-scaredy baby *Haaaaaaaaaaaaaw!*"

"Stop!"

But Bridget went on rolling around in the dirt, hiccupping
with laughter, and as Hannah watched, her embarrassment
faded, replaced by something new. In the pit of her stomach. A
hot rumbling, gathering force, rising to her chest until she
couldn't contain it. "Know what? You're a liar," she said.

Bridget froze in the dirt, and peered up at her. "A what?"

"You say you're my best friend but you're not—you make
fun of Sandi and Sue-Sue but you lie, they're really your
friends." It was all spilling out, no stopping it now. "You told
them where you hid when you ran away, you told them but you
didn't tell me, and then you pretend like we're best friends again,
liar! Liar!"

Bridget sprang to her feet, her eyes narrowing, growing
fierce, and the rumbling feeling in Hannah was gone as fast as it
came. She cowered, taking a step backward.

"You're a fuckin' fraidy-cat that's why," Bridget spat. "You'd
tell your stupid mom and then I'd be busted."

"Nuh uh, I wouldn't," Hannah said, shaking her head, taking
another step backward, then another.

"See? A fuckin' fraidy-cat."

"Nuh uh."

"You're gonna ditch out on me, you don't want to run away
'cause you're a fuckin' fraidy-cat."

"I am not!"

"Prove it!"

"Fine!" Hannah shouted, "I will!"

Bridget studied her. "Fine," she said, huskily. Then she leaped over the low stone wall and ran off down the street, toward Jan 'n Joe's.

Hannah grabbed her turtle and left the garden in a huff. She stomped up the staircase to her apartment, no longer caring about her ritual of stepping on the black tar strips at the edge of each stair. When she reached the top, she realized what the hot, rumbling feeling had been when she looked at Bridget rolling around in the dirt laughing at her.

Hate. The feeling came in a brief flash, faster than an eyeblink, and then it was gone. But she'd felt it. She'd pictured Bridget lying there in the garden, dead, next to her dead guinea pig.

That night, Hannah lay awake in the dark, her jaw clenched. Waiting for the signal from Bridget. It would come, any night now. It would be in threes: three owl hoots, three firm kicks against the metal fencepost, three handfuls of pebbles against her window—she didn't know which, and Bridget wouldn't tell her. It was a secret. Where they were running away to was also Bridget's secret.

Daisy snored her soft, wheezy snores. Farther off, there was the gentle sputter and crackle of the power lines outside, a sound that on other nights lulled her to sleep. But tonight, she thought of electric snakes, pictured the ropey cables snapping free and slapping around on the pavement, as Bridget said they did in earthquakes, imagined what it would feel like to be burned alive: a quick, sizzling flick against your skin was all it would take.

She sat up, heart thumping. Daisy squirmed, mumbled something. The shadows in the room took on menacing forms, faces—pointed teeth and hairy beast bodies and skulls and blood splats and yellow demon eyes. She clenched her muscles so she could remain perfectly still; they must not sense her presence, or they would come alive. The closet door was half-open, a long, gleaming fang hovering inside.

She kicked the sheet off her legs and dashed out of her room. Four steps down the short hallway and she was facing her mother's bedroom. She flung the door open.

"What is it, honey?"

Without a word, Hannah squirmed under the cotton blanket and nestled into her mother's thin, soft arms. She didn't want to run away—not now, not ever.

Her mother stroked her hair. "Shhh, now. It was just a silly bad dream. Go to sleep." The room was smaller than hers and Daisy's, it faced the schoolyard and held a different kind of night: no shadows, no buzzing from the streetlight, just a thick and velvety stillness. She breathed in her mother's warm dough smell. Yes, here she could close her eyes.

There was no recipe for Drink, which was the best part of the game. That, and watching your friend's face squinch in disgust as they swallowed.

The person who made the drink was called the Drinkmaker, and the person who had to drink it was called the Drinker. The Drinker was not permitted even a drop of water to wash away the taste in her mouth. That was how you lost.

Or you lost the other way: by throwing up.

As the Drinkmaker, you were allowed to use anything in the kitchen for ingredients. For a glass you had to use the smallest one in the cabinet; this rule had been established by Sandi when Bridget, as the Drinkmaker, made Sandi a drink in a Big Gulp cup, and Sandi threw up before she'd even drunk half of it.

Since there were no recipes, not one drink was ever duplicated, although there were certain combinations of ingredients that were especially popular—pickle juice and raw eggs, for instance. But if someone had written down what the kids at Sunset Terrace drank that summer, these would be some examples:

1 raw egg, scrambled
1 c. apple juice
3 tsp. Tabasco sauce
1 Tb. raspberry jam

* * *

1 c. milk
3 Tb. pickle juice
1 c. orange juice
2 Tb. peanut butter (crunchy)

* * *

1 c. orange juice
1 Tb. creamed corn
1 Tb. Dijon mustard
1 tsp. curry powder
1 tsp. sugar
1 tsp. dried basil
1 tsp. salt
1 tsp. cinnamon

You needed two people to play Drink, but three was better—that way, one could guard the kitchen faucet, and the other could guard the bathroom faucet. If the Drinker begged you to move so she could get a drink of water, you counted to twenty while she stomped on the floor, sticking out her tongue and making fake—or sometimes real—barfing sounds.

If the Drinker threw up, or drank even a drop of water before you reached twenty, she lost the game.

Then the Drinkmaker could shout, "You lose!"

You played until one person was left who hadn't begged for water or thrown up. That person was the winner of Drink.

* * *

*Drink,* Hannah said.

Daisy took the glass out of her hands. In three halting gulps she swallowed the drink, a mixture of pickle juice and ketchup and milk. Her face squinched up.

When Daisy lunged toward the kitchen faucet, Bridget shoved her back. "Guard the bathroom," she ordered Hannah. Hannah raced down the hall. Standing in front of the sink, she waited for Daisy to run up and beg her for a drink of water.

But Daisy didn't come. She heard Bridget in the kitchen, counting to twenty. Running back, she saw her little sister crying by the kitchen sink.

"...fifteen, sixteen..." Daisy squirmed past Bridget and stuck her mouth under the faucet, whimpering in between long guzzles of water.

"Aaaaaa, you lose you lose!" Bridget chanted. "Okay now I'm the Drinkmaker and Hannah has to drink."

Bridget took her time deciding on the ingredients, making a thorough inspection of the refrigerator and the kitchen cabinets. Hannah watched her make the drink, already feeling queasy. When she brought the glass to her lips, she tried not to think about what she'd seen Bridget put in it: mayonnaise and orange juice and mustard and cinnamon.

"Wait," Bridget said. "I forgot something." She added a spoonful of creamed corn to the mixture, grinning devilishly.

*Drink,* she commanded.

Hannah forced it down, cringing. She felt a watery clump of creamed corn slide down her throat. The phone started ringing.

It was her mother, Hannah knew, calling from the restaurant where she was eating dinner with Sam. She felt a gurgling in her stomach, and a sudden sharp taste rose at the back of her throat. Praying for Bridget to turn her back so she could sneak a glass of water, she reached for the phone. But Bridget grabbed it out of her hands.

"Hello?" Bridget said into the phone.

Hannah felt the sharp taste rise up at the back of her throat again, and swallowed hard. She lunged at Bridget, trying to wrestle the phone away from her, but Bridget shoved her back.

"Give it!" Hannah shouted.

Bridget gleefully wagged her tongue and shoved her again, this time harder—this time making Hannah stumble backwards and whack her elbow against the corner of the kitchen counter. She shrieked in pain.

Daisy ran up to Bridget and reached for the phone, saying "Give it! I want to talk to my mommy, give it!"

Bridget, her eyes blazing, reeled around and smacked Daisy across the face so hard Daisy fell to the floor. She wailed, curling up into a ball, clutching her cheek.

Bridget looked down at her, laughing *Hawwwwww!*, then put the phone to her ear. "Hannah just hit me and Daisy," she calmly announced.

Hannah grabbed the phone. "Nuh uh, she's lying!"

"What's gotten into you, Hannah?" her mother said. "What on earth is going on? Why is Daisy crying?"

"It wasn't me, it was Bridget!"

"Look, I don't care who did what, I want you all to stop fighting right now! I'm coming home. No more fighting, understand?"

"It wasn't me!" Hannah cried, but her mother had already hung up.

Daisy was still wailing, lying on the floor. Hannah rushed over to her. "Mommy's coming home," she soothed, stroking her head, feeling suddenly protective of her little sister. She hated Bridget, there was no doubt about it now, the feeling was so powerful she even forgot about the sharp taste at the back of her throat. She hated Bridget for hitting her little sister. She hated Bridget for telling Sandi and Sue-Sue and not her that she was hiding in the cabinets. For making her play Stripper. For scaring her, for making her feel so small. And most of all, she hated Bridget because her mother loved her—all those nights her mother made fried chicken for dinner because it was Bridget's

favorite, all the times her mother didn't see how bad Bridget
was, how dangerous, how cruel, how she didn't care about
anyone else but herself.

Hannah rinsed the glass in the sink. She would make this
drink undrinkable.

Now, she decided, it was Bridget's turn to be the Drinker.

Now, it was Bridget's turn to lose.

"Half a cup of milk," Hannah said, measuring with her
mother's Tupperware measuring cup. She spoke the ingredients
out loud, hoping to disgust Bridget before she took her first sip.

"A quarter cup of pickle juice, a third a cup of soy sauce."

Hannah felt the sharp taste again at the back of her throat.
The Drinkmaker was not supposed to get sick, only the Drinker.
She swallowed, feeling a churning in her stomach. "Half a
teaspoon of—"

"*Aaaaa,* you lose!" Bridget sang, as the lumpy pool of orangey
vomit spewed out of Hannah's mouth onto the kitchen floor.

\* \* \*

Flustered, Elaine returned to the table. Sam was giving her
order to the waiter, fettuccini alfredo, a glass of white wine,
small salad, house dressing.

"We don't have house," the waiter said. "Ranch, Thousand
Island, blue cheese, vinaigrette."

"Never mind the salad," Elaine said. "They're fighting,
Daisy's crying. We have to go back."

\* \* \*

Crouched over on all fours, Hannah coughed, watching
Bridget dance around her, flailing her arms in the air.

"*Haaaaaaaaaw!* I won!"

Then Bridget ran into her bedroom and yelled out the open window. "I won! I won! Everybody, I won!"

The laughing was what made Hannah do it. Bridget had left the room for only a minute, but it was long enough for Hannah to open the cabinet under the kitchen sink and shake her secret ingredient into the glass—not too much, just enough ant poison to make Bridget throw up.

Even though Bridget had won, she would take the glass anyway and drink it down. Bridget never turned down a dare.

She would drink it and wag her tongue and laugh her dumb laugh, but then she'd throw up. And Bridget would understand, once and for all, that they were not friends anymore. She'd run away again, but Hannah wouldn't go with her. Her mother would miss Bridget terribly at first, like she did when Bridget had run away before, but slowly—as the months and years went by—she would forget her. Until at last Bridget would no longer be her mother's favorite.

Bridget ran back into the kitchen, and Hannah held out the glass.

*Drink,* she said.

It all happened so fast, in quick pictures, like the poker cards in Mrs. Grover's hands as she shuffled them.

There was Bridget's face turning red.

The coughing, the choking, Bridget's mouth opening so wide Hannah saw the pink splits in her chapped lips.

Hannah rushing to her, panicked, pouring glass after glass of water into Bridget's open mouth, the water spilling out of her mouth and onto the floor.

Daisy crouching in the corner, wailing.

Bridget slipping on the water, falling to her knees, gagging.

And after, the men from the ambulance barging through the door.

Heaving Bridget onto the stretcher.

The siren fading away.

Then Hannah racing into her bedroom to hide under her bedsheet, shuddering, pressing her turtle against her throat.

And then there was later, when her mother returned from the hospital and lay down next to her in the dark bedroom. Holding Hannah in her arms, rocking her back and forth. Hannah cried for hours, until the tears ran out, and then she kept on crying, her eyes so swollen they were almost shut. They were eyes that no longer belonged to a child, the lurking shadows in the corners no longer fangs or goblin claws, just shadows, plain shadows. With the relief came something else, the dull pain of loss, since her new eyes gave her a new blindness: the glitter and mist of childhood vanishing with the goblins.

*Hannah, Hannah,* her mother whispered, rocking her. Through the open window, Hannah could hear the sprinklers in the playground go off, a lonely put-put-putting.

And suddenly her mother's arms felt very thin, like they'd snap if Hannah leaned back.

Mrs. Grover came back from the hospital, having recuperated from her stroke, but there was no homecoming party at Tanya's apartment, as was originally planned. No one noticed, in fact, that she was back.

The party would have to be postponed, the mothers in the building agreed. This was no time for parties.

Joan, red-eyed and shocked into silence, stood in the far corner of Tanya's living room, smoking one Virginia Slim after another. Every now and then she reached down to touch Mim's cheek with the hand not holding the cigarette. Ned stood behind her, shifting his weight from side to side, his hair still mussed from his morning mo-ped ride, when he circled the graveyard for hours. A shy, balding man lit Joan's cigarettes, brought her clean ashtrays. He introduced himself to the neighbors, "I'm Ricky, hello," in a meek voice. Her boyfriend from Culver City, everyone knew.

If it hadn't been a wake, you might have overheard Tanya whisper that even though opposites attracted, she wouldn't have guessed that a vulture and a field mouse would have hit it off. But circumstances as they were, Tanya kept her opinions to herself, and not just because she thought it was the Christian thing to do. Opening her mouth meant that the tears might burst through, thinking about how Bridget was so young, and then it would take a good ten minutes before the crying ran its course.

God must have had His reasons, she reminded herself, which only made her feel a little better. That, and having volunteered her apartment for the wake, as a gesture of charity was a way to Love Thy Neighbor, to show Him another example of why she was a good woman—and on the off-chance that He was planning on directing His wrath at her children, too, He might take note of the good deed and reconsider.

Tanya saw that the ice bucket was getting low, and edged her way through the crowd to the kitchen. She opened the freezer door and took out a bag of ice. By the sink, Mr. and Mrs. Hamilton were fighting, Mrs. Hamilton trying to wrestle a plastic cup and a pint of whiskey out of his hands.

"What did you promise?"

"I didn't promise nothin'. It was you that did the promisin' for me."

"Three, you said three was all you'd drink."

The ice bucket went tumbling to the floor, knocking over the vase of sympathy flowers Tanya had bought for Joan. The glass shattered.

"See what you've done?" Mrs. Hamilton shouted at him, as he dropped to his knees and fumbled with the flowers. He set them on the counter and went down again to collect the shards of glass.

"I'm sorry, Tanya," he said, looking up at her with drunken remorse in his eyes.

*Love Thy Neighbor*, Tanya reminded herself. "It's all right, now, it's nothing," she said, biting her tongue before anything else came out.

Elaine glanced around Tanya's living room, wondering if

she should have insisted that Hannah and Daisy stay downstairs with Mrs. Grover, for fear that the occasion would be too morbid, too trying for her girls, who had already been through so much. After all, everyone else's children had come to the funeral and were here at the wake, *their* mothers had let them come. The children weren't exactly with their mothers now, though—they seemed to be taking refuge in the back bedrooms, running out every now and then for a handful of chips or a can of soda. If Hannah and Daisy were here, they would most likely be with the other children in the back bedrooms, where she couldn't keep an eye on them. Maybe it was best that they were with Mrs. Grover.

Or had it been Mrs. Grover who had insisted? She remembered Mrs. Grover standing in her bedroom, remembered Sam telling Mrs. Grover that she'd taken sedatives for her nerves. She was as spunky as ever: the only signs she showed of having had a stroke were a slight downturn to the left side of her mouth and maybe a little stiffness in her left arm. When Elaine asked her how she was feeling, the old woman sat down at the foot of the bed and said "Fine, fine," with gruff impatience.

Sam and Mrs. Grover talked for a while, and every now and then she would awaken long enough to tell Mrs. Grover what she wanted her to know, that Bridget's dying was her fault. It was important that Mrs. Grover know this. She'd left her girls alone before, when it was a matter of necessity, and they'd always been responsible, they'd never gotten into trouble. When she was Hannah's age, her own mother had let her run around the neighborhood or stay home when she was out running errands or playing Bridge with the neighbors or what have you and it was never a problem, never a problem, that's what people seemed to do in those days. But all this was her fault and she knew it and there was nothing she could do about it, she left her girls and Bridget alone in the apartment and now Bridget was dead.

At some point, she felt Mrs. Grover's wrinkled hand clasp

hers. Drifting in and out of sleep, she felt Sam holding her other hand, stroking it, heard him mention something to Mrs. Grover about the wake, and Mrs. Grover told him she would watch Hannah and Daisy. "You and Elaine go to the funeral and the wake and leave the girls with me," she said. "You don't mind missing the funeral, too?" Sam said, and Mrs. Grover said, "I'll be at my own, soon enough."

Elaine glanced around the room now, looking for Sam, and spotted him at the refrigerator, putting ice cubes into two glasses of water. She saw Joan in the corner working her way through her pack of Virginia Slims, saw Ned with his windblown hair, saw Mim, all three of them looking sad and stunned. Their grief was her fault, her fault. Her mouth went dry and her legs buckled. She moved toward a chair, struggling to keep her composure.

"You look like you need a hug." It was Alma approaching in a black, drapey dress. Alma's arms enveloped her like giant, flowing wings, and Elaine started to sob.

"Relax, you'll get through," Alma murmured, "just breathe, don't forget to breathe." Elaine pressed her face into the gauzy folds and inhaled Alma's sweet sandlewood incense scent.

"Come on," Sam said, touching her shoulder. "Let's get something in your stomach."

He steered her toward the huge television with the crack running across the screen that Tanya used as a refreshments table for the chips and dip and cookies the neighbors had brought. All through the funeral, Sam had kept squeezing her hand and stroking it, whenever the sobbing came over her. And now he kept his arm tight around her waist, as if to keep her upright. It was an unfamiliar feeling, a man's steady grasp on her. She felt grateful for his strength.

There was a flag salute, first in English, to start off the day. The white kids in the class said it while the Mexican kids stumbled their way through. Then they said it in Spanish.

*Yo juro solemnemente a la bandera de los Estados Unidos,* the Mexican kids said, and it was the white kids' turn to jumble the words.

After the flag salute, they counted the numbers that were printed on a plastic banner above the chalkboard, first in English, then in Spanish. *One Two Three,* all the way to fifty (*Ooo-no Dohs Trays,* Hannah heard the Mexican kids say, all the way to *Sin-quen-tah*). Then they went through the alphabet: A, B, C (*Aaah, Bay, Say,* all the way to *Zay-tah*).

Hannah said nothing, no English words, no Spanish.

At ten o'clock, a woman from the cafeteria came by with trays of orange wedges, and announced that it was Nutrition Time. She distributed to each student two wedges on a torn-off brown paper towel. Hannah watched the kids around her eat the oranges and put the rinds in their mouths, turning to their friends to smile orange smiles. She ate her oranges quickly, and threw the rinds away in the trashcan by the pencil sharpener.

During Journal Time, Mr. Gonzalez told everyone to put

their heads down on their desks. *You're walking into the woods,* he said, *you see a lake, there is a boat there, you get on the boat.* When he was finished with the story he told them to open their eyes. He handed out fat pencils and brown, newsprint-like paper.

"Write what you saw, where you went," he said. "You have fifteen minutes. Write in English or Spanish, it doesn't matter right now."

Hannah stared at the newsprint-like paper. She wrote no English, no Spanish.

"Time's up," Mr. Gonzalez said. "*Paren de escribir.*"

At lunchtime, Hannah walked to the far end of the playground, past the rusty monkey bars and the swings with their cracked rubber seats, until she reached the chain-link fence. There, sitting under the shade of the eucalyptus tree, the patchy grass felt thick and cool. There, with the apartment building on the other side of the fence, she could look to the second floor and see her mother's milky blue curtains hanging in the kitchen window and remind herself that her turtle was close by, waiting for her.

She lowered her eyes to the first floor. There was Bridget's apartment. She felt her throat clench, and looked away.

It had been four days since Bridget's funeral. Since then, Hannah hadn't left the apartment until this morning, hadn't seen anyone in the building. Her mother had stayed inside, too, mostly in bed. Sam came by every night with take-out food, and he slept in her mother's bedroom, getting up early to set out cereal boxes and milk on the kitchen table before leaving for the day. The school where he taught started next week, but he had to go there anyway to get things prepared, he said. Daisy spent all day in her mother's bedroom, playing with her dolls at the foot of the bed; now was not a good time, her mother said, to play with Mim. Which left Hannah alone in her bedroom with her turtle. Which is how she wanted it to be.

"Hey Beaner!"

Hannah looked up, and spotted Trevor on the monkey bars, sitting on the top eating a bag of barbecue corn nuts. He was flanked by two other boys, who looked just a little bit shorter and younger than the boys in her fourth-grade class—probably third-graders, she thought, which was what Trevor was. It was strange, seeing the kids from the building at school with their classroom friends.

"Beaner!" Trevor shouted again. He threw a corn nut at a Mexican kid running past, kicking a muddy soccer ball. The corn nut hit the kid's temple.

The boy stopped. "*Cabrón!*" he spat back, and pelted Trevor in the face with the soccer ball.

Trevor threw his bag of corn nuts onto the sand and jumped down from the monkey bars. A stream of blood trickled from one of his nostrils. He wiped his nose with the back of his hand, making bloody smears across his face. Then faced the boy, clenched his fists, and puffed out his chest like Danny always did when he was mad. "You wanna start somethin'?"

"You wish you could," the boy spat back.

"Aww, suck my dick."

"Take it out, *maricon.*"

A burly woman stormed over, her hair drawn back into a severe ponytail, waving her jiggley arms and blowing fiercely into the silver whistle that hung from her neck. "Ooooo, Mrs. Thermometer, busted!" the boys on the monkey bars shouted.

"Mrs. *Thal*ometer," the teacher corrected them. She caught Trevor by the collar of his T-shirt and the Mexican kid by his belt loop. "Cool down, you two, we're going to have a visit with the principal."

Hannah watched them go, struggling and spitting at each other while Mrs. Thalometer held them in her firm grip by collar and belt loop and marched them across the playground.

The grass under her legs was starting to feel itchy. She

brought her knees to her chest and leaned against the trunk of the eucalyptus, looking up again at the milky blue curtains in the kitchen window. In a few hours she would be inside, in her bedroom with her turtle, away from all of this. She unwrapped the plastic from her sandwich and took a bite.

*I met a boy*
*A biscuit*
*He was so cool*
*A biscuit*

A cluster of girls by the swings were playing hand-slap games. The bread stuck in Hannah's throat as she swallowed; her mother's sandwiches had hardly any peanut butter or jam.

*Just like a swimming pool*
*A biscuit*
*Ten times ten is the funkiest beat*
*I said it*
*I meant it*
*I even represent it*

One of the girls shouted that it was her turn, that she wanted do Miss Mary Mack. Hannah recognized the name: it was the one Daisy sang when she took her bubble baths, the one Mim had taught her.

*Miss Mary Mack Mack Mack*
*All dressed in black black black*

She did not want to hear the song now, did not want to think about Mim, because then she'd start thinking about Bridget. She dropped her half-eaten sandwich on the grass and ran away, hearing their voices grow fainter:

*With silver buttons buttons buttons*
*All down her back back back . . .*

She took refuge in the girls' bathroom, hiding from it all to narrow her eyes in the mirror, daring her reflection to change into a face wickedly deformed and red-eyeballed. As far back as she could remember, she was convinced this would happen one day, not because she believed in the power of her will, but because her child's imagination was convinced that the transformation was inevitable.

When her father did strange things, screamed savage words, she would run into the bathroom and stare at herself in the toothpaste-flecked mirror, imagining the monster transformation in her own face. Her father's voice did not belong to him but to someone he was turning into, someone who no longer plopped her on his lap and read aloud to her from his books—a stranger who wanted her and her mother and baby Daisy to stay out of his sight. And when he screamed at her mother, she became someone else, too. No longer was her lap a soft pillow you could sink into—she was all sharp bones and sudden starts.

And now—now that Bridget was dead—her mother did the same thing her father had done: shut herself up in her bedroom the way he shut himself up in his study. Her mother wanted to be left alone, too. When Hannah visited her in the bedroom, her mother would hold out her arms and say *Come here.* But after a few seconds her mother would forget her, and her eyes would close, or look out the window. Bridget was there in the room, too, and it was too small to hold the three of them.

After the lunch bell, Mr. Gonzalez stood outside the hall and told his class to wait while all the other kids followed their teachers back into the classrooms in single-file lines. The seagulls had already begun circling above, diving down at the crusts of bread and cookie crumbs the kids had left behind. The playground was quiet now, except for the seagulls' lonely shriekings.

"Everyone look up," Mr. Gonzalez said, adjusting the thick-framed glasses on his nose. "Those are cirrus clouds."

There, in the sky, Hannah saw the faint, white wisps.

They are very high, he told them, higher than seagulls can

fly. Back in the classroom, he instructed them to put their heads down on their desks and close their eyes. Imagine you are floating on the clouds, he said.

Hannah kept her eyes open, breathing in the small, hot space between her folded arms, watching wet dots of condensation form on the desk's surface. Mr. Gonzalez distributed fat pencils and sheets of newsprint paper. Write about what it felt like, he said gently, and what you saw. You have fifteen minutes.

Hannah did not write about whiteness everywhere, or how small things looked on earth when viewed from such a height.

She wrote no English, no Spanish.

"Pencils down," Mr. Gonzalez said. "*Paren de escribir.*"

There was no language, there were no words to explain. It was an accident, Hannah told herself, though she did not know if this was true, exactly. She did not know if the words were right. She'd wished Bridget were dead, once. But it was not what she really wanted to happen.

Bridget was just supposed to throw up. That was all that was supposed to happen. She had worried that people wouldn't believe her, but they did.

To offer a translation: They—meaning the paramedics, the police, the neighbors.

They, meaning all the adults who said Bridget was a troubled girl, who had been found as an infant, abandoned in a Von's parking lot. The story fit. Here was a girl who was already a runaway at the age of nine, who received poor marks on her report cards and couldn't read, a fact supported by the California Test of Basic Skills. The girl's CTBS scores ranked her in the fourteenth percentile.

Here was a girl who, therefore, did not possess the skills (a fault of the foster parent? the System? The general opinion was mixed) to read a label, a girl who wouldn't have the sense or adequate reading skills to know that ant poison should not be ingested.

Who drank the poisonous substance, according to her friend, Hannah Kierson, aged nine (transcription of Detective Mark L. Jackson interview 9/10/83), on "a dare," "in a game."

*Witness's mother not present at time and place of occurrence,* according to interviewee, corroborated by interviewee's mother, Elaine Kierson (transcription of Det. Jackson interview 9/10/83).

*Victim accidentally ingested poison at t/p/o,* corroborated by interviewee and interviewee's younger sister, Daisy Kierson, aged five (transcription of Det. Jackson interview 9/10/83).

*Victim pronounced dead* 9/9/83 11:23 PM.

The story fit. A tragic case. A child's game gone awry.

Elaine did not want to did *not* want to but she had to.
Get out of bed.
Boil the water.
Dip the tea bag in.
From there, the steady rhythm of ritual could set her on course: wake up the girls, pour the cereal, make their lunches. Knife on bread, swipe, swipe, peanut butter, raspberry jam. She made sure to swipe thinly: money was running out.

Money was running out, but she could not accept what Sam pressed into her palm, his hard-earned teacher's salary, could not allow herself to be that to him, not now, not yet. Money changes things, yes, but in this case for the worse. She knew the resentment he felt toward his ex-wife, the outstretched hand of alimony—a woman's prerogative, even while sitting pretty, living off her city planning commissioner's family's old money.

She did not want to become Jeanine. She did not want to become a burden, dependent on someone's charity.

Roger had said the same thing when, in a rage, he tore up the checks his mother secretly sent, which came without a note three or four times a year after they'd eloped to Spokane and cut ties with his family. And now, here she was, folding up her boyfriend's checks and leaving them in the drawer with the

Lucky's coupons, when she had mouths to feed.

Money changes things—Sam's words, Roger's too, here, they would agree. But change in political relationships was what Sam meant: *special interests, Contra cash, blood money*. Change in personal relationships was what Roger meant, *blood money* he said too, but he meant something different: money from *his* blood, *his* family.

Elaine climbed back into bed and closed her eyes. She did not want to think about Roger now. She was so tired.

She felt herself drift, remembering the night she sat with Sam in the emergency room at U.C. General, planted in the hard plastic orange scoop-chairs lined up along the walls. It was just past eleven-thirty when Joan came in, running down the hallway with slippers flopping and bathrobe ties flying. At her heels were Mim and Ned and Ricky, Joan's boyfriend from Culver City. The attending doctor gave them the news, staring down at his clipboard as Joan's shriek filled the room.

The shriek was in Elaine's ears when she awoke. In a cold sweat, she gazed around her bedroom until the familiar shapes reminded her where she was. The shrieking, she realized, was just the sound of children playing in the playground below, coming through her open window.

She glanced at the neon numbers of the clock on her nightstand. It was just after one o'clock. She closed her eyes again, listening to the high-pitched shouts and squeals. Her girls were there in the playground, too. It was nice to have them so near.

She drifted off again. In her dream, the children's laughter became Bridget's laughter. She awoke with tears running past her temples, forming cold pools in her ears. Oh, she was to blame for Bridget's death, there was no getting around it. Countless times she'd rehearsed her confession to Joan, and though the idea of facing Joan filled her with dread, she simply could not back down. She had to do it. Now, when the momentum of her decision could sustain her.

* * *

The door to apartment one swung open, and Elaine found herself staring at a woman with wispy copper-colored hair that barely covered her scalp. Red-eyed, clutching a crumpled Kleenex.

Elaine faltered, then realized: it was Joan, without her wig.

She threw her arms around her. Joan stiffened. Elaine was sobbing now, and she took a deep breath to steady herself. When she could speak again, she told Joan what she'd come there to say. "I'm not asking for you to forgive me. I just wanted to tell you that I'm sorry. I left my girls and Bridget alone in the apartment. It's my fault."

"What the hell are you talking about, you're not her goddamn mother," Joan snapped, she slammed the door.

Elaine stared at the door, shaken. She pressed her hands on her cheeks, then against her mouth—it was as if Joan had slapped her there. How *awful*, how *rude!* Wearily, she walked up the stairs to her apartment and returned to her bedroom, pulling the bedsheet to her chin.

And in another moment she was filled, surprisingly, with gratitude. Joan had released her from her guilt. Joan had spoken the words: *You're not her goddamn mother.*

Instead of relief, she felt a crushing fatigue. It was two-fifteen, she saw, glancing at the clock. Soon, Hannah and Daisy would come home from school, and they would want a snack. She had barely eaten all week: just a nibble here and there when she mustered up the energy to go to the refrigerator, or when Sam came over with take-out pizza for dinner.

The grumbling in her stomach confirmed the hollowness she felt, a hollowness that could not be filled. Roger was dead. Even if she had known before his death that he was suicidal, there was nothing she could have done to stop him. And now,

now Bridget was dead. Forgiveness, she'd told Joan, was not what she'd wanted, but even as she spoke the words she wasn't certain they were true.

Now, she knew they were. But what good was absolution? What she'd wanted, truly wanted, was not forgiveness, but something that could not be granted. A treading-back in time, an impossibility, a miracle: *Bring them back to me.*

Her miracle took the form of Sam, taking care of the grocery shopping, helping her make the girls' lunches, lying next to her at night and stroking his fingers along her bare back. She stayed in bed, her window cracked open so she could hear more clearly the children's hoots and laughter in the playground.

One evening, to her surprise, Sam ushered Mrs. Grover and Tanya into her bedroom and left them alone. Tanya gave her a large box of frozen hamburger patties. "The manager gave this to me at a discount," she explained. "I thought you might want 'em—my freezer's stuffed full."

Mrs. Grover produced a deck of cards. "Seven card stud always cheers me up," she said, and dealt them onto the bedsheet.

The three women played twenty hands, Mrs. Grover winning nearly every time. Finally, Tanya laid her cards face-down on the pillow, shaking her head.

"I know when I'm beat—time for me to call it quits. You take care now, Elaine," she said, standing up. "If you need anything, come right over and knock on my door. And Mrs. Grover, I'm still expecting to see you one of these days at a PWP dinner. Elaine here nabbed the best one, but that just gives me hope that there's more where he came from."

"PWP," Mrs. Grover grumbled, once Tanya was gone. "Meddlesome, isn't she? But I suppose she means well."

Elaine picked up the cards and sighed. "I used to think so."

"Not anymore?"

"These hamburger patties, she's just trying to apologize for doing something." Elaine was on the brink of telling Mrs. Grover about Tanya calling Social Services, but she decided against it. Mrs. Grover was so close to her girls; there was the possibility that the old woman wouldn't side with her.

She shivered. The window by her bed, she saw, was still open, and the evening breeze carried a faint tang of mown grass, a smell she associated with children romping in the playground below. She shut the window, remembering what Tanya had told her about Mrs. Grover—that she had once had a husband and a baby. She thought of asking Mrs. Grover about the car accident, about how she'd coped with the tragedy. But she decided against that, too: better not to dredge up memories that would only cause pain.

Every night that week Mrs. Grover visited Elaine in her bedroom to play poker. Not once did she chide her for her lengthy stay in bed, and for this Elaine was grateful. Sometimes Mrs. Grover told stories about her childhood—wild, wonderful tales about her father's speakeasy and the shady characters there—but most times they played cards in silence. There was a comfort in the steady slap of cards, the exchange of coins, clattering on her bedsheet in the cycle of losing and winning and losing again.

Boys ate sunflower seeds and spit the husks out onto the floor or at each other when Mr. Gonzalez wasn't looking. They spit other things, too, fingernails and wet wads of paper and the pink bits of bitten-off pencil erasers. Some boys blew little clear bubbles with their spit when they were bored, or wanted to make a girl squinch up her face and shudder.

Girls' games were all whispers and tricks. They turned a single string into a cat's whiskers, a cat's cradle, a grandma's bra, a witch's broom. Or folded a piece of paper into smaller and smaller triangles until it transformed into a little package. Hannah saw the girls play with them under the table, whispering questions and counting and peeking under the folded triangles to read the secret message written there.

During Language Hour, the girl sitting next to Hannah whispered *Say four places.*

Mr. Gonzalez wandered from table to table, calling out "*El bebe, el bebe.*" Everyone repeated what he said.

The girl was looking at her, waiting. Her pencil was poised over a piece of paper hidden under her Spanish workbook. On the paper she'd drawn a square with four lines sticking out of each side. *Four places, like Los Angeles, you know,* the girl whispered. *Or even like a mountain.*

What is this game? Hannah thought desperately. Mr. Gonzalez passed by her table, and she looked up, feigning attentiveness. "Not *el bay-bee*," he was saying. "Listen carefully everyone, look at my mouth as I say the word. It's *el beh-beh. Beh-beh.*"

*Come on,* the girl whispered fiercely. *Just think of places where you've been before.*

Her mind racing, Hannah whispered the first four places she could think of: Taos, Florence, Casper, Amarillo.

*Real places,* the girl whispered.

*Those are real places,* Hannah whispered back.

*Fine,* the girl sighed again. *Spell them.*

Hannah spelled the places for the girl. The girl wrote each word on a line sticking out of the left side of the square. She moved her pencil to the bottom of the square, where four more lines waited to be filled.

*Now say four boys' names.*

Easy, Hannah thought. *Trevor, Danny, Davy, and Ned.*

The girl wrote the boys' names on the bottom lines, then moved her pencil to the right side of the square.

*And four numbers.*

Hannah whispered her answers, *one, two hundred, twenty-five, eight,* while Mr. Gonzalez said "*La pelota, la pelota, los niños, los niños.*" The lines at the top of the square were the only ones that remained.

But the girl didn't ask her a question for these. She wrote the letter *M* on the first line, *A* on the second, then an *S*, and finally, an *H*.

*Now tell me when to stop,* the girl whispered, and drew a spiral that kept getting bigger.

*Stop,* Hannah whispered.

*Okay, one two three,* whispered the girl, counting the number of times the spiral had gone around. *Ready?*

Hannah nodded, wondering what was coming next.

The girl tapped her pencil on the *M*, the *A*, and the *S*, counting *one two three*. She crossed out the *S*.

*One*—she tapped the *H*.

*Two*—she tapped the *M*.

*Three*. She crossed out the *A*. Then counted to three once more, skipping over the crossed-out letters. *Three* was *H*. The *M* was the survivor; she circled the letter.

She moved on to the names of places. *One two three*, she counted, and crossed out *Casper*. *One two three*, and crossed out *Florence*.

The girl kept counting and crossing, moving around the square, as the class repeated "*La leche, la leche, el papel, el papel*," after Mr. Gonzalez. When she finished, she whispered, *Wanna hear your future now?*

Hannah nodded, intrigued.

The girl tapped her pencil on the crossed-out *A*, *S*, and *H*. *You're not gonna live in an apartment, shack, or house.* The pencil tapped on the *M*. *You're gonna live in a mansion!*

*I am?* Hannah whispered back excitedly.

*Yeah, in Tay-yoos or whatever you call it,* the girl replied, *and you'll be married to Danny and have twenty-five kids.*

Hannah frowned at the girl's prediction. "Nuh uh," she protested.

*Itty-bitty-titty,* a voice whispered then.

Hannah reeled around, knocking her Spanish book to the floor. But there was nobody there. She picked up her Spanish book. She could have sworn it was Bridget's voice. The whole class, she realized, was staring at her.

"Are you all right?" Mr. Gonzalez asked. He consulted his seating chart. "Hannah?"

She nodded. The girl peered at her strangely, scooted her chair several inches away.

*Itty-bitty-titty,* came the whisper again. *Haaaaaaaaaaaaaw!*

Hannah leaped out of her seat, terrified. Mr. Gonzalez

called after her, but she kept running—out the door, down the hallway to the playground, all the way to the chain-link fence. She jabbed her foot in a hole and hoisted herself up, climbing the fence in five seconds flat, faster than ever before.

When she ran past apartment one, she heard Bridget's voice again: *Certs! With Retsyn*!

Sam was unloading groceries in the kitchen when she came rushing through the front door, slamming the door so hard the wall shook. The Lucky's bag was on the floor, and on the table were neat rows of canned soup and apples and a stack of frozen Hungry Man dinners.

"Let's try not to make too much noise," he gently scolded. "Your mother is resting." One by one, he set the apples into a bowl.

Hannah had never run so fast in her life. She opened her mouth, gasping for air.

Sam moved toward her. "What happened?"

She put her hands on her knees, trying to catch her breath. Then she felt his arms. He was leaning over, hugging her. "Tell me," he said.

*Bridget's ghost, Bridget's ghost, she won't leave me alone,* she wanted to tell him. But she stopped herself. He would not believe her.

* * *

When Rich Jr. came back from juvie, everyone crowded around him. He told about bunk beds and knife fights and teardrop tattoos that meant you killed somebody, about how some punk from V-13 almost slashed him.

"So whatchu been up to?" he asked Danny.

Danny shrugged. "Nothing much, just working on my breakdancing. Check it out." He dropped down to the pavement and flailed his legs in the air.

"That's some sorry-ass moves," Rich Jr. observed.

Hannah was there, watching from a distance, crouched in the garden behind the tall, chewed-up cactus. Hoping they wouldn't see her, she crept away, stepping over the ice plants and dandelion clumps. She tripped, and looked down. There was the circle of rocks, where Bridget had buried her guinea pig.

Bridget whispered *Porky, like the pig, not the movie.*

This time, Hannah did not run away in fear. Finally, she understood what Bridget wanted her to do. She was alive, and Bridget was dead, and Bridget would not stop haunting her until a part of her died, too.

In the apartment, she opened the cabinet under the kitchen sink and grabbed the bottle of ant poison. She tiptoed down the hallway to the bathroom, put the rubber plug in the drain and filled the sink with warm water. She turned the bottle upside down and shook the white powder into the water.

Three tiptoes it took to leave the bathroom and enter her bedroom. Another six to reach the aquarium. Her turtle sat on a rock, next to the jam jar top she used for a water bowl. She stroked its cool, bumpy shell. "Bath time," she whispered. And for the last time, she brought her turtle to her throat.

After, she picked her way over the ice plants and dandelion clumps in the garden out front, clutching a shoebox, a dull weight rattling inside. When she reached the old cactus she dropped to her knees. Crying, she dug a little grave there.

Elaine chose her outfit carefully: black slacks, a plum blouse, a chiffon scarf in her hair. It was Saturday afternoon, and she squinted in the daylight as she walked down the cement pathway to the parking lot; she hadn't been outside in what seemed like months.

In her car, she took the map book from the glove compartment and studied it. Thomas lived in Pasadena, a forty-five-minute drive, she estimated. Enough time to compose her thoughts, figure out some way of persuading Thomas to write a check. Calling him was out of the question—she risked the possibility that he would hang up on her. If he wasn't home when she arrived at his house, well, she would just wait in her car until he returned. Alma had taken Hannah and Daisy to the beach for the day, so she had some time to spare.

As she drove, she found her resolve strengthening. The traffic was light on the freeways, and she moved in a swift stream of cars. The sun shone brightly, hard to believe it was September. A perfect day for swimming in the ocean. She would remind Thomas that she had children to raise, that Hannah and Daisy were his nieces. If she appealed to his sense of family obligation, how could he deny her at least some money? She was willing to bargain—two thousand, one thousand five hundred even, just enough to put down a deposit on another apartment. Not too far away, because there was Sam, of course. Just someplace else, away from Sunset Terrace. They could not stay there, that much was certain.

She parked the Datsun in the driveway and took a deep breath before getting out. Straightening her blouse, she walked up the cobblestone path to Thomas's house, a modest split-level with an overgrown yard, much less imposing than she had imagined it to be.

She rang the doorbell, waited, rang it again. Inside, a dog barked.

A series of heavy footsteps, then his voice: "Yes, what is it?"

"It's me, Elaine," she called back, adding, "Roger's wife."

The door cracked open, and Thomas peered through, one hand on the doorknob, the other gripping a leash. The dog appeared, growling—a sleek black Labrador. "Of course, of course, I know who you are. Elaine, yes. Well, what a surprise."

"I was wondering if I could talk to you."

"What about?"

He wasn't making any move to invite her in. Although she wasn't sure she would want to now, with that dog of his. She fidgeted with her keys, stuffed them back in her purse. "About my daughters, you'd mentioned your father's will—"

"Haven't we done this already?" he sniffed.

The chiffon scarf in her hair was slipping, but she didn't want to fuss with it now. "Yes, but I thought—please understand that we desperately need the money, my daughters—"

"Let me repeat myself, since I obviously didn't make myself clear the first time." He coughed into his fist. "My father cut my nutcase brother out of the will, remember? We discussed this. There is no, I repeat, no cache of money with Roger's name on it, waiting for you to claim it. I'm very sorry if you've deluded yourself into thinking otherwise, and I regret whatever distress this causes you. Roger caused our family a considerable amount of pain, so believe me, I empathize."

"Please, we need—"

"Now, don't call me or come by here again, understand? If you'll excuse me." The dog started barking, and he yanked on the leash. Then slammed the door.

Elaine tore the scarf from her hair and walked down the cobblestone path to her Datsun. Her hands trembled with rage as she dug through her purse for her keys. In the car, she rested her forehead on the steering wheel, trying to collect herself.

Elaine spent the next week circling job openings in the *L.A. Times*. She found one for a hostess, and another for a fry cook at some fast-food chain, but now was not the time to be picky. She filled out the applications and drove home. At the end of the week she called to follow up, and was told that they wanted someone younger for the hostess job and the fry cook position hadn't yet been filled because the manager was still reviewing applications.

*Charlie Forrest* Alma had written in looped cursive on the notepaper, and underneath, an address. Elaine folded the paper and put it back in her purse. She thought again of what Alma had said about the lawsuit the owner had won against the landlord—that the new parking lot would mean more business. And more business meant more employees.

She spotted the construction crew as she pulled up to the curb. Her list of references in hand, she walked to the restaurant, with its silver sign that spelled *Charlie's*.

It was after three o'clock and the restaurant was empty, except for a college student in jeans sitting at a barstool with a bottle of mineral water, studying some papers. She approached the young woman.

"I'm looking for the hostess, someone who works here?"

"I'm the owner, Charlie Forrest," she replied curtly.

"I'm sorry, you're so young, I thought you were—" Elaine began. She held out her list of references, and pressed on. "I'm here to apply for a job."

Charlie took a sip from the bottle of mineral water. "Business is slow, I have a full kitchen staff, and no one's leaving, as far as I know. But I'll keep this on file, in case an opening becomes available. Thank you for coming by." She took another sip and returned to her paperwork.

"But isn't that a parking lot you're building in the back?" Elaine persisted. "Don't you think your business might increase after you won your case, don't you think you should expand your staff?"

The young woman eyed her suspiciously. "How did you know?"

"The construction crew in back, I saw it as I was walking in—"

"I mean about the lawsuit, how did you know?"

"Please, I need this job, I need to work, I have two—"

"The case was appealed, if you want to know," Charlie said, her voice growing shrill. "I'm selling the restaurant if you're really interested, the construction crew is there to turn this place into a clothing store."

"Oh, I didn't—"

"How the fuck did you know there was a lawsuit, are you a friend of Fred's? Did he send you here? I'm paying it off, look, I've got the paperwork to prove it." She smacked her hand on the mess of papers scattered on the bar. "It's all there, so get out of here, get the hell out and tell him that, why don't you."

It was all too much for Elaine. She turned and ran, holding a hand over her pressed lips.

Back in the Sunset Terrace parking lot, she climbed out of her car in a daze. Rich Jr. was performing gymnastic maneuvers on a cardboard box opened up and laid flat on the asphalt, spinning around on his head and flailing his legs to the beat of an enormous radio in Danny's arms.

She made her way up the cement pathway, wondering if her mail would be safe now that Rich Jr. had returned. Once she got through the front door, she headed straight for her bedroom. Sam had left the mail at the foot of her bed.

She stripped off her clothes and climbed under the sheet. Any other day, she would reflect on how lucky she was to have a man in her life who was so thoughtful. But today, all she could think of was how everything was falling apart.

She reached for the mail and settled back on her pillows. A flyer for carpet cleaning. A letter addressed to Resident, which turned out to be another advertisement. An electricity bill. A letter from the school, about the candy bar drive to raise money for the library. And finally, another letter. She stared at the return address: T. Kierson. 225 East Brook Avenue.

Alarmed, she tore the envelope open.

> Please understand what this is. This is not charity, nor is it a legal disbursement, as Roger was written out of the wills of both my parents (which I've made clear to you).
>
> This is purely a selfish act, on my part. To alleviate my conscience.
>
> Roger caused our family considerable distress – I don't think I need to elaborate. He was a nutcase but he was a good man. And besides that, my brother. Which I suppose carries some responsibility—the onerous entanglements of family, etc. What I mean is, he would have wanted me to do this.
>
> Put it to good use, will you?
>
> — T

She laid her hand over her mouth, staring at the check in her hand for a full minute. Then she threw off the sheet and leaped out of the bed.

If someone had peeked in the bedroom window through the milky blue curtains right then, they would have seen an odd sight: a woman jumping around the room in her underwear. It was the dance of a woman who had seen misfortune and tragedy, whose burdens had finally gotten the best of her, chipping away softly, slowly, until they cracked the fragile carapace and released her to the consolations of mourning. Who'd dreamed the dreams of everyone else at Sunset Terrace: those that remain rare, faint clouds in the sky, lucky if you remember to look for them.

Now, finally, there would be money. To move into a new apartment, to start over. Not a windfall, exactly. But enough.

# VI. AFTER

*Pathway: an epilogue*

Why Hannah went back to visit Sunset Terrace the day after her college graduation, she did not know, exactly. She drove there in Sam's Tercel, which he let her borrow whenever she came home to visit from back East.

The reason, she told herself, was to walk down the cement pathway, to read the names and messages of the kids who had lived there, as she once did. Walking past *Ruben '68* and *Josh '74* and *T.M. sucks C.L.'s dick* by the mailboxes—past *SxMx* and *Danetta 1962* and *RD+JS =4-Ever* and *Hot Tuna Rocks!* and finally, in front of the laundry room, *Bridget '83*—she would have some sort of feeling, she thought, she would reach some sort of conclusion.

She remembered the pathway because this is what you store up for a later date—this is what is preserved in your mind as you look back and ascribe meaning to the details belonging to a time long gone, when the seconds and minutes and hours and days lasted so much longer, when you did not know then the deep imprint these names and messages would make.

But enough of this philosophizing, she would say—and said to herself then, turning onto Pico Boulevard. Four years of college had made her impatient with ponderous theories. She reminded herself: I am only going back to walk down the cement pathway, to say *I lived here once.*

There were so many other places she had lived. The memories were scrambled in her mind, all the musty motel rooms where they'd stayed after her father's suicide, during her mother's crazy flight across the country.

She knew that now.

She was old enough to say it: her mother's crazy flight.

But at Sunset Terrace—there, her mind had stored up the details, one by one. It was not a jumble of flowered bedspreads and Bibles in the drawers and motel managers with their racks of room keys. Sunset Terrace had made its imprint. She could calibrate the minutes and hours and days.

Her mother was married to Sam now. He was a natural teacher, her mother often said, which could be taken as a compliment or a complaint, depending on her mother's tone of voice. As a teenager, Hannah had become skilled at interpreting the subtle inflections of her mother's speech to glean her tacit meaning. Sam was pedantic, her mother meant, and the world was his classroom. An evasive woman married to a pedantic man, who says they can't be happy?

Sam had finally consented to sell his house in Venice to a real estate developer. He couldn't decide whether the sum of money the sale brought was an embarrassment or an outrage, but in the end he considered it a blessing. With it, her mother had done what she'd always wanted to do: open up a restaurant. Hannah remembered the day her mother called Charlie Forrest with her proposition, how her mother had gleefully thrown her head back after she and Charlie had signed their joint ownership—remembered the utter amazement in her mother's expression when she read aloud to her and Daisy the restaurant review in the *L.A. Times*, which called the restaurant a Cozy Hot Spot with Mashed Potatoes to Die For.

Hannah drove past the graveyard, past Jan 'n Joe's, and made a left turn. She had exactly one hour to spare. Her mother was throwing a party at the restaurant to celebrate her college graduation, and she didn't want to be late. Daisy and Sam would be there, too, with Mitchell, now living in Long Beach. Every now and then, when Hannah had been on break from school and come down to visit, she'd go to a dingy club to hear Mitchell's band. He played lead guitar with fanatical intensity, and kept breaking strings, forcing the band to stop while he wound on new ones and re-tuned his guitar. The band was awful, but Hannah cheered anyway. Daisy was Mitchell's biggest fan, and plastered her dorm room with his posters.

She slowed down the car, and parked next to what had once been the empty lot. Gone were the stray cats, the piles of old tires and trash: now a brand-new condominium stood there, with a salmon-colored awning and a burnished steel gate. An image came to her then, of Mrs. Grover padding in her pink slippers across the street on her morning trek to feed the stray cats.

Hannah pulled up the emergency brake and sat for a moment, her hands resting on the steering wheel, stung with the realization that Mrs. Grover was probably dead by now, after all these years. What a wonderful, generous old woman she was— a cranky, poker-playing saint who had descended into their lives just when they were unraveling.

Well, she amended, almost a saint. After all, Mrs. Grover had been the one who had called Social Services. She recalled the morning Mrs. Grover had confessed. It was the day they moved out of Sunset Terrace and into Sam's house—Sam had insisted on it, even thought her mother had put down a deposit on a nearby apartment. Her mother had been packing in the kitchen, wrapping plates in newspaper, when Mrs. Grover came marching through the front door and announced that she had to set the record straight: she had called Social Services, and once she did, she'd bitterly regretted it. Her mother was so overcome with shock that she nearly fell at the old woman's feet. There were so many times that she'd tried to come clean, Mrs.

Grover quickly explained, pressing a handkerchief to her mouth, but she could never muster the courage. Her mother hugged the old woman and laughed and said that it was so funny, she'd convinced herself it was Tanya.

Hannah took the keys from the ignition and stepped out of the car. A construction worker in soiled jeans and a Dodgers cap walked past. He crossed the street, heading toward a tractor with enormous, mud-caked wheels. A wrought-iron post lay underneath one of the wheels, the *No Vacancy* sign crushed into splinters. Hannah gazed at the pile of dirt and broken concrete where Sunset Terrace had once stood. Gone was the cement pathway; gone was the garden, with its animal bones. Now there was only rubble.

She felt her breath catch, and had to lean against the car door to steady herself.

The construction worker mounted the tractor and settled in his seat, flipping up the brim of his Dodgers cap. It was an indifferent gesture, almost a tic, something the man obviously did a thousand times before driving the tractor over the remains of someone's house. *Here we go*, it said.

The tractor drove back and forth, its saw-toothed shovel plunging into the rubble, carrying away what was left of Sunset Terrace, exhuming voices she had long since tried to bury.

*Oo Ah Oo Ah Maleenie.*

*Quit it.*

*Ditch 'em.*

*Miss Mary Mack Mack Mack.*

They all rushed toward her, a motley parade waiting to be summoned. *Allie Allie All Come Free.*

Tanya, with her curled pigtails. Joan, flicking the ash from her Virginia Slim. Ned in his mo-ped helmet standing next to her, and Mim too, clutching Daisy's Skipper doll. Mr. and Mrs. Hamilton and Rich Jr., sitting on the plastic-covered couch. Alma, in a drapey, incense-laden dress, smiling down at Trevor, with his bag of corn nuts. Danny jingling a pocketful of quarters. Davy swinging around his arm with the cast like a propeller. Sandi flipping back her feathered bangs, Sue-Sue giggling, jabbing her sister in the ribs.

And there was Bridget with her chopped scramble of blonde hair, perched on the chain-link fence. A nine-year-old girl kicking the post with her heel.

Hannah felt her throat clench. She could not help it— couldn't stop wondering, as she often did, what Bridget would have been like as she grew older, went through junior high, high school. She imagined Bridget standing before the bathroom mirror, rimming her eyes with frosted blue eyeliner. Wrinkling her nose at a pimple on her forehead, picking at it. Cutting class and smoking under the pier at the beach, running into the water and flailing her arms as a wave came crashing down. Kissing her boyfriend between classes in the hallway as the other students rushed by, clamoring to class.

She climbed into the Tercel, trying to push the images out of her mind.

She rolled down the window and breathed deeply, filling her lungs with the warm air. Now that Sunset Terrace was reduced to wreckage, she resolved, it would no longer have the same resonance in her memory.

*It can't haunt me anymore.* The words reassured her, and she repeated them.

It was a silent but futile prayer. Driving to the restaurant, she ran three red lights, remembering Bridget's wide, chapped-lip grin.

# ACKNOWLEDGMENTS

I am indebted to my agent, Jennifer Carlson, for her persistence and unswerving support, and for making everything possible. Special thanks to my excellent editor, Anika Streitfeld, who read draft after draft and still managed to see straight.

For their inspiration and encouragement, I am grateful to Nicholas Christopher, Michael Cunningham, Gordon Haber, Dani Shapiro, and Jessica Shattuck.

And most of all, thanks to my husband, Erich, whose boundless supply of love and patience still astounds me.